Swampoodle

A Sullivan Family Saga
of a 1920's Irish Crime Family
in Philadelphia, Pennsylvania.

DP Curran

Swampoodle

DP Curran

ISBN: 9781520543369

First Publishing: February 2017

Acknowledgments

Colleen M. Curran

Melanie Fountain

Chad Dayton

Scott Phelan

Muse

Editor

Cheryl Walker Castela

Dedication

Jonathan A. Hirsch

1961-2016

Friend, teammate, brother.

R.I.P

BOOK I

O'Suilebhain

Port Donegal, Ireland. 1900, sixteen years before the

'The Rising' . . .

Better the trouble that follows death than the trouble that
follows shame.

~Irish Proverb~

DP Curran

CHAPTER 1

Whistles split the moan of fog horns and the odious sound of hounds filled a man up with thoughts of capture, followed by torture. The eventual firing squad by English soldiers would be a welcome respite in the end.

A boy, Seamus O'Suilebhain, made his way by night through the remote passages he had known as a child to the Port of Donegal. A ship bound for America would be waiting for the survivors of a raid on an English encampment, hours before. The voyage was a commercial venture, bought and paid for what would later become known as *Bráithreachas Phoblacht na hÉireann.* '*The Irish Republican Brotherhood'* founded in 1918. Money raised and held in coffers for bribes and favours of English Loyalists. Merchants and landowners in Ireland. Their love of money outweighed any notion of being hung for treason.

Upon reaching the port, a blackened ship creaked with the twisting of its line. An English patrol snuck about the empty ship, waiting. Their crouched bodies made the stiffened lot seem more loathsome.

Bodies of boys, no older than Seamus, were being dragged lifeless into the pines that grew in random patterns along the rocky shore. Each body still between that of boy and man, each one, Seamus had known from the first days of school. Before that even, in the back gardens and along the sea and glens of green, that now swallowed him whole. He watched as another swam to the port side and climbed into the waiting arms of English soldiers, eager to stifle and slice the throat of all who boarded, unawares.

Seamus watched until the shock of remorse had left him. He rose up and headed for home to gather any information he could from his father, a leader and organizer for *'The Brotherhood'* since it's conception in 1858, a secret oath-bound fraternal organization dedicated to the establishment of an independent Ireland. Freedom from the cruelty of the British.

Ulster Unionist infiltrated the IRB and fingered several dozen members for the English High Command in Kilcar, County Donegal. A trap set, Seamus being the one person to reach the ship and not perish. His sickness turned to anger, not in that moment for the English, but for brothers, though not related. How could they not have noticed? Did they not sense the danger of the desolate ship, the dead sea captain tied to the helm? The signs were clear to see, but they were blind to it all and now . . . now, they were dead. A hardness encased his mind and body as he walked, watchful, senses heightened with rage and cunning.

This was the home of Seamus O'Suilebhain, the oldest of five children born alive to Padraig and Sinead O'Suilebhain. Four boys and a daughter, Lilly, struck dumb at the age of two by an unknown illness.

A raid that night was thwarted, though several fires set, caused non-fatal injuries to English soldiers, already tipped off by the Unionist.

The father, Padraig, his sons, Kieran, Daniel, and Rory O'Suilebhain were lined up against the stone wall of their home as Sinead was questioned about the whereabouts of Seamus. A mere formality was all for the record. The results would be the same for all that were lined up already. A fine catch, the O'Suilebhain Clan. An onsite death warrant procured by the sworn statement of a man who was now neither English or Irish. The English considered, Peter McCall, their paid informant, now useless. Given that his name was attached to the statement which was shown without hesitation to all that questioned it. He had been used and paid a considerable sum, including the deed to a small house on a fertile piece of land more than suitable for farming and the grazing of livestock. The property was not transferable and would be relinquished at the time of his death back to *'The Crown of England'*. All of this, so thought agreeable and secret in its binding. Not a terrible deal for an unmarried man the same age Padraig O'Suilebhain's.

He had given up people he had known and fought beside his whole life. His fate was now sealed, a dead man, but not by the English themselves. They posted the man's name and likeness for all to see, in the town square at nightfall, as was their custom to arouse men of action and track their whereabouts. The posting added that there were more like him amongst them, perhaps their own children or lifelong friends. It was a tactic that served but one result, the death of Peter McCall as he left the pub that night feeling that he had gotten away with it. Having spent the evening with people who knew different, but said nothing to raise any such suspicion. His body was to be found intact, though impaled on a long iron lance, through the arse and out of his mouth, with bloody precision. He faced the English posting that gave more rise to the belief in *'The Ghost'* and the legend of Aengus O'Boyle.

Rory O'Suilebhain stared off into the salted wind and took a deep breath, tasting the sea mixed with fire, knowing his death was nigh. His eyes following the pieces of thatched roof, blown above the torches and into the moon, before disappearing behind racing clouds.

DP Curran

A question without sufficient answer produced a single shot, first Padraig. Shot through the back of the head by a soldier's rifle. Sinead rushed toward her husband only to be knocked unconscious by the butt of a rifle. With each denial came another shot until there were no more. Left with a warning after being revived by the urination of the English Captain Edmund Wainwright, known as *'The Lion'* for his ferocity and absolute devotion to *'The Crown'*. Sinead O'Suilebhain rose to her feet in defiance. Her unbraided blond hair soaked in blood and urine. She stood and soon found herself wrapped in the arms of an old woman. The English mounted their horses to ride off, laughing. Not, however, before a heed from the captain.

"You do your son no favour here this night madam. You, I am afraid, have guaranteed for him a slow and agonizing death. It will not be by single bullet or even the impassiveness of the hangman. All here had every chance to save themselves, as this old useless woman can confirm. Look at what all this bloody violence has wrought on this once beautiful woman. I will see to your son's death myself. From beginning to end . . ." He nodded and tipped his cap as that of an English gentleman, high atop his stead. *'The Lion'*, as he was known, looked down and steadied himself once more. The arrogant man had streak of overwhelming love for his station in life.

He continued, "On the other hand, widow, you will live out your days with the comfort of a retarded daughter you feel compelled to hide from the world. Lilly, is it? Such a pretty name to waste on a throw away. Look as she peers from the shadows. She will now have all of your love, love you once had to share with so many." The captain did not tip his cap this time, but smiled. The leather saddle pinching beneath him, along with the sound of the horse's bit froze Sinead. She stared long after the men and horses were gone.

Seamus O'Suilebhain returned home in the shadow of the full moon. Thin clouds moved about the sky as spirits.

Bodies laid in rows in front of the house, shrouded in linen. A candle burned in the window, covered in a red globe of fine tempered glass, reserved for the dead. Neighbors, women all, now appearing to console the inconsolable.

The words of Seamus's mother, Sinead, drifted into the night without meaning. The bodies told Seamus all he needed to know.

Partings were said without recollection of words to people he had known his entire life, as all, save a few, remained out of fear for their own families, young and many fatherless by now.

The woman, though tested with hardship and loss, still produced a natural beauty. She would stay the night with Sinead O'Suilebhain. Orla O'Boyle was no stranger to the English having been the one person to stand beside Sinead in the presence of 'The Lion'. Orla's husband and four sons taken, never to be seen or heard from again, twenty years prior. Australia some said and so said Mrs.

DP Curran

O'Boyle herself, in hopes others might believe it. She herself did not, the fire of pride and purpose kept her silence. Orla had one of her children later in life, a daughter, as a precaution for the future, so she thought. Bridget O'Boyle, was born four years after Aengus.

One thing separated Bridget from all others, she was conceived and born unawares by the English authorities. The girl was moved south to County Cork, after being weened. She lived with cousins in the south, the Morrison's. She was closest in age and mindset with her cousin, Owen, who protected her, and saw to her every move, that she might be happy. Seamus O'Suilebhain, knew not of the existence of Bridget O'Boyle.

The Morrisons were known for their sheer size and strength, though they were not known for agitation of any kind. Thus, they flourished without suspicion or reproach. This was calculated, and much money was given to the Irish cause, under the guise of their outward appearance of compliance, and ambiguity.

The English themselves stopped all inquiries concerning the youngest son, Aengus, more than a decade ago, who may have escaped, or so the story went. Aengus O'Boyle was seen all over Ireland, more of a ghost than a living person by now. The vicious slaying of English soldiers, often left for dead without various body parts, taken at horseback by a medieval lance made of iron. Soldiers started riding in no less than groups of four, but the slaughter continued in the same fashion. It was concluded that one man was not capable of such an undertaking, no matter how vengeful he might be or skillful in his craft. The fact that the boy's father was a blacksmith continued to fuel the myth of the iron lance. The boy himself skilled in the art.

Stories to tell of heroism of a boy long since dead. A legend of a boy turned into tales told about a man. Legend in any sense is hope and hope they did need. Aengus O'Boyle had been that hope for many, whispered as truth though tales was all, for it could not be so. Aengus's mentor, as it were, was Neil Corrmack. He was known as *'Death'* to English soldiers, by horseback, boat, or foot. He lived amongst the pines that surrounded water, always the sea. Corrmack, left Aengus to himself, and headed for America with his luck and head intact, or so it was said. Another story, perhaps.

Howbeit, Seamus, his father and all his brothers knew better than to think any of these things as myth. They had seen the carnage many times. Strewn body parts collected as quick as possible by the English. They had special patrols of soldier's who went about the Irish countryside for the single purpose of collecting body parts and valuables, wedding rings and photos of children of the slain soldiers. Soon, they not wore nor carried any such personal articles in Ireland. No matter, heads on sharpened branches would do fine for *'The Ghost'*.

DP Curran

Blacksmith's would be hung in public squares if found making lances of any sort longer than the blacksmith's right arm. Still, bodies continued to turn up impaled on the long iron lance. Chilling to even the most seasoned English officer.

Silence was Orla O'Boyle's dignity, her strength, though suffer she did in that silence. Orla, was strength itself. She handed Seamus a canvas pouch with a drawstring, weighted with gold coin. They embraced without words, the eyes of the old woman were of certainty to Seamus. No question of the money left the mind of the tall, lanky boy. A boy who had become a man, but did not himself know it yet. Orla O'Boyle did, all too well, and she prayed in that moment to God for Seamus's safety and that he may smite his enemies.

Arms and ammunition, hidden beneath the floorboards were retrieved with the methodical mind of a sociopath. Seamus was more comfortable in this mode of thought than any other. The natural chemicals tantalized his brain, giving a paganist pleasure known but to Seamus himself.

Seamus's pleads for his mother and sister to come with him were of no consequence, there was no coming back after tonight. They would serve but to slow her son down ensuring his death. She had at this point no regard for her own. Something Orla O'Boyle would instill once more in Sinead, in time. A hug by mother and son were said in forgotten words in Irish.

Seamus kissed his sister, Lilly, as she sat unawares. She tried to speak, but managed no words. The girl, now eleven, was not retarded or the slightest bit dangerous, as the English had claimed. Hearings were held to determine the girl's mental fitness. Being judged too unstable to live without oversight from a sound minded adult. A relative, of immediate family no less. Without the kindness and gold coin given to men of influence by Mrs. O'Boyle, such a judgement would not have been reached. Lilly would have been taken away to the sanitarium, but because of her beauty, more than not sold to sex traffickers at the highest bid. Mrs. O'Boyle would pay more than once for the sparing of Lilly O'Suilebhain. Everything done unbeknownst to Lilly's mother. Sinead O'Suilebhain attributed these blessings an act of God, brought forth out of resolute prayer. This, Orla O'Boyle knew, and she would not take that from Sinead—for Orla believed that God worked best through people, and that she herself was just one of many.

Lilly was in fact, beautiful to the eyes, long red-blond hair with the oval green eyes of an angel, not of this world. She was dressed with mindful purpose in plain clothing, her hair often covering her face when amongst strangers of any kind. The girl was kept from sight while English patrols took place. Unannounced house inspections, to search for weapons or large amounts of undue monies. Harassment led to beatings and rape, meant to terrorize those most suspected of revolts against '*The Crown*'.

Lilly's deficiency was in her speech and at times her mind. Lapsing into the mental state of a small child, unable to reason.

Seamus died in separate little sections each time he thought of his sister. He had wished her beauty could be hidden on the inside, so that men, evil men would not want her.

"I will be back for you, Lilly. I will be back for you and Ma . . . of this there is no doubt." His sister put her mouth to Seamus's ear, before sliding down in silence. Seamus nodded and rose without another word or glance.

"Mo mhac is sine, mo mhac . . ." His mother repeated, until her lone boy was out of sight. "My oldest son, my son . . ." was all she had left to say.

Mrs. O'Boyle's presence was a cold comfort to Seamus, but it held him steady, as he walked from his home and family, both that were intact less than one day before.

CHAPTER 2

A bonfire lit the English encampment revealing each face as they ate and drank, filled with laughter and stories of murder and rape. Visions of the starving and ravaged played over, again and again. Seamus sat and rocked himself into a trance, listening, brimming with a hatred that drives a man to such violence as he was about to do, though still conflicted by his faith in this moment. The Gospel, which served as comfort to him when other families were killed, was of no comfort to him now. He knelt and asked Jesus for forgiveness, his last act of any connection with the Lord, as he had known Him.

A light in the small barracks hidden within the trees, a gift of the full moon, illuminated a makeshift office of sorts with a short interlude from the moving clouds. Officers' quarters, Seamus figured. *'The Lion'* would die this night, he would lose himself in order to do it if necessary. There would be no more listening, no more pious reflection on God's will. The Old Testament was in his blood, the taste of it on his gums and lips.

In a volley of grenades and rifle fire, he killed and dismembered every soldier outside and he waited with a rifle for anyone coming from the single door to the small barrack.

Three figures emerged, dazed and fumbling for their side arms. Seamus seeing this, reloaded and made himself known. The men were blinded with concussion, as Seamus O'Suilebhain shot each man at will, in the smoke and flickering fire, without utterance. He would speak just one word while leaving, *"Ceartas."* Meaning justice in the Irish tongue. Shooting any that wheezed or moved in the clearing surrounding the carnage, amplified with the rage

Young men appeared from the wood line and showed their hands and spoke in the language of their fathers to Seamus. With his weapon still on the men, some no more than boys by all accounts, they began to make sense. Seamus hadn't killed, Captain Wainwright, he was not in that encampment, nor was he ever so said the boys.

There was no time for further action, a ship was waiting now in the Port of Derry and they would take him there if need be. Seamus picked two men of similar stature to accompany him to Derry. He gave the other's pieces of coin and entrusted his family to them, as well as Mrs. O'Boyle.

"I shall return one day—be careful to do my will . . ." Seamus spoke, still ravenous in body and tongue, his sincerity was evident.

To this there was no argument, given what they had witnessed and heard here this night. A hero was born, though just fourteen years of age himself, Seamus was. His size and actions told another story.

The ship, laden with a cargo comprised of linens, livestock, countless cases of distilled whiskey and many hundreds of barrels containing various brews was bound for ports unknown to Seamus, along the Eastern Seaboard of America. Linen, wool and livestock was to be discharged in England. The ship itself inspected, then the long voyage to America. Seamus's thoughts of reaching America would first depend on a successful departure from England. This was arranged by the IRB, though no guarantees could be given. The voyage was folly at best, but Seamus had no doubts of his own, nor choice. Confirmation by a reluctant, but well-paid captain was not enough.

Seamus boarded, each step echoed beneath him as he ascended the wooden foot bridge. His mind, black as the soot from an English torch that pierced the salt air.

He stood alone as instructed at the ship's stern, all the while waiting for the horn to signal departure. No sense of time or common sense came to him, though he did try to summon his wits. Seamus was lost when not in motion, without a looming plan. The boy doubted himself and fought this with hope of an encounter, even if it meant his life.

A scheduled ship it was, bound for England and New York City, USA. False documents and papers would be waiting for Seamus upon his arrival on deck, or so he thought.

A white bearded man gimping with advanced age approached Seamus, dangling a corn cob pipe from his toothless mouth. A mouth no stronger than the stranger himself.

"A strike of a match has ye', boy?" The old man was Irish alright, but of what allegiance, Seamus pondered, as was his nature.

"*aye*" Seamus quipped, producing a wooden striker.

"*buachaill Padraig s*" asked the old man, as he drew from the flame.

"Whose boy I am is of no concern of yours, *daideo*." Meaning grandpa.

"You've answered my question, Seamus." The stranger said, leaning in close enough to reveal his tobacco stained teeth and rancid breath, "Come to the rail now so more might be said." The old man continued, but this time in the voice of a much younger man than his appearance would have one believe.

Looking about first, Seamus went guided now by the arm with a gentle, but purposeful grasp of the stranger.

"Listen and speak no more, boy. There is little time to explain."

The horn had sounded, and the ship pulled from port, the moon separated from the clouds that circled above the island. The deck of the ship now lit with a sense of physical respite for Seamus. The happenings of the last hours could be written about in a manner of days or weeks having transpired. Tobacco, Seamus thought. The man, teeth stained in the same, he would have plenty, for sure.

"Tobac?" Seamus asked, his head searing with pain that took him from time to time.

The old man stared at first before rolling two cigarettes in silence, then filling a pipe, much different than the corn cob pipe used earlier. The stranger spoke then in the English words.

"We're flyin' under English *colours*, boy. Best to not look up—and better still to use their language than lose a tongue and then, be hung from a yardarm in a British port. Understood, boy?" The man's tone now that of a stronger, upright sort who stretched before handing Seamus his bag of tobacco and papers, knowing of his sparseness of personal effects.

"And your answer?"

"aye, a dhuine uasail." Meaning yes sir.

"I see you take direction like the ignorant feck I had you figured for, boy. Last chance, no warnins', no nothin' for you. That simple." A crowd of a dozen men filled the space afforded the two until now. Knives and rope was plain to see in the ambiguous light of the moon.

"Yes, sir" Seamus answered, in a calm voice reserved for the brave who have much to do, despite whoever this man, this stranger was.

"Good then." The man spoke, striking a match and nodding so the others knew to take their places once again. He lit his pipe, a fierce piece of wood it was, knotted with the sharp natural spikes of a walking stick, that no other man might want it.

"There is much to do, and I know, willingness is not your trouble. I heard firsthand what measures you took tonight and your commitment to the cause since you were a wee boy. Your da couldn't shake ya' for tryin'. A natural, he'd say. More men, innocent men will die because of what you've done this night" His dialect of English told Seamus the stranger was from the north as he.

"Many a brave and even innocent men have died at the hands of the English, including me da and brothers all. Women . . . girls, little girls raped and left dead or worse to carry an English baby. So, why do you tell me this? If that's not enough, kill me now, so I can take a few of ya' cowards with me to heaven or hell, dependin'."

"Dependin' on what, brother?" as the man stepped to Seamus.

"Dependin' on who's confused and who's deliberate. Make your move then." Seamus dropped his duffle and let the knife slide from his coat sleeve to his wrist.

The stranger, instead of engaging the boy, began to remove his filthy hat and peel the ragged beard from his face, eyebrows as well. His gloves last, used to wipe the grime from his face and mouth. His disguise.

The most wanted man in Ireland stood in front of Seamus, still hidden by ragged clothing and the remnants of burnt ash rubbed into his face. Standing in front of him, to his shock was *'The Ghost.'*

Seamus himself used to pretend to be him in games of war in the trees of Dublin, before his father took the family to Donegal, though he knew it not.

"Well, now, Seamus O'Suilebhain. You're not afraid to kill or even die yourself, but you're too ignorant to go on livin' much longer. The choice is now, do you want to learn, do you want to know your purpose in this life? That's a question you need to ask yourself now, and be quick to answer or I can tell you, you'll die having never known. That will not concern me a wee bit, because a man who is ignorant of his purpose gets more than just himself killed. And that I cannot abide."

"I want to learn to do whatever you need of me, sir." The removal of a certain disguise disarmed the boy. Words did not come so

19

easy for Seamus. He stood with the sharp blade against the tender flesh between the joints of his fingers, unable to right the knife to the cuff of his shirt.

"It's not easy to be questioned about such things when everything you hold dear has either been murdered, starved or raped. Give yourself credit, boy, you've put others ahead of yourself here this night, on both land and sea. Come below where we can speak without our words repeating themselves in the wind. For me thinks the salt air makes any man thirsty and with a drink comes a tongue of betrayal which lends itself to death."

The stranger turned to his men, "Trust is an illusion, boy. Actions, whilst a man has reason to betray you for his own advancement, will tell you more than any talk swearing of allegiance can. That will be your first two lessons, boy. There will be many more based off those two that I've spoken aloud for all. Put the knife away, you'll not be needin' that for now, boy."

The two went below to a compartment fit for a Captain of the Royal Navy, not an Irish rebel, no matter his infamy. So, Seamus thought. There was much to learn, indeed.

CHAPTER 3

A short drink of whiskey was placed in front of young Seamus O'Suilebhain. A much larger one sat in front of the stranger. The bottle rested near.

"Do you know of me, boy?"

"Everyone in Ireland, Scotland, Wales and England knows of you, sir. In America, too. Folks say as much, anyway, sir." The boy spoke with certainty now. This produced a laugh from a strange man, indeed. As though the devil himself might laugh, so the boy thought. Seamus gulped the whiskey, it slid down hot and sat in his gut as hot lead, giving the boy, some needed courage.

"Then, who do you say that I am, boy?"

"I wouldn't want to say aloud, sir. No, I wouldn't."

"Whisper it to me then, step over here now." Seamus took three steps and leaned into the man's ear, looking about first.

DP Curran

"The Irish Robin Hood, *'The Ghost'* with, how should we say', an unquenchable thirst for English blood? More, *'Vlad, The Impaler'*, me thinst." His laughter now coursed through Seamus, as if he had taken another shot of whiskey.

"All of that, sir," Seamus said, as he straightened.

The man stood and faced the long windows that revealed the blackness of the sea.

"No family claims a man such as this in all of Ireland. It is said that the father and sons of the O'Boyle family are suffering in Australia. Or perhaps to America were the streets are paved with gold and every woman beautiful. Is that not the rest of the story, Seamus O'Suilebhain?"

"I believe it is, sir."

"You, believe it is, so it is. Am I correct in your understanding, Seamus?"

"Yes, sir." The whiskey produced a deeper voice.

"Yes, you say, but your answer provides no Christian name." He held up his hand anticipating a quick correction by the boy.

"The truth, boy, is a thing that scares men, as does the name of Jesus, no matter a man's religion, faith or the lack of both. The truth in our case will, as is said, set us free. As a people and a country, but not before I die. Of this I have no doubt, though I wish not to blaspheme. Some must live if possible in order to achieve our freedom. I pray that you might be one of those men, Seamus. This being a time for truth, I doubt you will be, but again, I blaspheme. God knows your time, boy. We'll need more of your seed in the New World, in America."

"Someday, I'll come back, back to Ireland . . . to '*The Brotherhood*' and fight again." Seamus said.

"Grand plans ye' have."

"Aye, sir."

"Pour and drink as you like, that you may be comforted by it. A toast to illusion perhaps, no? Better yet . . . to Ireland. To our Emerald Isle." Glasses raised, electricity charged through the sound of the chime, as rims touched. Seamus's eyes darted about until they locked onto cold blue magnets above the steady glasses, darkened in half with light brown whiskey.

"go h Eirinn," spoken aloud by the most infamous man of Seamus's youth.

"Good then," said the man, with eyes now closed, enjoying the effect of the whiskey.

He rose once more. "Pour again for the both of us, boy. Go on . . ." Seamus poured heavy out of respect for a hero. Who would believe it, he wondered? A calmness was about the ship now, out past the buoys. The sound of the sea being breached was all to hear . . .

"My name is what you thought, but could not say, boy. Aengus O'Boyle, the son of Nevin and Orla O'Boyle. Brother to Declan,

Finbar and Lorcan. Mrs. O'Boyle, bein' your neighbor, the woman who gave you a sack of gold coin. Are you hearing me boy?" The man snapped his fingers in the boy's face to lighten the moment more than anything else.

The boy could do nothing, but nod and drink from the glass in hand, his eardrums ached with confusion and fatigue. He spoke unknowing.

"My allegiance is with the quickly coming of the Irish Republic and you, sir?" The empty glass slid as the boy put it to the table. A rogue wave had raised and lowered the ship from bow to stern.

"Don't ya' think I know that, Seamus O'Suilebhain . . . don't ya'?

"Aye," was spoken in a deep whisper.

"Then listen up, boy . . ." *'The Ghost'* turned to the sea and began to speak in an even tone.

"Da is dead, sure as the fuckin' English hung him from a tree, not a walk from the house me Mam still lives in, the house we all lived in. Me brothers and I got loose and survived in the cliffs of Donegal Bay, though Finbar was shot through the shoulder and scores of other Irishmen shot dead, still boy's most. Finbar's left arm useless, nerves were damaged. It serves as a disguise for dignity sake, now, I suppose, never a whimper out of him, though. I believe he aims to feather his own nest for the injustice done to him by God, Himself . . . so far as Finbar believes. I believe a man that blames God is weak, boy. Make your peace with God now, if ya' haven't done so already. Anyone lookin' for sympathy in a cruel world as this is prey to the wolves."

"You mentioned, not a whimper out of him, sir," Seamus spoke, with the full measure of the whiskey bridling his thoughts.

"Self-pity, silent scorn, call it what ye' may. A man can be vindictive and sorrowful without the need for words, boy. Actions is what gives a person their due, be it man or woman."

Seamus sat in quiet wonder, at what was being said. Aengus drank once more, from the bottle now and continued.

"We doubled back with the sound of the hounds off to the south. I cut da down and we washed him, before layin' him to rest in the high tide of the bay. Ma was threatened, and the house watched for years, some say still. She had nothin' more to lose and the English knew it. They didn't want the blood of a childless widow makin' the situation worse—they concocted a story about Australian penal colonies and the like to save face. They had Ma swear to it on paper and she gave her word on the souls of her sons not to deny it. But, no matter . . .many more families were killed in my family's name. So, ya' see, Seamus . . . not enough English can be slaughtered to wash that away. What we need is power and that means money and arms. This can come from one place and that place, that place is America."

DP Curran

"Yes sir, Mr. O'Boyle, sir."

"You've never seen nor spoken to anyone by that name, son. You don't call me anythin', anythin' whatever. Shut the fuck up, for Christ's sake and the sake of Ireland, if not your own ma and sister."

"What of my ma and sister, sir? The English will be their end, and my sister . . ." Aengus quieted the boy.

"We have men there who will choose money over a crown, boy. Keep your mind on what you need to do, and I'll see to your kin and my own ma, the best any man might. Oh, me ma, she is a fistful that one, tougher than me own da—in intestinal fortitude alone mind ya', God rest his soul, the bugger."

"Thank you, sir. I feel the coward, leavin' them behind, a shame that must be worse than death itself . . ."

"Aye, boy . . . but your stayin' would be their death, and the death of hundreds more, for you would have killed more soldiers in the process. This time there would be a face and a name to use against others of the same ilk. I feel your hurt, boy, that I do. Dyin' is easier, it's livin' on and makin' a difference that's hard. Many a day and night I thought of riding rough shod through an English camp and takin' out as many as those cocksuckers as I could before bein' killed myself in a blaze of glory. That's all bullshit though, isn't it, boy. That would be no more than an escape, an abandonment of my duty and the promises that I have made is all."

"I believe that you are right, sir, and I thank ya' for it."

"I believe your right, sir? Enough of that shite talk, let's just assume if I say it, then it's right. For fuck sake, now, let's get down to business and no more of that whiskey, it's makin' ya' daft or bringin' out the real you. Don't know yet which be worse. How old are ya' anyways, boy?"

"Fourteen, sir. I'll be fifteen before long."

"You just might at that, you just might. Feck sake lad, you're a long stretch of wood for fourteen years. Forearms of a woodsman or blacksmith, maybe."

"My ma's side is as big as they come, so I'm told, sir."

"I don't give a fuck about your family tree, next you'll be wantin' to show me pictures of your Aunt Blowme . . . Jesus help me, if this be another test, Lord, then I'm woefully unprepared." Aengus O'Boyle took off his cap and looked up, as if to the heavens . . .

Aengus O'Boyle continued on into the night, as he went about the task of trimming his red beard, before taking a bath in water that was boiled and turned his skin as any cooked lobster. He was nothing at all resembling an old man, for which he disguised himself. Aengus was solid, muscles, grew from muscle. His shoulders stacked high between shoulder and neck, he stood at 183 centimeters, and weighed a good 14 stone, absent any fat whatever.

DP Curran

Though just four years his senior, Aengus O'Boyle, just as well could have been ten years his elder. The age of a warrior cannot be measured in years alone.

The morning sun lit the horizon, as Seamus was at last given final instructions.

"My brother, Finbar will show himself to you in the future . . . careful there, boy. I can't say that I envy ya' by any stretch, but until they figure a way to kill me, my decision about you is final unto death. You may come across a few others, but don't count on it, boy. Pray it isn't Declan, the eldest, he's fucked in the head. Finbar has him wrapped. Declan is not daft, so much as unpredictable to a fault. I fear we'll be dealin' with him sooner than later. Tis' a hellava thing for a brother to say. Speakin' murder of your own kin . . . brothers, no less. Life's a mother fucker, Seamus, but we are not monsters. We are men, sons, brothers, fathers, committed is all, there can be no in between." With that Aengus O'Boyle, thrust a dagger that he unscrewed by the handle of his walking stick into a pristine wooden table. "Believe all that I've told you, Seamus, on the soul of my mother. Remember this above all, trust no man, except yourself and your own judgement, from this day forth."

"Aye, sir . . ."

"Don't count on anything more than I tell you, for now. The time will come when you will be the one to make the decisions from your end. You'll have your orders for a time, like everyone else, of course, but you'll be left to your own judgement when I feel the time has come. I'm exercising my judgement now, as you will in the years to come, but until that day, remember the truths that I have told you here this night. For the good of our families and our mothers and kin in Ireland."

"Will I have to change my name, sir?"

"You'll not bastardize it for the sake of the English, but we have taken the liberty of making it, shall we say, more American. Not so bad, boy."

"Me da hated this happening more than death itself, sir, he did."

"Well, your father, Padraig was a great man, Seamus O'Suilebhain. You will be no less of one, for this I'm sure." Mr. O'Boyle handed Seamus folded papers, identification documents and American currency. A hefty sum at that. "I'll be needin' the gold coin, boy." Taking the boy by surprise but he handed it over without hesitation or question, as instructed.

"Good, then. Here, take this and hide it until you need it. Not when you want to use it, know the difference and you'll be fine as rain." A smaller sack pulled tight by a drawstring was handed to the boy.

"Thank you, sir."

"There's one other thing, concernin' my family, Seamus O'Suilebhain, something more important to me as anything I've said so far. I have a sister by the name of Bridget. She is by my memory the same age as you. Don't become attached to another, if things go well, you two shall meet. Don't speak a word to me about her this night. Just know this, you'll not be disappointed, just don't disappoint me."

"Again, I thank you." Seamus spoke, without completely understanding, his thoughts scattered.

"Don't go thankin' me now, boy . . . you'll be cursin' me soon enough. Responsibility will be your burden. Carry it each day with dignity and without complaint, though at times it will be heavy. Pass it on to your own, that they might learn to carry it well."

"I will, sir. You can count on it." This forced a grimace from Mr. O'Boyle, as the boy's heartfelt sentiments were not welcomed or in his nature.

"Don't go soft on me, boy. You're tempered ruthlessness gave you this opportunity. Discipline where needed, but death to those who get their number punched. Leave examples for all to see, but carry yourself with control. There are few things scarier to a person than a large dog that's trained to attack, but remains calm until called on to do so. Dress well, but never over dress, unless it applies, and you'll know when."

"Will we be safe in England, sir?"

"We? There is no we, boy. Look at your identification papers, you'll see but one name. That name will be yours to the end. Do ya hear me talkin' to ya'?"

"Yes, sir."

"More like it. Now, read the card out loud as so you can hear it in my presence and not fuck up and use any other name, least you'll see my face and think better of it. Always think of me as just near, boy. That will serve ya' well. Go on, now . . ."

"James Sullivan." The boy said in a brogue that made it for what it was a foreign name.

"For feck sake, some effort, boy. You'll be a Yankee before ya' know it. Your father, God Bless his soul, he'd be on the floor laughin' at that tongue of yours in the States. That ya' can believe." And Mr. O'Boyle laughed for the first and last time in the true sense.

He began the process of applying the disguise of the old man once more. A man who killed more Englishmen than anyone in modern history. This right before the boy's eyes and it was not lost on him, for he stared as if to emblazon the true face of the greatest man he would ever meet, save his father for whom he loved though not having ever said the words.

The old man began to speak. "Commit this name to memory, boy, for I cannot put it to paper. Liam Donnelly. Just remember the name, don't try to spell it out. The same was done for him which was done for you. He'll be your American Sponsor. You'll take an Irish wife, of course. That will be arranged, but I promise you, boy, you won't be disappointed."

"England, sir?"

"You'll be shown a compartment. Don't leave it, until you hear three knocks. *'The Father, Son and Holy Ghost.'* Use that in the future, but with pause after each knock. Commit the knock you hear tonight to memory as well, James Sullivan, and use it in all things business. For whatever reason.

You'll be called upon to kill a man within days of settling in Philadelphia in Pennsylvania. A section known as *'Swampoodle'* when you find out what that means, tell someone who gives a shite. For the life of me, I don't know a lie from the truth in that country. In some ways, it will feel familiar, in other ways more foreign than I could ever explain. The first-generations Americans will test you. Put those that need it in their place, straight off. Examples, examples, examples. You get the idea, do what you do best. Besides, once you fill out, nobody in their right mind will fuck with you and them that try, kill the sons of bitches." The old man fixed his tattered brimmed hat and waved the boy to follow. He then stopped. "A man without a name, will deliver the three knocks. Ask no questions of him. He will see you through the immigration inspection port of Ellis Island and your short journey to

Philadelphia. He is a man of considerable power, observe him, but never interfere."

"Aye, sir," said Seamus.

"Oh, and boy. You'll have your chance at revenging your family, most of all Lilly." *'The Ghost'* spoke in a way reserved for a man with feelings for family alone.

"How long in the compartment, sir?" His whisper echoed, the hollow sound of change.

"Until you hear *'The Trinity'*. When you reach New York." The reticent voice of an old man sent a chill through the boy. Those were the last words spoken by Aengus O'Boyle. *'The Legend of Ireland'*, as he was known.

Enough food and water for ten men sat before James Sullivan. He stared as the door shut behind him with the unemotional clasping of a lock. Young James glanced at the hammock that swung with the silence of an owl in flight, before using his sleeve to rub the sea stained portal which gave the boy the hope that he would need.

"James Sullivan." He repeated, each time with more confidence. Over and over again, while he rummaged through the duffle bag the old man had had him carry without explaining. A clunking sound was made as the bag was lifted and set down. In the bottom was a revolver, taped on the butt of the weapon, as was the newly formed custom in Ireland to preclude any fingerprints. His first decision, should he take a chance on carrying the gun or leave it behind, was it a test or a necessity to have?

Young James Sullivan hid the gun behind stacks of wedged dry goods. He had chosen well. He was as his father had said . . . a natural. He took a bite of a fresh, cool apple and waited for *'The Trinity'*.

BOOK II

Swampoodle, 1912. The Irish Immigrant
Section of North Philadelphia, Pennsylvania.

"In Swampoodle, there is no call for rumor. A whisper of
truth will do . . ."

~Elizabeth Sweeney~

CHAPTER 4

James Sullivan Jr., waited on the front porch of his family's row house. His worn boots were laced tight, as he looked down the long chain of porches that stretched out to the end of the block.

The Sullivan's had moved from a flat brick front row home with three steps to the door. A feat regarded as amazing in a neighborhood where people and their circumstances seldom changed for the better. Within ten short years of James Senior reaching the shores of America, the Sullivan Family had made it. A house with a porch came with its advantages, with Shibe Park, America's first baseball steel and concrete stadium, just a block over. The street, porches and rooftops were packed with people willing to pay less and watch the ballgame from the rooftops just above the bleachers.

All except for the Sullivan's house, living in the corner house, no one sat on their roof or the next one down. Something that made the

Sullivan kids different from the start in Swampoodle. When he asked his da why, he told him it was because he paid extra for the privilege was all, but in time James Sullivan Jr. came to know better. For now, though, he and his best pals watched many a game on their roof.

An orange summer sun rose behind the houses, each porch permeated with the vague smell of its inhabitants. Trains rattled off in the distance. Shibe Park across the street was desolate, not a baseball game to be played today. No friends allowed at all near the house as Jimmy, the oldest of soon to be six children, waited for his mother, Bridget, to give birth to a brother or sister just upstairs in the front bedroom. This would be the seventh, for no one dare say different. Little Alice, the first born, died during childbirth. Bridget, screamed to the midwife to give her the child, no matter her condition. An experienced midwife that wanted to spare Bridget the sight of the baby born before her time, in a state of momentary death. Bridget held and whispered to the infant as her slight breath slowed to a stop. Blood, along with the pains of labor and loss that covered Bridget, made the moment as beautiful as it was tragic. An angel, her mother said, she would be part of the family whether anyone could see her or not.

The younger children sat in the kitchen, eating breakfast made by Deirdre who went from kitchen to bedroom at the beck and call of a midwife and her mother. She was the second in charge to her mother, being younger than to Jimmy by little more than a year.

DP Curran

There was James Jr., an only daughter named Deirdre, Shane, Padraig and Rory for now. All no more than thirteen months apart, save Alice. "Irish twins" as they were known by *'The Natives'*. Deirdre was nine years of age with the same workload of a married woman with children of her own.

And then, over the muted murmurings from the kitchen, came the cries of a baby. The wailing of another pain in the ass, something to make the old man go further away in his mind and further away from Jimmy and the rest. James Sr., didn't speak of baby Alice—their first born. He spoke but a few words about Rory getting the polio, but it was there for him to see every day, the leather and metal leg braces that were either strapped to Rory or resting on their own in the dark of the boy's bedroom each night.

Jimmy hoped it was a girl, a girl he thought, would be better. Less competition, hell it might even make the old man happy for a time . . . thoughts shattered.

"James Sullivan Jr., go and fetch your father and be quick about it now," said Mrs. Byrne. She never said a word like there wasn't something wrong, no matter what. She was the self-proclaimed midwife. Her husband, Oliver, had been shot dead back in their homeland in an old wooden boat, painted black in order to fish at night off the Irish coasts of Derry. The waters were dotted with black boats on the nights of the new moon. The English soldiers would single out a few boats and take aim. Every man in the sea knew someone would not come in alive. They had just the one boy, Stephen, a friend of Jimmy's from the beginning of all memory, ever since Felicity Byrne paid with her body the voyage to America for she and her infant son. She never remarried, a promise she had made with the Lord to atone for the sin of fornication, to secure their voyage. She gave herself to life, as her mother before her, as a mid-wife. If anyone's mother in Swampoodle knew the Widow Byrne, and they all did, she delivered your brother or sister, dead or alive. A woman who took the death of Alice Sullivan as a punishment herself, though there was nothing she could have done for a baby born so soon.

"Is it a boy or a girl?" Jimmy yelled, as he ran from the porch, the wind filling his ears with the sound of large seashell held to your ear.

"A boy and a big one . . . hurry now." Mrs. Byrne's voice split into Jimmy's side like a knife.

"Shit . . ." was all Jimmy had in him, running over three lines of train tracks and across the field behind the warehouses and smokestacks that let out plumes of black smoke, day and night. Dodging cans, broken bottles and rocks, Jimmy made it to the clearing where he and his buddies had made their own baseball field. Mickey Doyle, Bobby Burke and Stevie Byrne were putting the bases down from flour sacks filled with straw and dirt. Home plate was white, in as far as it wasn't as brown as the dirt it rested on.

Story was that the home plate in their "Dust Field" was taken by Cornelius Finn, known as Old Saucy, right out of Shibe park itself, after a night of drinking in "Sweeney's Taproom" with boastings and then promises of the very act itself.

People stood and watched the grounds crew shaking their heads in disgust the next day, before the A's were to play the Red Sox. The game was held up for over an hour just to replace it. Saucy would be a hero. He would forever cement his place in Swampoodle history.

In the mind of a drunk, this was pure genius. The world of a taproom was a fickle thing though and each uneasy patron gave up the ghost, as if it their duty. Every man kept his honor and they did tell one another so, when questioned by one of Donnelly's men. Any lack of cooperation would mean a fate worse than death itself, no booze. Jack Quinn, was not an enforcer, though more than capable. He was a private detective who had one client. Liam Donnelly.

Word had come down from Mr. Donnelly, that stealing home plate from Shibe Park was the equivalent of stealing from the poor box in church. The old home plate sat on the high ground in the field behind the garment factory, where the children played undisturbed. Perhaps a lesson was to be learned for them as well. In the boys of "Dust Field", the story lived on and was told time and again.

Saucy had stolen from the church and was found, after missing for two weeks. His body lay on the railroad tracks, found by three men, working the rails. Beaten to death, the bloody baseball bat lay at his side. And it was said in every quarter, that Old Saucy, clenched a blood-soaked baseball, signed by his own hand. Saucy was now, forever famous. His wake consisted of seven people, including undertakers. Mr. Donnelly, paid for his funeral and tomb stone. Which read . . .

Cornelius Finn

Friend

The sound of a homerun was in every tap of the old broken bat, filled with nails discarded by an opposing player in Shibe park. Bobby Burke, king of all things brilliant, hung out behind the stadium and nagged old Mister Flannery into helping him with the trash after each game. He didn't get paid in money, he got paid in what he found. Bobby found plenty, watches and other valuables including clothes left behind in the visitor's locker room. Years later, Bobby, would be one of the greatest sign stealers ever to work inside the scoreboard. This under the tutelage of the master, Eddie "The Eyes' Casey.

"Yo, Jimmy, where you goin'?" asked Mickey, as Bobby and Stevie just laughed and watched him running as fast as he could.

"Gotta' find the old man . . . Ma had the baby . . ." His voice fading as he ran.

41

"Boy or girl?" Bobby yelled, but Jimmy wouldn't answer.

Mr. Donnelly's shop was a brick building, surrounded with a metal fence. Jimmy hit the fence and climbed over it, without so much as ripping his pants on the sharp top row of the chain link fence.

Out of breath, but feeling the adrenaline of a long run, he made his way around the building to the front. Men . . . large men stood at the door.

"Jimmy boy, what in the hell are you doin' lad, lookin' like the coppers are chasin' ya'?" said the thick brogue of the redheaded man, his Irish cap tilted up a bit. "Cause' if they ever are chasin' ya', don't' be leadin' em' here, now." Both men laughed.

"Lookin for me da . . . Ma had a baby just now and Widow Byrne sent me after," Jimmy said, standing straight, his head tilted back and breathing through his mouth and nose.

"Go on then, son. Go in and tell Mr. Donnelly, he'll know where your da is for sure. Come on, I'll take ye, I will," said the darker haired man. "Remember Jimmy boy, we were aimin' to help . . . don't forget that if your da asks and be sure and tell him, it was me that did the helpin'. Not a finer man than your da, no sir," the man said, in a voice that sounded more like Blackbeard the pirate than any Irishman Jimmy had ever heard.

A knock on a heavy metal door, was met with the sliding of a small slat, high above Jimmy's head. Without a word the door was opened and in walked Jimmy with the dark-haired man. "Young James Sullivan is here to see ya', Mr. Donnelly, sir."

"I can see that, Mulligan, take your place out front," said Mr. Donnelly, his eyes never leaving the boy. The metal door slammed by another man with the blonde hair, the same as Jimmy's father. A man he had not seen before, not ever. A thought that wasn't lost on the boy. The man was even bigger than the two out front.

"Well, now, Jimmy Sullivan . . . let's have it." Mr. Donnelly pushed a bowl of hard candy toward Jimmy. The boy took just one. "That's good, Jimmy, not too greedy, that's just one of the traits that I love about your da."

"Thank you, sir, for the candy and the kind words." Cap in hand, Jimmy knew how the game was played and he played it well. James Sr., had taught his son chess and cards, not for leisure, but for the sake of strategic advantage. Reading the signs and meanings of another man's face and tendencies. Jimmy was calm as he read the face of Mr. Donnelly.

"I think I'll have one myself, now . . . what brings ya' here, James Sullivan Jr.?"

The hard candy rattled around in Mr. Donnelly's mouth as he spoke.

"Ma just had the baby, sir, and Mrs. Byrne sent me after Da, she did." The root beer barrel in Jimmy's mouth shot through him like a drug. The sugar and taste of the root beer was a powerful thing as any boy could have.

"Of course, she did, that old woman's been tellin' people what to do since before she left Ireland and I don't see it stoppin' anytime soon. Told her husband to go fishin' one evening, as I recall. Is it a boy or a girl, now?" Mr. Donnelly rose to his feet. Thick as a horse was he.

"A boy and Mrs. Byrne says he's a big one for sure, he is." Jimmy hated that he said the last part, but he lost control of his tongue and it hurt.

"Another big boned Sullivan, tis' good news boy, come on let's go and get your da. Drew get the truck, you know which one." And the man with the blonde hair led Mr. Donnelly and Jimmy through another metal side door into a covered garage with black Ford Model T trucks in various stages of alteration.

The smell of paint filled Jimmy's lungs. Each new truck was being detailed by hand. Industrial fans blew all but the most gratifying of smells out through wooden hatches in the walls that could be shut and locked at night. The train tracks ran along one side of the warehouse. Large, thick sliding doors on rollers were left open during the warm months. They were there to load and unload all manner of roofing goods and lumber. This included the very trucks that lined the garage portion of the vast warehouse.

"Donnelly Roofing & Masonry were being hand painted on the doors of the trucks that were dried, in gold lettering, outlined in white. Little men with brushes, like leprechauns, Jimmy thought. But there were solid black trucks too, black as ink. Some were bigger, like the moving trucks on Lehigh Avenue. Not a name or marker on any.

Jimmy followed the two men without looking where he was going. He couldn't take his eyes off the trucks and the little men that painted each one . . . never stopping or changing their pace.

The smell of fresh cut pine brought the boy's attention to a section relegated for wooden crates with piles of packing, like shredded rope. Grates being brushed with a clear stain or lacquer. A smell stronger than the fresh paint used on the trucks. The longer Jimmy stood, the more smells hit him. Tar, lumber, paint, exhaust fumes. The popping of a welding torch, followed by a tinge of metal that stayed on his teeth.

"Hop in the back, now, come on, James." Donnelly ordered, noticing the boy's interest.

"I'll bet you'd like a tour of the shop or better yet to explore on your own, eh, young James Sullivan?" the old man asked, eying Jimmy with his first realization that the boy would one day soon be as sharp as his father. Tutored by him for years now, perhaps. The thought angered Mr. Donnelly for not thinking of the boy in those terms sooner.

DP Curran

"Ya know what makes these trucks special, young James?" Donnelly asked, spitting out the last of the hard candy before climbing into the most beautiful thing Jimmy had ever laid eyes on. One of the black trucks, with the wooden bed and rails. A new smell filled the boy's mind, a newness he had not experienced before, but it was a physical feeling as much as anything he had ever imagined. Toys, even real trucks and motor cars he had seen before, but nothing like this, no nothing so beautiful as this. His head spun with want.

"No, sir," Jimmy answered, with his hands on the leather bench seat of the truck. He had never felt leather like this, just the worn harness of horses that pulled carts and wagons. "They're mine, everyone single one," he said, standing straight with his legs spread a bit.

Jimmy started to climb into the cab of the truck.

"Think again, young James. Not up front, not just yet." Mr. Donnelly brushed off the seat that Jimmy had pawed with the sweaty hands of a healthy boy. Donnelly laughed, as they drove from the yard to get James Sullivan Sr., and bring him home to his new boy.

Jimmy laid flat in the bed at first, before sitting up against the cab. The smell of fresh black lacquer made light of his head. He sat up, as to be seen by any and all who might catch a glimpse of him in the back of the truck with the likes of these two men. Men who put fear into all, but his father and he was proud, at that moment, for many did see him. There was nodding and tipping of caps along the way.

CHAPTER 5

"Site number four, Mr. Donnelly?" Andrew Laing asked, in a brogue thick with whiskey and tobacco. And the boy wondered how long had he been here to have such a strong speech still about him. One that sounded so different to all others. No questions were ever asked, no questions at all. Thinking about one for too long raised suspicion among the Irish.

"*Is ea Andrew.*" Donnelly answered, yes in the Irish. Jimmy both spoke and understood, but knew never to respond to any adult speaking in Irish, unless being spoken to direct by his parents, relatives or a few older neighbors. The thought of the wooden sign with the script #4 painted on it stayed in the boy's head, with the sweet coating of the root beer candy stuck to his teeth like the enamel of the new truck.

"You will speak American, learn of them and you will succeed. Never be bested out of ignorance." James would tell his son again and again, but when the drink was present in the home for a baptism, communion, wedding or funeral and the like, Irish, or *Gaeilge,* as the outsiders called it, was spoken by all within an hour.

James Sullivan Sr., was the foreman over every roofer, chimney sweep and mason who worked for Liam Donnelly, but there was another side to Mr. Donnelly. He ran all the betting that went on in Swampoodle, baseball and the ponies. He was known as, *'An Lochannach, The Viking',* in the Irish. With brutal, sociopathic precision, James Sullivan took men apart, men bigger in stature and reputation than James went down as all the rest. At times, to the shear amazement of Mr. Donnelley, who for the life of him could not come to terms with his man's gift, as it were. There were days on occasion that his white overalls would be covered in tar, never to be seen again. Replaced by new ones. Whatever time of day or night he was called upon, the results were the same. The night though was reserved for even more ruthless dealings, resulting in murder. Something James Sr. mentioned to no man, not so much as Mr. Donnelley, who at this point relied on a diamond hard stare and nod from James.

Jimmy watched his father turn the corner at six o'clock every night during the week. He could tell if he smiled or not when he got close enough if it was going to be a meal that included humor or one in total silence, where no silver had better touch tooth or plate. Supper was on the table for six-fifteen sharp, giving his da time to wash the grime from his body in a bath already drawn by his wife.

Just as sure as he came home every night during the week, he dressed after supper on weekends and collected for Mr. Donnelly. James was big, big in the sense of height and muscle, the forearms and shoulders of any heavyweight prizefighter that he could have been. A heavy bag hung in the cellar, nicer than that of the one at the local gym, where Jimmy and his brothers went to box. Some nights the house shook for hours as James Sr. pounded that heavy bag, the air expelling from his body with each blow. "Blowing off steam," Jimmy's mother would tell the children.

Jimmy loved it every Saturday afternoon, when the A's played a home game, his da took the boys across the street, right through the turnstiles they went without having to pay a dime. Everyone knew who James was, better yet, what he did for Mr. Donnelly.

Jimmy was introduced to men in real suits, expensive ones, not the kind you wore because you had just one, for church, funerals and weddings. They mingled through the crowd on their way to the first row, first base side. No matter who was there in those seats, they got up and moved. No one said a word about it. Bigger than life, some said for the old man to hear, but to Jimmy, he knew it was true.

There his father was, just as Jimmy always imagined him when he whispered the stories of beatings and even the suggestion of murder at the hands of his father for Mr. Donnelly.

Square shouldered, with the suspenders that clipped to the heavy pants his father wore. Blonde hair, tinted with red that matched his eyebrows.

James Sullivan had earned the nickname *'The Viking'*, due to his blonde hair and barbaric tendencies when given the order, though no one dare mention it aloud. His tactics were of a brutal persuasion. Men feared to be in Donnelly's debt, knowing of the quiet rage that lived inside of James Sullivan, the man that would dole out justice to those who had it coming.

The newness of the truck wore off when Jimmy neared his father. Nothing compared to the exhilaration and safety that his da gave him. He jumped from the truck without it slowing down. "What the *fecking* hell? And another bigger one already born, waiting at home," Donnelly said.

The smell of fresh cut lumber and tar filled Jimmy's nose and head with a sudden awareness of everything around him. His hearing, sight and limbs having an extra feeling. The boy's lungs filled with strength, a feeling that left as soon as it came at times. The one difference was that today . . . young James realized it to be so.

DP Curran

"Good news, James." Donnelly yelled from the truck, as if to defuse any potential ideas the elder Sullivan may have, seeing his boy with the two men.

"What might that be?" James asked, sleeves rolled to the thickest part of his forearms. Sweat and blond hair mixed and glistened in the sun. His father's scent, familiar to his son.

Jimmy spoke first, this was not lost on the three men. "Ma had a baby boy, Da." James did not take his eyes from Andrew, knowing of the boy's oversight.

"This is cause for celebration, James. Take your eldest son and I'll stop by later this evening for a drop or two," Mr. Donnelly spoke, without ever getting out of the truck. Andrew, Donnelly's body guard, was no match for James, few men were. Donnelly would take his respect by way of an unpleasant task for James soon.

The truck drove off, leaving the father and his son to walk home.

"You spoke out of turn, boy. Do you know that, do ya?" James asked, still looking at the truck growing smaller.

"I'm sorry, Da. I didn't want him to be the one . . ."

"There is no fear in ya' concernin' these men, is there son?"

"No, sir, no fear."

"Good enough. You'll not do it again and that is by my orders and mine alone. Do well not to forget that. *Thuiscint?*" A slight pause with the sound of a train's whistle and rattling.

"Understood . . ." Jimmy answered, looking up at his father with the sun stinging his eyes, just out of the shade provided by his father's back.

"Good. The man known as Andrew Laing is a Scotsman, don't forget that. Now, then, tell me about your new brother."

"A boy, Da. A big one says Mrs. Byrne."

"Must be so then, son. It must be so . . ."

The two walked together with the same stride across the construction site, into the brightest of suns. Jimmy walked backwards in front of his father at times. Not missing a step of the old man's cadence as he spoke in volumes about what little he knew of the baby's birth. The boy spoke into the red and blond stubble on his father's face, locked on it and the father filled his chest with the morning air, not looking down as he walked.

There was a bond between father and son, more so than any of the other Sullivan boys. A certain comfort and calmness the two felt for one another. Different in every way from the other rest of the Sullivan boys, though not shown in action or words except when alone. And different they all were, in each one's abilities and talents.

DP Curran

CHAPTER 6

News spread fast in Swampoodle, Mrs. Byrne left nothing to chance. This included the live or dead babies that she delivered. Each with equal enthusiasm, though she treaded with light foot with the likes of James Sullivan.

The smell of the tar pitch roofs pinched the air, as father and son reached the top of the block. The summer sun would soon make the scent permanent all the way into an Indian summer, later in the autumn.

Everything heated up and provided its own smell in summer. The concrete and the tomato vines that grew in small back yards. Shibe Park was a mixture of odors that filled the mind of young with the thrill that a carnival brings. Hot dogs, cotton candy and peanuts by day and the dew of fresh cut grass at night. The smells danced in the bellies of every kid in town before the unknown day that comes to all and erases such things from the forefront of one's mind. It becomes an elusive feeling, a fleeting thrill that returns, if just for a moment, to the oldest of Swampoodle inhabitants. And that, enough to sustain them.

"What will ya' name him, Da? The boy asked, squinting up at his father.

"Michael, after The Archangel. We'll take all the help we can get, son. Not a word of the name, as if you ever knew beforehand. This is between the two of us, *athair go mac.*" which meant father to son in the Irish. James Sr., stopped as did the conversation for a moment, before speaking once more.

"Are you ready, son?" The question posed with a smile.

"Ready, Da . . ." And the two strode up the steps past Mrs. Byrne, who rattled on without ceasing to the consternation of both James Senior and his younger.

The voices of the other children spoke in turn, as they saw and touched the newborn for the first time, save daughter Deirdre, who saw more than any boy might ever see.

The weakened voice of ma, raised above that of the children, as James entered the room.

"Seamus . . ." was all she said.

The room quiet now, James leaned down to his wife in a way that both silenced and moved the children to near tears, for this small amount of affection was as rare a thing to be seen. He whispered the name Michael to her, before kissing her cheek.

"That's a fine name, a fine name, indeed." She mouthed back, their lips and ears touching with the gentleness of seagrass.

James would not deny himself his first lustful thought of Bridget years ago. He drifted back to the reception hosted by his American sponsor, Liam Donnelly, just days after his arrival in land of the free. The steel that was in James Sullivan's blood melted once more at the mere thought of Bridget's strawberry blonde hair pinned at the top. Two long tresses flowed over her large breasts that showcased her tiny waist, giving her an air of modesty. Howbeit, her sly grin told otherwise. Their eyes locked, love bound flesh and soul in that single moment.

All the Clan of Sullivan knew of the respect and bond that existed between their parents, but to show it bonded all of them in those rarest of moments. These times would be few and out of solidarity, more than an outpouring of love, which was never spoken of. They were Sullivan's and that meant, stoic, in all things. Neither death nor tribulation shook those present.

"Let others cry and complain, but not one of you dare." That was hand carved on the smooth hardwood plaque above the front door, for all to see. It was the first thing they were taught to read, and it was recited by every child, regardless of their understanding and long

before the age of knowing. A high tolerance for pain, both emotional and physical was a trait best learned young. So far as, James Sullivan Sr. was convinced.

The smell of cabbage soon filled the house. Mrs. Byrne cooked and ate more cabbage then any person that ever lived. She boiled it with the urgency of a doctor. Small pieces of lamb were cut into strips and mixed into a boil. No one ever saw the actual lamb, more like rabbit in the mind of most, including the Sullivan's.

A small bowl was brought first to Bridget Sullivan, as James took the baby from the grasping hands of the Widow Byrne.

"I'll be taking my new son along with the other boys for a meeting of sorts, Mrs. Byrne," said James.

"He won't understand a word, sir, if you don't mind me saying, Mr. Sullivan." Forgetting herself in the heat of her duties.

"He won't talk when all he needs to do is hear the sound of my voice, Felicity. Something he is sure to get accustomed to sooner than some," said James.

Mrs. Byrne stood in shock at the sound of her first name, for which she hated, and after all she was a mid-wife, a woman of purpose, who should not on any occasion be called out by her first name, in front of children, no less.

Her shock turned to fear at the thought of her loose tongue. A tongue she so wanted to keep even more than a limb, perhaps. An apology was in order and she would craft the finest sincerity known to man before nightfall.

A small amount of laughter was permitted by their father, as the boys descended the stairs behind their father and into the front parlor.

"You'll all have rabbit and cabbage when we're through boys, no worries." The father said, straight faced, what everyone already knew about Mrs. Byrne's lamb and cabbage for which she was famous for in Ireland. With the scarceness of lamb in Swampoodle, the plain widow was resigned to rabbit, caught in her own traps behind her house.

Snickers were herd in the secret meeting of the Sullivan men that afternoon.

"Your new brother's name is, Michael. What name comes to mind when you here that name, boys?" their father asked, holding the crying infant.

Now, all the boys, except for Padraig, due to his tender age, thought first of Michael Shanahan, who was shot dead by the police after robbing the Erie National Bank on 6th & Erie Avenue.

That thought held for a moment, before the boys blurted out in staggered succession, "Michael, The Archangel."

"Good boys, you've done well, despite the many nefarious choices of the name in this neighborhood. Padraig, you'll do well to remember the same." The old man was keen to end the meeting and bring his wailing son back to an awaiting Mrs. Byrne, hovering not far from the closed pocket doors of the parlor, before one last question, the most asked question of all.

"What is it that I ask most from you boys, Sullivan's all?" Their father's face was that of another man, a man Jimmy knew of for certain and he answered without hesitation in his voice.

"That we protect one another from oldest to youngest, top to bottom, no matter what the cost. Never to start, but always to finish." Jimmy was sincere, and his father knew it.

"Do the rest of you understand? Tis' better to handle things yourselves outside this house, rather than come home without your honor and to have it beat back into you. Well, then?"

"Yes, Da." Their words were unanimous.

As the pocket doors opened to Mrs. Byrne, Jimmy knew the responsibility was his concerning his brothers. Lanky and big footed as he was, Jimmy could box better than all his brothers and any kid his age or older in the neighborhood. And then, there was Shane, quiet and wide as a mule. His rage and strength did not lend itself to boxing, but to street fighting. The likes of which was legendary, already by the age of seven. Jimmy could take him by getting off first, but the worm would soon turn, and Jimmy knew it. They were the closest of the Sullivan boys. He looked up to Jimmy and a bond was formed over the years that did not include more than a few skirmishes. All in all, the Sullivan's were thick as thieves, but Shane, he was dangerous in a way that weighed on Jimmy and he carried that weight always.

Young Deirdre and Mrs. Byrne, took turns rocking the newborn, between feedings, as Bridget Sullivan slept on and off, through the night.

James Sr., and his boys ate and spoke of baseball and the conversation soon turned to the church carnival at Saint Columba. It was the most fun the boys had with their da in some time. And then came a knock at the door. Gaggles of women were sure to come by tomorrow to see the baby and bring food for the family, but this was a knock that James was familiar with and the lightness of the evening became heavy.

"Evening, James. Thought I'd come by and pay my respect to the wife and lay my eyes on our newest boy. The future, so to speak." Donnelly was drunk, and James confined him to the porch. Locking eyes with Andrew, who was embarrassed in his own way.

"There will be no visiting this evening, Liam." James said, straight.

"Liam, is it now? No, James, Mr. Donnelly is I and I'm here to pay a visit and have a drink. That's how it's going to work, understood? Now, let's have a look see."

"You'll not pass through my door tonight, not as Liam or Mr. Donnelly, sir" James stepped to him. Andrew took his place now, on the porch.

"Easy, Andrew. If he spits into his hands, they'll be no turning back for any of us. Give my regards to the babe's mother for me and congratulations, again, James. We'll take our leave out of respect, a subject we can discuss in the morning. We'll need to make things right, James. I can't afford to lose Andrew and then have you lurking about. No, much too dangerous, I think, for all. In the morning, then," he said, as he turned to walk away.

"Fan airdeall . . .," said James, as to say stay alert to Andrew.

"That will do, James. Good evening to ya', friend." Donnelly was under a different spell than that of just whiskey. Being disrespected by James Sullivan and his eldest son, be the boy young was unsettling at best. Something not even more whiskey could remedy.

There would be a reckoning come morning.

That night, James slept in the parlor, clothed and ready for what may come. He did not drink when business, as he knew it, was at hand. He gripped and loosened his fists unknowing in the darkened room, as his family slept above, the frequent cries of his new son, under the watchful eye of his Deirdre.

DP Curran

Sleep did not come to James, nor did he need it when pressing matters were at hand. He was a man of instinct, someone that showed up and did what happened. James was as unpredictable as the situation, no more, and no less.

A man that met violence without a pension for emotion. Whether it was violence by orders or by happenstance, emotion did not strengthen or weaken him. He proved to be the sociopath in all things pertaining to family . . . his family.

That night he sat, eyes fixed on the street lamp and waited for first break of dawn.

CHAPTER 7

A crisp dollar bill evoked a smile from a tired Deidre, who sat in a nightgown on the bottom step. Her bare feet and ankles shone the budding signs of a young woman, the picture of her mother she was, minus the brashness.

She watched as her father left without a word into the pre-dawn blur on 22nd Street. The fading light of streetlamps mixed with the hidden sun illuminating the horizon.

Brass knuckles and a blackjack were standard issue for James Sullivan. As well as a Colt Revolver, though he seldom used it, except in matters of being out numbered or ambushed in the course of his duties. He hoped his timing was right as he crossed the open field, known by children as "Dust Field" The one spot on high ground that made baseball possible in a town of low lying pools of water.

DP Curran

James checked his watch, plenty of time to enter the warehouse before Donnelly. The watchman treated James with deference, opening the gates and doors without question or suspicion.

"Good mornin' to ya', Jimmy," said the old prize fighter, "Pug" Moran, who was still capable of knocking out anyone who might underestimate him, regardless of his advanced age. A formidable man with champion's stature. He owned a small gym, and worked a taproom by the docks part-time. Pug had saved more kids than a thousand honest priests might ever hope to. Many a boy ended up in *Pug's Gym*, by word of mouth and results, a legacy . . .

"Mornin', Pug . . ." And the two spared, in jest.

"Early today, Jimmy . . ." Pug was not one for many words, but he knew the score.

"Early bird catches the worm, champ." James said, as keys jangled each door open, all the way to Donnelly's office.

"Or the hawk catching the snake today, is it, Jimmy?" Pug shook his head.

"One way to put it . . ." James lent his eyes.

"Careful, lad, the snake, he is poisonous." Pug and James hands met in a deadlock of friendship and strength.

"Careful, it is then . . ."

"Shut and locked, Jimmy?"

"Aye, Pug . . ." And James Sullivan sat in a wooden chair in the corner behind the door of Donnelly's office and waited.

The office was bare bones, nothing special about it. There was a reason for that and James knew it, but the thought that he could do better bolstered him in a way he hadn't thought of before this morning. The power rested in the man, himself, not in a sparse office with a railroad safe anchored to the floor.

What was Liam Donnelly's strength, who kept him in power, if not for people like James Sullivan? These thoughts were more important than what James was there for in the first place. What, a few toes being stepped on, two proud men and a boy with the balls of his father? The whole reason for being there seemed unimportant now. The real question was, who needed who the most.

No doubt, James Sullivan could be replaced, but so could Liam Donnelly. Sullivan's head raced with opportunity. How would he play this overblown meeting? The fact that he was already sitting in Donnelly's office made it all the more problematic. But his mind was made up, James stayed put and waited, his thoughts just fleeting perhaps. He summoned his blind pride once again. Ambition be damned.

Loud voices echoed in the empty outer rooms of the warehouse. The deep sound of mangled vocal chords, cut with whiskey and tobacco, like a mighty river can do to the hardest of any rock in its path. Another monotone voice accompanied, Donnelly's. The smell of coffee was in the air, Pugs last chore before leaving each morning.

A single key turned the lock and the door swung just to the feet of James Sullivan, who sat, elbows on knees, fist clenched. Blood engulfed his forearms, his sleeves rolled like tourniquets around massive, blonde, freckled limbs.

Coffee cups clanked in the background, as James glazed over with dispassion and a certain limberness which often proceeded unspeakable acts of violence.

Two men entered, unawares. Talking of matters that did not concern James.

Donnelly took his place in one of the chairs, facing his own desk. A sickness fell over James, by a man so easy to submit.

Miles Finnegan, a man with specific credentials, a man with one purpose. Miles was called *'The Negotiator.'* A man more important to the balance of things than any crime figure or elected official. He mediated problems, dilemmas, misunderstandings, premeditated understandings. He was paid and paid well. Miles Finnegan's ruling was final, this was agreed on by the most powerful men in the city, perhaps on the entire coast. It was not important to know anything more about Mr. Finnegan, just to know that when he made a ruling, it was the end of any further discussion.

First the finest of tweed hats, then a light suit jacket, taken off without haste by the slight, short man with impeccable hair. Red at one time, now a lighter amber shade of grey. He sat in the large chair, more wood than leather, behind Liam Donnelly's desk and took out pencil and paper from a tan brief case. The snaps of its brass fasteners made things, all the more official.

Mr. Finnegan looked up, with neither surprise or anger at James, sitting in the same pose.

"Good morning, Mr. Sullivan." In that moment, Liam Donnelly, turned to see the most dangerous of all men he had ever known—the death he had dreamt of the night before. His heart heaved, a man on the verge of vomiting.

"Good day, Mr. Finnegan." James spoke, without moving his frame.

"*Comhghairdeas,* Seamus. And my respects to your wife, at this special time." A rare deviation from business by Mr. Finnegan, but his congratulations was much appreciated by James. Thus, proving once again the man's prowess for impartial negotiation.

"Thank you, Mr. Finnegan, sir."

"Now, let's get down to it then. Your performance thus far has been exemplary. Your methods sound and to the letter. We even forego your penchant for the extreme at times. Given your nature, that is excepted, without question. There are those in much higher positions in this world who, let me say, admire your extra flare, as it were. With that being said, there are subordination concerns, nothing serious mind you, James, but concerns none the less. Check your compass, James. Be sure to stay on course is what I'm obliged to tell you, sir. Perhaps, pass along the same to your eldest son and his youngers. We welcome you all, Mr. Sullivan, but there must be order. Keep that order and there will be more in it for you than . . ., well, this." Finnegan, paused before, looking over his bifocals at the meager office conditions.

"Temperance, James . . . not so much as a beating over this. Should Mr. Donnelly turn up dead, you will be contacted. Otherwise, you'll not see me again, except in passing, sir. Now, out of pocket, five hundred dollars or gold coin to Mr. Donnelly and a handshake, to be witnessed and noted. For you, Mr. Donnelly, an apology and a sober and sincere visit to the Sullivan home out of respect for his wife and the blessed birth of their son, Michael Sullivan. You'll not visit there again, for any reason whatever." A full sheet of penciled paper was presented to James. He skimmed through it, as Mr. Finnegan, uttered one short name, "Ian" and summoned with his hand toward the doorway.

The tallest, widest man James had ever seen shone himself for the first time. He lit a wooden match and without a sound let the papers burn to his fingertips, until there was nothing but ash, for which he smeared on the wooden floor with a shiny boot in front of James, now standing. James surmised that Ian, as it were, was a good four inches taller than himself. He was impressed but, in that shortness of time, thought of how he might kill the beast, if need ever arise.

An apology was given by Liam Donnelly, in the time it took to shake hands in the middle of the room. Witnessed with a surprising amount of attentiveness on the part of Mr. Finnegan. James retrieved five gold coins taken from five different pockets and handed all to Donnelly in a stack, heads all facing down.

"Duly noted, for the record, gentlemen. Take a few days with your family, James. See yourself out through the garage. A new truck has been assigned to you, a company truck, mind you, but for your own use as well. You need not walk home again, unless if by choice, of course. Take your pick, as long as it's unmarked, which, of course, is black."

"Thank you, Mr. Finnegan, sir."

"an-mhaith . . ." which is to say very good. Mr. Finnegan lapsed in and out of two worlds and his speech was proof of it.

James Sullivan chose the ink black Model T truck, without the added notoriety of Donnelly's logo. A caveat not lost on James, given his extra work at nights.

In the end, Donnelly decided to go to the bosses and have *'The Negotiator'* settle his dilemma with James Sullivan. It seemed to be a smart move for all involved.

DP Curran

A brand new, black truck pulled up to James, as he stood in the garage. A man of small stature slid from the seat. He pulled with him a clean white cloth that covered the long bench seat, revealing the leather upholstery that his son felt with the sweaty hands of an inquisitive boy, just one day before. To the chagrin of Liam Donnelly, who was now, perhaps, getting more than he had bargained for, after all, having called for *'The Negotiator.'* And James, without ever knowing until this day, was more valuable than he knew. He had seen the other side of the coin now. And he would be a better man for it.

The matter was not mentioned between Donnelly or Sullivan. A cordial visit by Mr. and Mrs. Donnelly was the last remnant of the incident. It was not spoken of again and general sense of autonomy was afforded James from that point on. Though James did not trust or ever take light the possibility of Donnelly's penchant for revenge. A particular eye was kept on the Scotsman, Andrew Laing.

CHAPTER 8

The baby, Michael, was not so much as to be taken out onto the porch to escape the stuffiness of the house that summer. No self-respecting Catholic would dare take a newborn from the safety of the home before a baptism was performed. Noisy house fans gave the mere allusion of coolness for the children, along with a rhythmic humming sure to put one to sleep at night. A block of ice was delivered late in the day just to be put into a tray behind a large fan in the front bedroom of James and Bridget where baby Michael slept, as well.

The iceman came and went without payment just as the milkman, breadman, paperboy or any other delivery that might incur a routine payment. The mail didn't come to the Lehigh Avenue house. That was sent to the home still owned by James on Taylor Street. The mail was brought by an apprentice of sorts and delivered to *'The*

Lehigh House', as it was known. Not one piece of unwelcome news, be it in the form of letter or package ever darkened the doorstep of Bridget Sullivan. No, not ever.

Preparations were being made for a Catholic Baptism at Saint Columba Church, with a huge party to follow at Dunleavy Hall. As after every such gathering, the regulars would march back to the Sullivan's home. Every man, swearing his allegiance to the IRA a dozen times each, without a trace of the English language to be heard.

Every woman for blocks would make their signature dish to bring to the celebration, though friends of Mr. Donnelly sent catered food in from the central business and government district known as Center City. Even the Honorable Harry Mackey, the Mayor of Philadelphia had sent his regards to James Sullivan himself, by courier. To Taylor street, of course. All of this for a man that James had never met. The writing was on the wall for Liam Donnelly. He knew all along the time would come, but never did he imagine the actual day. He failed to plan what was to come.

James took everything in stride when it came to whom or what his extracurricular activities affected. Be it, good or bad. He had put those thoughts of worry out of his mind long ago as a boy in Ireland. His father and brothers, killed by the English, as his mother and sister Lilly watched. He was hardened with a sense of duty. He did not give or look for sympathy in a cruel world. Such was his relationship with

God Almighty, life on life's terms, though he did pray or talk to God, as he put it. It was a mutual understanding, a knowing James thought that things as they were, he would take care of his family. God would have to explain the rest when they came each . . . face to face in the end.

Every detail was thought of. Safety for the Sullivan family and close friends. Not to mention Donnelly's own security detail. Which, by far, was much greater than that of James Sullivan. Not so much because of Donnelly's value or importance, but anyone involved in the rackets feared James more on a personal level. Any attempt on James's life would bring the ire of the Italian factions, as well. James was held in high regard by the Italian families. A rare feat for an Irishman, let alone one off the boat. He had performed duties for them without consequence or suspicion, all with the approval of '*The Irish in Center City*.' This served two purposes for James's bosses. They made money from James's attention to detail and any specific requests other men might find objectionable were done to the letter. Also, it was proof to the Italian's that James would be a terrible adversary in a war. It was well known that the Italian's were, first and foremost, family men and did not involve civilians. A baptism was sacred, and any violence was considered an infamia. A disgrace.

The other Irish rivals, the first generation American-Irish did not share this virtue.

DP Curran

Sullivan had been protected more than he knew up to this point, but any unsuccessful attempt on his life would mean a personal vendetta for James. Certain rules did not apply to him. Due in large part to his gruesome efficiency of his work. He had dealt in brutal fashion with the first generation Irish, those born in America. *'The Natives'* or *'The Firsties'* as they were known as in Philadelphia. He had taken the advice of one, Aengus O'Boyle, as gospel and carried out his words with unprecedented violence. No calling cards or warnings, just total annihilation. James took a page from his heroes' book on justice. Bodies were left impaled when deemed necessary by James alone. Any type of an example needed by Donnelly or the big bosses meant impalement or dismemberment. The latter being the rule for anyone high profile, that James had no discretion in whatever.

The sheer fact that the Pennsylvania Railroad blacksmiths and their apprentices hammered out iron spears that James kept in long crates in boxcars in the fenced section of Donnelly's shop was enough to keep all in the know sharp and loyal.

This along with the unmistakable power shift made Donnelly nervous and he went to the bosses in Center City one too many times about the fact. When all the while James's career did not parallel Donnelly's in the least. His discontent led to a visit by the most interesting of men after being shown the door not a full day before in Center City.

It was afternoon, James had been given a letter to be delivered in person that morning. No doubt to prove the sincerity of its content. This was rare, but orders were carried out not questioned. The change in routine would keep him all the sharper. He looked at everything as a possible hit, a test at least. This delivery was to a butcher shop on Lehigh Avenue, his pursuit of the intended recipient was the head butcher and owner.

Otto uttered the words, "Thank you," as he took the envelope with a look of a man beaten down by circumstance. His eyes fixed on the envelope. James took no pleasure in the ruin of a working man, but it was speculation, something James Sullivan could not indulge in.

The heat from the concrete and slate sidewalks cooked a man's feet in his boots in summer. Something James had not experienced in Ireland. He walked to the shop alone each morning, leaving his truck inside the gates of Donnelly's warehouses and out buildings. The long section of railroad track that aligned to meet the loading docks were gated, also. All deliveries were made at night under dim drop lights and the cover of a vast darkness that stretched well into the abandoned fields surrounding the building and its operations. Land owed on paper by Donnelly. Much like everything else thought to be his including his home, cars, horses and several speakeasies. More like whorehouses with liquor than anything resembling a night club.

DP Curran

Liam Donnelly played his part and was paid well for it, but every man or woman involved could be eliminated and things would go on. That's just how things worked, and they did work. Anyone got too greedy or had thoughts of self-advancement was wise to keep it to themselves. Though Donnelly . . . well, Donnelly had been runnin' his mouth so long he had lost all sense of consequence. His use of Big James Sullivan to settle personal scores became a liability to those above him. There was too much money at stake to lose a man like James on the personal whims of Liam Donnelly. His loose lips and the drink had made things worse, word of his drunken visit to the Sullivan home came at a cost. In the financial sense and a visit from a man no one wanted to meet, not even by happenstance at a gala event, where one might enjoy the illusion of relaxation or brevity.

It was clear which man was more valuable for the future. Donnelly's mention of James Sullivan Jr., as brazen and loyal to his father, sparked the interest of powerful men, as well. What was to be an admonishment by Donnelly, served to endear the boy's size and spirit to many. The apples did not fall far from the tree, not for Jimmy or his brother Shane. Yes, the future was in the Sullivan's favor. All without James's knowledge. He was a man who took orders and did the hard things, the dark matter that keeps any organization of this kind in the black, and out of the red. The scales must be tipped in one way alone, and James Sullivan made sure of that.

Something for which he was unaware of in his duties, he was a perfect instrument. His value could not be measured in terms of one quality alone, for this he was protected on high. Every level of power had James Sullivan earmarked for a position. He thinned the herd, kept those that would upset the balance of business in Philadelphia shifting and moving to safer, easier, marketplaces. The term outskirts of town had a new meaning, reserved for low life hoods, petty thieves, or the grandiose hot shot looking to do the impossible.

There was but one man standing outside of the front of the shop this morning. Not a large man per se, but a serious one with the sharp features of a hawk. He wore a light-colored suit with a derby hat, revealing blonde hair and a clean-shaven face. The man looked away, but never down, as James entered the bulletproof glass front showroom façade that faced the street.

The smell of fresh scones filled James with the flames of his youth in Ireland and he did follow that aroma to the back office. Three sharp knocks before entering shown an all but gruesome sight. That of Liam Donnelly still seated in his chair behind his desk. His throat was sliced from one ear to the other, which gave the illusion of a smile, clown like. Blood ran down a leather bib of sorts into a pan, not unlike the ones James used for the ice blocks that were delivered like clockwork for Bridget and the baby Michael for the hot and humid nights that Philadelphia provided all who lived there.

DP Curran

There was something missing in the midst of such a scene. One which James took in stride, still not knowing who the two men were in the office. It was the smell of burnt coffee that mixed with the ever-present fumes of paint and lacquer used in the shop. Being just two men, fear had not entered into the mind of James Sullivan Sr. Though a quiet increasing rage boiled like the kettle on the black iron stove in the corner. Then the silence was broken, with a gloved clap, against the desk with one hand.

"The knock of *'The Trinity'*—Good afternoon, Seamus. Come in now, and be good enough to shut the door. Mind you, this is no reflection on you whatever, but it involves you, none the less. Your reputation proceeds ya', so . . . let me get to the point, as so me and Amin here don't end up worse off than this big mouth, self-aggrandizing mother fucker ya' see sittin' before us bleedin' out. And his boy Andrew, ya' won't be seein' the likes of him no more. Scotland lost a son before dawn, Seamus." This said, with the second man, a tall man holding a shotgun with the barrel cut down.

The talking man stood and looked square into the eyes of James Sullivan, looking for something that wasn't there, fear or concern for the man with the shotgun or the dead man in the chair, covered in blood. James's light blue eyes against his rope thick blonde hair, provided a pale fear that could not be ignored, for it was the face of death itself. From his eyes and the pores of his skin, James exuded death, he had a certain musk to him. What was attraction to a woman, was as death to a gangster. Seconds seemed as minutes, with the red second hand of a greasy silver clock hung high on the wall, keeping score.

In that moment between life and death, a man notices things . . . things that are so acute and important in that moment. Inexplicable in its way, known by many, spoken of or remembered by few. The man's left arm hung lifeless at his side. He had gone so far by habit, perhaps to lift it with his right hand and place it on the desk as if to balance himself as any man might.

"I'm Finbar O'Boyle, Seamus. My brother told you we would meet one day when it was necessary. Well, it is necessary, and I wanted to make a good impression for you, given my little brother's trust in you. Notwithstanding the fine job, you've done here without one complaint. Not one, in how many years now, twelve it must be, twelve if it's a day, Seamus O'Suilebhain, no, or be it more?"

Seamus did not answer, he looked at the man with the shotgun with a look reserved for the new dead.

"We can do without that now, Amin. Is that not correct, Seamus? After all, we are brothers-in-law. Aye, you've be given the finest export ever yielded by Ireland." This produced a slit eyed grin, that exposed a row of small teeth. Finbar continued.

DP Curran

"Liam Donnelly had a purpose, like you, me . . ., like all of us, don't ya' see? There is no room for selfishness and disrespect, not when you've sworn otherwise, no, not when you've sworn otherwise, Seamus. You . . . well, you understand that better than most. Better than all, and that's what we need, Seamus. That's what we need, commitment. Not this piece of shite, one of those who start out at their peak, never any growth, just lies. Men as this lie to themselves every day, long after anyone else is listening. Ya' don't always know at first, but when ya' do, ya' have to end it. End it before it grows in others, like that Andrew he brought over, without even so much as a mention. Forget permission. Many men, some innocent, no doubt died because of it. Chances are for suckers, Seamus. We can't afford it, no matter the cost at times. But, in the end, when we looked at this man as a whole, the thing that bothered me most was him going to your home, your home Seamus. The very thing that was taken from us both once before. The thought of one of our own stealing the peace you've created in your home was his death sentence. I told him so myself, gagged he was, as so I would not be interrupted. I told him, I did.

You've not interrupted me once and your calmness is, I have to say Seamus unnerving as hell, man. Am I right, Amin? Jesus, Mary and Joseph it is unnerving." Finbar blessed himself and the three men sat in the presence of Liam Donnelley, eating fresh Irish soda bread with tea as hot as any man might ever want. And the spirit of Ireland was upon them, a feeling Seamus O'Suilebhain had longed for. And he was Seamus O'Suilebhain, if for one day, so be it.

The thought of returning to Ireland felt a possibility for the first time in twelve years. A longing in his heart for the rolling green hills of his Emerald Isle. A possibility he dared not dream of before now. He had not asked of his mother or sister in all this time, but today he would.

With the sound of '*The Tinkers*' hard at work behind a metal door, the memories of sea grass of home sprouted up around the men, as they slipped into Irish tongues and the splendor thereof.

And it was made known to James that he would return home to Ireland, so that he might gather up his aged mother and see for himself the condition of his sister, Lilly.

Mrs. O'Boyle had past not four months prior, at the age of fifty-five or says this, her eldest son, Finbar. The woman herself was a legend, a rock to all around her, for she offered more than herself. Orla O'Boyle gave all a sense of what it was to be Irish, to be worth something more than what the English had tried so hard to kill inside of all that they could not kill outright. She was dignity, strength and hope. With her gone now, it was thought best for all concerned that James gather up what remained of his family. Peace of mind would pay dividends and with prohibition looming, the Irish would need

James Sullivan more than ever. That would be discussed more in detail upon his return from Ireland after the baptism of his son, Michael.

'The Night Cleaners', as they were known, would be at the shop at dusk. Any remains of Liam Donnelly would vanish like a short thunderstorm in the humid night air over Swampoodle.

Talk rose from the shop and turned to whispers, then to nothingness into the passing hours that led to a new-found friendship.

"Tomorrow evening at seven, James. Will that not be an imposition?" Finbar asked, popping the lid of his derby.

"It would be an honor, sir," James said.

"Refreshing is this man who stands before us, Amin. Not a first name, nor last, this whole time we've spent together. When my brother is right, he is right and that, well, that hurts a bit, it does. All for the best in your case Seamus O'Suilebhain. Enjoy the sound of that name in your mind now, for it won't be spoken of unless it's ceremonial, yet we understand it being used as a term of affection by those close to you . . ." Finbar paused and turned, before speaking again.

"Lock everything up tight, but let *'The Tinkers'* finish their shift. You'll see *'The Night Cleaners'* in. You'll know them by their knock and gold coin is the preferred method of payment. One for each man, including Mr. Donnelly, of course—a generous tip is common place." Two stacks of gold coin were placed on the desk of Liam Donnelly, in a last act of official business. "Goodnight then, Mr.

Sullivan." And the man with the decorative arm and sharp wit left with tall Amin. As tall a man as James had ever laid eyes on. He thought again of how he would take the tall man apart, if the need ever arose. Such was the mind of Mr. Sullivan.

Not a man of keys, for good reason, nor spare change in his pockets. Lest anyone hear him coming. James was, however, prepared. Rather than sit with his lifeless sponsor, whose body was now showing signs of transformation, James took to the shop after securing the front. It was clear that no man would be using the front door for business this day.

No one spoke to James unless spoken to first. Some men in the shop had not uttered to him a word in Irish or English, ever. One man in the shop was as close to what one might call a friend than anyone. The one *'Firstie'* in Donnelly's employ. Tom Kirkpatrick, his family steeped in revolution history against the English. Known as Tommy to all but James, Tom it was.

Tommy was a truck driver, a delivery man for the Irish faction. He delivered supplies for the shop full of *'The Tinkers'*, as well, men who neither asked questions or even spoke English in the shop. Each one shanghaied from Irish factories and shipyards for their talents. The exceptions were those transferred from Northeastern Pennsylvania. Miners and rail workers for the Reading Railroad Company. Coal and iron, mined and transported across the country.

"Have ya' a cigar, Tom?" James asked.

"Hand rolled shit leaves is all." Tom replied, wiping his hands on a clean rag from the drum. He enjoyed his time with James.

"My brand then, Tom." James did not favor cigars, the thought of removing the stench of his former boss from his nostrils gave rise to the cigar. It served its purpose, and even had an agreeable flavor to it. Tom's trips down south produced the discarded leaves of tobacco fields that Tom brought back in bushel baskets.

"For the one honest man that I know . . ." Tom struck a stick match on his thumbnail, but James shook his head.

"A man should light his own smoke, Tom. Otherwise ya' give a part of yourself away each time another holds a match for ya' . . ." The big man sliced a half inch off the tip with a razor-sharp knife and drew his own smoke.

"A man in my position doesn't always have that luxury, James."

"Change your position, Tom. Opportunity is all about."

"For a '*Firtsie*', workin' with intruders? Somedays, I believe I'm neither. Expendable is all, just waitin' for the bullet I'll never see. That's not feelin' bad for myself either. That's the best I see it, is all. Not seein' it comin', that ain't so bad is it, James?"

"You're not Italian, Tom. The Irish always see it comin', we make a point of it with our own. Not a bad thought, but it won't happen that way."

"What do you suppose my options are? I have no trouble with killin' a man for cause, but what good could it do me in this country?"

"You attended school here, learned the language and ways of the Americans and Italians. You know all too well our ways, the Irish way. No, Tom—you're a valuable asset to anyone smart enough to recognize it. And some have—look at your connections down south alone. The Irish will make their mark there someday. I'd like to be part of that, your next run, ya' know, the next trip down, I'll come along to look things over. I'd like to run a boat of me own from here to there, Tom. Not so much for adventure as opportunity, it's endless . . ."

"Who that might be that thinks me a commodity, is a secret well kept, James. *'The Natives'* want information from me, as do the Irish and Italians. Time is counted in minutes for me, but I appreciate your faith in me, I do."

"Ya' haven't betrayed a soul, Tom. I would have been the one to tend to ya'. Face to face, not this behind the ear shit. Such mercy lay elsewhere, with the Italians."

"Either way, a matter of time. My hair is turnin' white all too soon, Big James Sullivan." Tom wiped the sweat from his right ear with the back of his hand.

"If ya' could work with me, Tom. With me direct, would ya' be willin'? My children, me daughter and me boys are no different than you, Tom."

"They're your clan, James. Your blood, no man set foot in their shadow. Ya' know that . . ."

"And why is that, Tom? Because they're protected by my word and deeds, same be true for you too. You'd be my clan . . . I don't say these things with a light touch, I need a man I can rely on, Tom. You've always been square with me. Plus, you're about the one man I can converse with who doesn't want bloodshed by my hands. Your family's commitment to Ireland is not lost on me, Tom. A man needs one friend in this place. Least that's what I've come to believe . . ."

"I said you were honest earlier, James. Honest in both life and death is how I see it. I'm your man to the end, be it at your word, sir."

"Sir won't do, Tom. James, from here on out, no matter the company we're in."

"For certain are ya' now?"

"It's the least I can do, you havin' the misfortune of bein' born on foreign soil and all . . ." For the first time in Thomas Kirkpatrick's life, he noticed a short smile on one, James Sullivan.

'The Tinkers' clocked out in the same precision in which they worked with molten metals making the necessary repairs to machines,

equipment and the like. Each man leaving out the back, without being told.

"Stay with me here tonight, Tom. You'll be seein' what ya' already suspect, but bein' in the same room makes you an accomplice, an accomplice to murder. You're a student of American history, Tom. A great famous man, an American once said, *'Either we hang together, or we hang separately.'* I'm of the same thinking, someday you'll tell me that man's name, for which I already know." The two men walked to the metal door and Tom entered the world of James Sullivan.

"Scone, Tom?" Tom, looked in amazement at what sat before him. His hands tingled and there was a lightness about him.

"No, thank you, James."

"Had to let ya' see it, Tom, death's flower is bloomin' here this evenin', let's wait in front. Close both doors, will ya' Tom?" James left the scone and made his way to the percolator, where a good half urn of coffee sat, burnt.

The two sat and talked of Ireland, places the two of them knew well. Places where children played, swam, and fought each day. Most of all they spoke of the Bay of Donegal, the hours past and each story sped the clock, as if they were paying for the time. Then . . .

Three distinct knocks echoed through the shop. The sound of *'The Trinity'*. *'The*

DP Curran

Night Cleaners' had arrived.

Seven men entered the building with the unconcerned gait of professional movers. Each in coveralls, carrying drop cloths at first. The last man closing and locking the door behind him.

Lights turned to darkness behind the shop. Three more raps at the back door, as one of the men unlocked it in silence. A covered truck coasted to the door in reverse. Mops, buckets and cans of chemicals were brought in. No man spoke a word, not a second wasted on thought or planning. James reached into his pocket, where ten cold coins were taped together in a roll. He had no way knowing when the day would come he may need the coins. James kept twelve taped together at all times, many a man knocked cold while holding the coins in his massive fist. Remembering the words of Aengus O'Boyle. This was the time. James considered the sizeable sum that Finbar had left, as an oversight. James would place it in the money safe at the Taylor Street house, he would let Aengus know of it.

One man in the crew pointed when needed and wore a flat tweed cap. James handed the man the coin. A tip of the hat was all.

CHAPTER 9

"Flowers—Plenty of flowers, that's what sets off a real celebration from a poor one, Bridget. Weddings, funerals, all of the sacraments concerning children and the like . . ." Finbar was adamant. Putting down the heavy bottomed crystal tumbler of whiskey.

A pause fell over the lavish parlor of Bridget Sullivan. She was no stranger to the O'Boyle's, though not raised with any. The marriage had been arranged as Aengus O'Boyle had suggested and he was right, James was not disappointed. Bridget was a natural beauty, with long strawberry blonde hair and skin like milk. Her lips gave the appearance of lipstick, though she did not wear makeup. She was as beautiful a person, sensibilities shown in every matter. Her love was unconditional, as was her husband's. The two spoke in a language known but by two hearts beating as one. This marriage was arranged, though in the minds of James and Bridget, not by Aengus alone, who visited his sister often and was close. He was, also, closer than any of his own brothers to his cousin, Owen Morrison.

"Fine, Finbar, but should you be getting too involved? This is a closeness we've not shown here in Ireland or America." Bridget was held in modest regard by her eldest brother.

"Planning is all, Dove. The future belongs to the children. Planning is all." Finbar smiled a true smile and nodded his head, as if to be contemplating something pleasant.

"Just planning?" Bridget sang.

"To plan is to pay, Dove. Nothing less than the finest, you make the list of what's needed or wanted. No holding back, you're as stubborn as your husband, you are. What Aengus was thinking, I'll never know . . . we have each other's word then?"

"Just to be contrary, I will agree, but I won't be makin' a habit of it, brother or no brother, mind you."

"That's our girl, now. Record the date, James, I've witnessed a miracle and, though I blaspheme, I consider it one, indeed." The laugh of a serious man is oft upsetting.

"Deirdre, bring the lot, dear . . ." Bridget raised her voice in such a way as it would soothe a person, child and adult alike.

The children lined up each in order of age to say goodnight to their uncle. With one exception.

"Goodnight, Uncle Finbar," said James Sullivan Jr., reaching out his hand and looking his uncle straight in the left eye, as his father had taught him. The first son took that honor, no matter his age in the world, different than most.

"Well now, Jimmy. We've heard nothing but good things about you and we are all proud of ya', know that. You've your father's face and build or the makings there of and a hearty handshake to go with it. Sleep well, boy and learn all that you can in and out of school. Be seeing ya' soon, James Sullivan Jr.," and the line followed with Deirdre, the spitting image of her mother, though a bit taller even now.

Each child was given by sleight of hand and respect, a twenty-dollar bill. Other than James Jr., Finbar could not believe the sheer size and comportment of Shane Sullivan. He was a sight to behold, closer to his mother than his father. Not by choice as much as a natural bond that was well known by his siblings and parents. James Sr., admired that and the way he looked after his sister and brothers. He was already feared by much older boys in the neighborhood, for good reason. He fought anyone and everyone. Finbar noted this in his notepad, in a shorthand code designed for himself alone.

Shane stood back from his uncle, staring with the disapproving look of a seasoned outlaw, an eye for such things, such men as this. He looked to his father who motioned him to his side. Finbar greeted the rest of the children, with a serpent's guile for Shane and his father.

DP Curran

With the children in bed, Bridget left James and Finbar to themselves. She pulled the pocket doors closed with eyes averted.

"Fine family, James. Potential in all, no doubt. I have to say it, James—Shane is the mightiest cross between an O'Boyle and O'Suilebhain than anyone might pray for. I've not seen or heard the likes thereof before this night. Takes reasonable thought out of a man seeing that, startling."

"Aye, the boy has his own way about him. A natural affinity for his mother, God help the one that gives him even the impression of dishonoring the woman. I see the boy watchin' men's eyes, delving into their hearts as he walks with her. Same with his brothers and sister."

"Best make your peace with him now, lay the cards on the table."

"That's my son, Finbar . . . we have an understanding, me and the boy. Do we, do you and I have the same?" A proud yet tired man stared up at James.

"*Teahlaigh, Seamus O'Suilebhain.* Family . . ."

"'Tis right and true, Finbar." James looked to the ceiling and sighed with heavy feeling.

"Better asked than to think wrong. We must all be clear in mind and motive, I trust you all the more, be it possible, Seamus. You've done more than anyone could expect of a man left to his own discretion. Aengus knows you've been loyal and patient. Not one problem, not one order not followed to the letter. You have proved invaluable. This, all this Seamus, your home, wife and children. Everything you've done since coming here, top shape. Order, discipline, loyalty, discretion. You've even managed the impossible for most . . . love. The single hardest emotion to admit for us, the Irish. You've shown it in a thousand ways, without ever saying it, yet you've asked for nothing." The stoic repetition of the grandfather clock mitigated any feelings of weakness, concerning talk of love. Something James found repugnant on its face.

"I was told of what was to be, I do these things out of duty and responsibility. The one curse of a good life, I believe Aengus once told me."

"You were told the truth and you have carried the load thus far. We've much to do, Seamus and you will be at the helm for much of it. Prohibition now, combined with our other interests, will enable us to allocate funds for our home, for Ireland."

"Aye," said James, with satisfaction.

"After the baptism of baby Michael, everything will be laid out in a meeting in Atlantic City on the Fourth of July, at the Blenheim Hotel . . ."

James interjected. "I was to go back to Ireland and tend to my business after the baptism, Finbar. My mind is set, this can wait."

"Seamus, you've waited out of agreement not argument. The time will be soon, and you'll be told when, just relax your mind and body. It's soon, that's all I can say for now . . ."

"By soon, no longer than the end of the year, Finbar. Is that what your promisin' now?"

"For both of our sakes, Seamus . . ."

"Be it soon then."

"The King of Swampoodle, thank you, for letting me be in charge. The meeting will include, Mr. Johnston, our host . . . enough of the English speak, Seamus." And Finbar and James talked well into the night of things to come, including Thomas Kirkpatrick's role. All in their native tongue . . .

CHAPTER 10

Saint Columba Church was a grand feat of architectural design. Inlayed with an Irish green tile, befitting the Lord. Adorned with every conceivable thought put into honoring not just God, but Ireland as well. A cathedral more than a church, ceilings to the heavens, artisan stained glass and statues surrounded the thick oak pews. Not one child might consider themselves bored with so much to marvel at.

The echo and perpetual sweet smell of incense made the church a refuge for all. From the most faithful of Catholics to the worst criminal element. Each found a semblance of hope in the shadow of the Lord's House. For some it was a daily or weekly respite for their misdeeds, through the sacrament of confession. Civilian and gangster alike.

James Sullivan did not share such views as these. He entered the house of God with a sense of neutrality, as if everything would be sorted out in the end. He did not scoff at religion, for his wife Bridget and daughter Deidre shared an abiding faith and devotion to Jesus Christ and the Catholic Church. This was not so apparent in all his son's, however.

The one exception being, Padraig. He was an altar boy and sang in the choir, his voice left little room for detractors, silent may they be. A tenor, at a young age, was rare, one with such range and talent even more so. Padraig managed the stables for the church, rectory and convent, his humble yet tough nature made him formidable among other children and adults alike. His knowledge of Catechism and interest in theology gave every indication of his becoming a Catholic priest. A fact that was held in high regard by his mother and teachers. Others kept their opinions to themselves. Including James Sullivan Sr., who would support his son in this endeavor, for no better reason of how the boy handled himself on the street. If this was the boy's calling, God had made him tough in all ways and this was pleasing to James, though not spoken of in private with his son, as of yet. The boy would have to pursue it with a passion if he wanted it. That's all James required of his sons, that whatever they endeavored to do in life, do it with passion and forthrightness for all to see.

Large cars filled the streets surrounding Saint Columba. The people of Swampoodle were not accustom to this. Those that owned a car used it for trips outside the city and those were few. Horses, still prevalent contrasted two different worlds, each defended with equal fervor. Families walked to church together, in any weather or season. These cars were driven by chauffeurs dressed in black in the humidity that claimed Philadelphia each summer.

Strangers to most were attended to as they exited the church. A gesture of helpfulness more than anything of a physical nature. The chauffeurs stayed with their cars, while thick men of fair complexion each escorted their superiors through the ornate oak doors of Saint Columba Church.

Stragglers from the High Mass gathered outside the church in what was an unprecedented scene of attention for a child's baptism in the history of Swampoodle. Newspaper men mingled with the crowd asking questions, hoping to get a salacious answer from one careless soul, but all knew better. James Sullivan Sr. was a quiet, generous man in his community. A man who settled disturbances with a mere look, a man who gave to those who had not. All any of these neighbors need think of was a Christmas made whole by the generosity of the quiet man who took care of his own and meted out justice to those deserving of it. No, there would be no scandalous remarks made, not by the loyal inhabitants of Swampoodle.

Police directed the flow of people and cars and it was now apparent who oversaw Swampoodle.

DP Curran

Councilmen and local organizers shook hands with the overflow of people, taking advantage of the boon that was gathered unawares. They were prohibited from entering the church by Lorcan Finn, the O'Boyle's eyes and ears. He knew everyone from the underbelly of the city to politicians, the useful ones and their opposites. Lorcan was public relations, a slight man who took it all in and was as much responsible for a man's fate as any. The sight of him sowed the seeds of common sense. One notation in a daily report from Lorcan Finn was oft times the difference between paying points or death in the extreme. A meeting was inevitable, if your name was in his most meticulous notes, all compiled from memory and prepared each night for the following morning. In cases of immediate importance, Lorcan administered the news with a whisper to Finbar himself. He did not once speak to James Sullivan—James was the Grim Reaper or '*An Reaper ghruama*' in the Irish. All from Ireland knew him as such, '*The Firsties*' called him the Viking at first, but that soon faded. He was '*An Reaper ghruama*' to all, even the Italians referred to him as such, il cupo mietitore. With all due respect given. Finn was forbidden to write the letters of his name, let alone speak his name, least it be worth his own life.

A full church for a baptism was unheard of in Swampoodle and perhaps most anywhere. Michael Sullivan was being baptized in the blood of Christ, anointed in holy water, just as sure as Seamus

O'Suilebhain was being baptized into death. Bridget Sullivan's brother, Aengus O'Boyle, stood as Michael's Godfather this Sunday. No words were to be spoken, other than to the priest in lieu of responses concerning the baptismal services. No interaction with anyone else would be allowed. Bridget's oldest cousin, Daniel O'Bannon, had made Aengus's presence a possibility, though be it brief and at the church only. Aengus was wanted by the authorities in England, America, and Ireland. The charges were many, murder alone meant the noose, itself.

Daniel O'Bannon's name and reputation were impeccable in both Europe and America. He was on the Board of Directors for the Chase Bank in New York. He helped balance the scales, as it were. Nothing left to the wind.

An Irishman in a top position, with a first generation Irish-American as his confidant was a gamble the O'Boyle's were not ready to take. A gamble that could pay dividends for decades to come, but it wouldn't be Thomas Kirkpatrick. Aengus would not sanction it, under any conditions, a fact that James was still unaware of. James had made his case in his home with Finbar and it was agreed upon, though tentative and still a few years away from ever being instituted in theory. Many contacts and political leaders from both countries had to meet and find James to be more than just '*An reaper ghruama*'.

The celebration after the baptism was more formal than anyone from Swampoodle had ever seen, including the Sullivan's. It was ceremonial and a necessary part of business at the next level, the highest level. For James Sullivan, it was the pomp and circumstance that he despised, yet did for his son, Michael, his family and for Ireland.

The reception was held at the landmark building known as The Bellevue Stratford Hotel at 200 South Broad Street. A playhouse for the rich and famous. The Sullivan's closest friends were in attendance, with many left behind in Swampoodle. Something for which James and Bridget would make up for the following weekend at Donavan's Hall in Swampoodle.

"Seamus, come with me. Follow my lead as I introduce ya' to the money men. Don't break any hands while shakin' em', for Christ's sake . . ."

"Shall I fetch Tom?"

"Fetch Tom? First of all, they'll be no more fetchin', not the word nor its meanin'. What the fuck, Seamus? We'll bring Thomas around in due time. Say as little as possible. Come now."

"Congressman Cahill, I'd like you to meet the man of the hour, who's son's baptism we celebrate here today . . ."

The rest of the day consisted of the same, Finbar's strategy was to introduce James to the most influential men in his pocket first. Then he would at another date announce the two being acquainted to other associates after the fact. All of this preceding the meeting in Atlantic City in less than one month's time. All at once, force feed them all. Everyone knew of James, now it was time to let the monster out of his cage. And James, was as real as they came, no pretense.

"Tell me again, how that son of a bitch took home plate out of Shibe Park one more time, James . . . and this time, this time tell it for my friend here, Senator Weston. Paul, come over here and sit with us . . ." So, it was with the Irish, a story for every occasion.

"Pleased to know you, Senator, allow me to introduce my associate and good friend Tom Kirkpatrick . . ." The reign of James Sullivan may have already started, but Finbar was still not pleased, for he thought James harder to handle then he ever expected. The matter of both James Sullivan, and Thomas Kirkpatrick would remain for now, at least.

The familiar face of a man caught the attention of James, as the coat check girl retrieved his wife's wrap.

"Give me a moment, dear, I'll be right back . . ." James strode toward the man, his heart beating through his head, a painless throbbing.

"They'll let anyone in this place, for shite sake. I'm discontinuing my membership. This establishment is for the satin and lace Irish not the pig shit variety." It was the voice of Aengus

O'Boyle. Tresses of reddish hair combed back with strands of white woven throughout.

"Sweet Jesus, I thought I'd not see ya' again, Aengus. The church was one thing, but here, out in public?"

"You wouldn't have, had I seen ya' first . . . oh, look at ya' boy. You're a giant, me sister is feedin' ya' well, I can see. You've done wonders, Seamus—you've carried the load for us. You're the King of Swampoodle. Ha . . . I swear on me ma' if it were anywhere else I'd stand and shake your hand and show you the respect you deserve."

"Standing as Godfather to Michael is thanks enough, Aengus. Something I'll not forget, and Bridget, bein' your sister, I had no idea . . ."

"Well, let's not get sloppy here, man. We've a lot of work to do, a lot of work indeed. Bringin' Kirkpatrick along showed good judgement, Seamus. No matter how things work out. That's when I told Finbar it was time to make our move. We'll meet again, this time, somewhere, the docks perhaps, you, Finbar and me self. *The Trinity'*, as it were, Seamus. Stick to what works, boy. Finbar will fill ya' in on when and where, now go, go home with your family and . . . your quite welcome for Bridget. Yeah, yeah, go on . . ." James wanted so much to grab the arms of Aengus O'Boyle in gratitude, but he stood nodding like a stranger and left for the coat check. He looked back after his exchange with the young woman and the man in Irish clothing was gone. Not a drink or napkin.

"My coats now, dear." James said, with an air of confusion about him. The dull headache that plagued him throughout his adult life.

"Mr. Sullivan, sir . . . Mr. Sullivan?"

"Thank ya' darlin'. This is for you and yours alone." James produced a twenty-dollar bill for the young Irish indentured servant or, so he thought. James placed a fur coat over his wife's shoulders and covered Michael himself with a woolen blanket.

"Sir, I cannot take that . . ." The girl whispered, as she looked around the ballroom.

"I'll be just a minute, Bridget, get the children to the car . . . no more than a minute." James reassured her. James ran his thumb and index finger about the corners of his mouth, before once again speaking in a measured tone.

"There is no one you need fear, believe me." James took a black pen from his coat pocket and put his name to the back of his coat check and handed it to the startled young woman. "If you are not happy in your circumstances, I will come here in person to discuss your situation, with a female chaperone, of course. Best not to delay, if you want my help. If for any reason you are unsure of me, ask people here, people that you trust. Few they may be." He nodded and turned for the door of the main entrance.

Such was James's way when it came to the servitude of young Irish women. A labour slavery system custom for which he and his wife both despised and fed their hatred of the English. A hatred which fueled James's resolve, his purpose in the world. "Who would be so foolish as to eat the food prepared by a slave, for if I were a slave to any man, better for you to kill me straight off or you would eat some foul excretion of my body each day." This is what James told his children, stopping short of his thirsted plan to kill every infant, man woman and child of his owners, had this been his fate.

He saw the American Negro as lost, save the children perhaps, in time. James knew that color meant nothing to the English and Dutch, it was a matter of dominance. Fear, shame and starvation that soon turned many a strong man to self-loathing and a tameness reserved for the living dead. Just as white men enslaved white men in Ireland, so too did black men in America.

He witnessed Negro men who outworked their white counterparts. He found his fondness for one such man as this, rise up to be free, not rich for his hard-earned material worth, but a free soul. James saw the grey areas in life and would make up his own mind what was right and mete out justice as he saw it. Moses Creed was the Negros given name. James used Moses in matters of Negro trouble, as it were. The same laws of the street applied to all who gambled or borrowed money for whatever reason. Moses Creed was not the man any Negro wanted to see who owed money by way of the Irishman, such as James Sullivan was known in that circle. Moses was paid, and paid well as any man as reliable as he. They had an understanding, each to themselves, they enjoyed a certain pride that oppressed men might feel. James left Moses to mete out that same justice in the black sections, something which felt right to James, though he had done it himself without concern before meeting Moses Creed. Satisfied in one another they were, each.

"Wait, Mr. Sullivan . . ." The voice of the young Irish girl caught his ear before the revolving doors. "The man, the well-dressed man you spoke with gave instructions to deliver this walking stick to you, sir. You struck me with your bluntness, what I mean to say is your kindness . . ." The girl bowed her head.

"Bluntness is kindness in disguise, dear heart. What is your given name?"

"Shala McNamara, sir."

"I'll be here tomorrow morning before nine. We'll discuss your future with your deed holder." He produced a fresh cigarette which made his words all the more definite. Shala McNamara spoke in a grateful whisper.

DP Curran

"Might I come to ya' on my own sir . . . out of my own volition?" She looked up with a confident smile.

"Aye, Miss Shala McNamara, just know that you are not kept here but of your own free will from this day forth." James turned, having made himself clear, the knowing of the girl carried him.

The walking stick was carved from the Sacred Irish Oak. The same walking stick used by his da in the Port of Derry, years before. Turning the top of the stick one quick turn to the left, produced a lethal dagger, the length of James's hand. Aengus O'Boyle had plunged that same dagger into the wooden table of the captain's quarters on their passage to America, years before, to make a point, a point that was now clearer than ever before.

James Sullivan climbed into the waiting motor car to the sound of his wife's voice.

"It was all too much, James. Finbar goes too far for the wrong reasons . . . James, I don't trust him. I never have, a terrible thing to say, but you are in his world now. Please do not dismiss my word on this, husband. Be cautious in your dealings with him . . ."

"Is there a specific reason, Mrs., something you haven't felt necessary to tell me until now, Bridget Sullivan?"

"Since I was a child, though he rarely visited the Morrison Clan who raised me, he scared me to the point that I would not be left alone with him. Perhaps it was the over imagination of a little girl, but it hasn't changed, all of my brothers, save Aengus. I felt safe around him, there was a certain goodness about him, always. Aengus is my brother, he alone, that's how I feel . . . God help me, for saying such a thing about my brothers. Though Declan is known for his ferocity, even he fears Finbar. Aengus is his mother's son, that's the best I can explain it, I suppose."

Bridget held Baby Michael, who looked like he might speak for himself, the massive brute.

"Everything is fine, Bridget. It's your brother's way, is all."

"I'm not naïve, James. I know what is expected of you, of us, but promise me you'll not forget what I've said or the friends we've made in Swampoodle."

"Never, I will heed your concerns. As far as Swampoodle, tis' the home of our children and your friends. I will not turn my back to a friend" And the two held each other's hand against the seat between themselves.

"We have to talk later this evening about Shane. He's become more aggressive with the older boys in the neighborhood, James. Their mothers have spoken to me out of pure fear and asked for my help."

"Aye . . . we'll get him on track, we will. Subtle with the bull, Bridget. And a bull he is. I'll be puttin' him to work at the shop or with the blacksmith's, maybe. I've been thinkin' on that. I'm not alone, that much is true. He'll be alright, we'll put that aggression to good use for all involved. Have the mothers rest easy . . . but not too easy, he is a Sullivan. Oh, and let's not forget the O'Boyle contribution to the boy's disposition . . ." James did smile.

"James Sullivan, you are incorrigible . . ."   And their hands tightened for a brief moment, before James let go as if it was the one thing he feared. Love and the pain of its loss.

That night, James and Bridget Sullivan knew each other as if for the first time and all thought of loss was gone. They had sex at will, there were no boundaries that went unexplored, they were each other's. There could never be anyone else, it too must be written in the Book of Life, so said Bridget.

For the first time in any detail, James spoke of Bridget's mother, Orla. The two lay together, naked beneath a thin sheet of white linen, as questions were asked and answered. The low voices, just above a whisper, gave their words the respect Orla O'Boyle was due . . .

CHAPTER 11

James Sullivan stood in the kitchen of the Lehigh Avenue House. Word had come down from Finbar O'Boyle concerning the meeting at the docks. It was eleven-fifteen at night. A large three-quarter moon shone through the lace curtains, casting a hue of green from the glass cabinets. A quiet tranquil setting for that of poets, but not for the rapid heart of James Sullivan.

Tranquility would come with death, when the score was settled, when the battle was over. He reminded himself of this as he raised his suspenders with formality. He toyed with the idea of the bulletproof vest locked in a steamer trunk in the cellar. Accustomed now to American coffee, he gulped from a hot thick mug. The daintiness of the tea cups placed inside the glass front cupboards gave James pause, just long enough to open the cellar door.

DP Curran

He took to the dark stairs that gave with each step of his thick frame. Thumb and finger slid down a smooth string ending in a metal cap. With a slight noise that felt connected to James's own internal wiring, a dim light lit the musky, but otherwise clean cellar. A smell that he associated with the steamer truck and its contents. A spot for every key, James reached to the top of the stone foundation and took down a loose stone, cut and hollowed. A single key lay inside—a hard turn and the steamer was unlocked. The lid was heavy, but opened with a welcome ease.

No guns, ammunition or knives were kept in the trunk, being no match for the young Sullivan boy's nature. The most dangerous of weapons were kept in hidden in gun safes at the house on Taylor Street. A folded pile of shirts, coats and jackets to conceal the vests themselves was all. His personal sidearm and a Tommy gun were fitted into the floor boards of his and Bridget's bedroom. The automatic machine gun was no secret to Liam Donnelly or his superiors, due to a full disclosure policy concerning such gifts offered by dead men to be. James Sullivan's reputation for such loyalty of disclosure was as frightening as the man himself. This particular overture was by one William Conway. The Blue Man as he would be forever known.

James was given the order to dispense of the mark due to back gambling debt and a pension for random threats against the late Mr.

Donnelly. This did not sit well with those in higher places, even *'The Firsties'* weighed in. A weakness on the part of Donnelly that put the Irish in a bad light given the numerous unanswered threats. The Italian's were also watching with rivaled attention, as any sign of weakness was noted and exploited.

James was brought in and Billy Conway knew it. His one chance was to reason with Sullivan. A quiet man often possesses such reason—James, however, did not. In matters of business, he followed orders to the letter. William Conway was to suffer before death, nothing less.

The door of a taproom called The Lantern creaked just before closing time. James took a seat in the back booth, reserved for few men. Once Donnelly's private booth, it now sat empty in a crowded saloon since the unspoken death of Mr. Donnelly.

Patrons filed out, tongues wagged without mention of the man who filled the rear booth.

Hennessey "Pug" Morrison ushered the last man out the front door before running a bleached white rag across the bar rail, then taking the narrow hallway to check the head for stragglers. Two latches turned, and the back door opened. Billy Conway would get his wish, he moved through the doorway, removing his hat—prepared to reason.

DP Curran

Sitting now opposite Sullivan, he was silent as Pug put down two shots of the whiskey. James pushed his across the small table and lined the two shot glasses in perfect unison, side by side in front of a now trembling man.

"Resign yourself, sir." James said, eyes fixed.

"It's a question of how my debt will trouble my wife and children . . ." Mr. Conway knew best not to utter his executioner's name.

"Shame and guilt can be a heavier price than money or one's life, that I do not deny. Though through death, your debt be paid in full in this life. Best to settle with God, sir—than to waste time with worry."

"I'm a degenerate, it's true, but my wife and children are innocent. Is there anything I might offer or say to ease their suffering?"

"No."

"Then why did you agree to meet with me, with all respect?"

"Your type fascinates me, sir. You are first generation here in America, you have the backing and full measure of a good Irish family that makes its way fighting in Ireland. Still, you send not one American cent to that family. One generation and you have lost yourself here in this country. Your parent's, though dead, gave their lives for you to be born here, but still you sit in front of me and ask for favors for your wife and children. Be they your one true contribution to this world. I will tell my sons of you and men like you, who have become lost, lost inside." James pointed to his own chest in a gesture of truth.

"I have left all of my weapons to you." Conway confessing as a schoolboy.

"I have no need of your weapons, sir."

"There is a Tommy gun and a full crate of ammunition to go with it. It waits for you under a tarpaulin in back, if you so choose. That may be all that may be of use to a man such as yourself . . ." The condemned man made every indication of rising in submission, but stopped short, leaving his hands flat on the table.

"I cannot deviate from how you are killed, sir. Any gifts even offered must be disclosed, on my honor. You've crossed into the short painful world of barbarism. Gird yourself. Your wife and children may find their way back to Ireland—your two young sons and an infant daughter would do well far from this place . . ." James Sullivan rose and in that second the air from the open back door smelled of freedom for William Conway.

"Bless you." Cried the condemned man.

"You have no such power, sir." And the two men left into the night.

DP Curran

The next morning, Mr. Conway's body was found hanging by the neck from a signal station at a major train crossing for all to see. His torso hung in the crisp sun of an Autumn morning, minus his arms and legs all. His face had turned a queer shade of blue, leaving onlookers in carnival amazement. James made passage for the man's wife and children. All that remained was a forewarning of the "Blue man."

Fitted with a bullet proof vest, James Sullivan Sr., drove his ink black truck to the Taylor Street house at midnight. Not a man for hats, his blonde hair took to the night air and invigorated him, as any free man might be. James took two grenades and two Colt revolvers, one which he strapped to his ankle with a leather holster. A serrated fishing knife, which he took from the hand of a dead man after a battle at Brady's Crossing in Donegal, slid along his belt to the back of his hip in a sheath of lamb hide. Aengus O'Boyle had mentioned a meeting at the docks, but James had a bad sentiment for Finbar. This was on James's mind and taking to account the warning given him by Aengus himself, years before on their voyage to America. "Believe all that I've told you, Seamus, on the soul of my mother. Remember this above all, trust no man, save yourself and your own judgement . . . from this day forth."

Across from the Sullivan's Lehigh House sat Thomas Kirkpatrick, perched in a narrow alley way. Donning a cumbersome bullet-proof vest and the Tommy gun. He watched the Sullivan House with cat like attention for all who might dare walk in its shadow.

James's judgement, not trust, committed Thomas Kirkpatrick to the world of Seamus O'Suilebhain. A *'Firstie'* at that.

The humidity waited above the river to produce clouds of fog that filtered the light of a full moon. Shrouded lampposts gave a shadow of the docks amidst the muffled sound of fog horns calling to one another. A play unfolding on an invisible stage, more beautiful to James than the symphony or opera to a refined, cultured man.

James knew every corner of the docks, every clear exit by motor car, foot or water. He parked in a section reserved for employees, for which he was. He had long since been on the books, though a longshoreman, he was not. It would not be unusual for his truck to be seen here day or night. James took this into consideration, in case some accident was to befall him this evening.

Dressed in a dark blue seaman's coat that covered a bulletproof vest and a pullover tweed sweater. He donned a black woolen hat and traversed the docks with the most lights out all the way to the foreman's shack. The long-barreled Colt was cold against his stomach, keeping his senses all the sharper.

Bodyguards dressed in cheap suits surrounded the shack, as James approached undetected, until he tossed a stone into the placid waters. He was faced with four men lined in front of him. "We'll have to search you now, without trouble." A man of little English graveled.

"*Gan anocht, cara,*" James replied, meaning not tonight, friend, in the Irish.

Finbar O'Boyle stood behind the wall of men, though there be more. "A bit underdressed, Seamus, are we?" Finbar asked, in his customary long coat and suit. The men parted, and James entered the shack, not to his surprise, there was no Aengus O'Boyle present.

"Just the two of us, Finbar?" James looked about, nothing of a meeting did this resemble. Not a bottle or glass in sight. No other counsel or person present. The backs of men's heads blocked each window from the outside. Except for one, a familiar man ducked into the shack without so much as a coat or sweater. It was Declan to be sure, red hair and beard as long as you will. Thick with the freckled skin of an ancient warrior.

"Either I'm wrong, Finbar, or more than one person will die here tonight," said James.

"Always death on your mind, Seamus. You should be more concerned about life than death, no? Perhaps not, who am I to say, after all."

"Declan, is it now?" Seamus asked, feeling a bit cumbersome in his present clothing, but he thought this would be no ordinary fight, not this night.

"A nosey fuck is ya' too, boy? Ya' kill a few Englishmen and marry my sister as a reward. They'll be no rewards this night . . ." Finbar interrupted his older brother.

"Declan, the man deserves respect, that much is true. Business this may be, but facts are facts. Wait just outside, brother." Finbar was stern in his voice.

Declan, still fueled by whatever Finbar had told him previous left him simmering with the stare of a madman. The one thought that occurred to James was that his own son, Shane, was infected by this same disposition. If he lived, James would make his son's actions a priority. It was an indelible fact.

"My brother, Aengus's methods, so to speak, are of no use now, friend. We have found our way here in America, though his thoughts and plans remain in Ireland. What did he think he might achieve there? A one-man revolution, two if we count you, Seamus. Even those sworn to help in the past are gone now, both here and in Ireland. The English killed off the main players, boy. You couldn't see it, not with Donnelly fillin' yer' head with shite. He was square he was, wanted the same as you and Aengus, all the while keepin' the coffers full for me and all the politicians at my disposal. You killed many a man, Seamus O'Suilebhain, but not for your ideals, not for Aengus and never once for Ireland since your arrival in America. You were a loyal friend to my brother, Aengus, and I respect that. I envy that in a small way, but I, for the life of me, do not understand it. Two men to be reckoned with to be sure, Aengus and yourself . . . The good Lord knows that to be fact. It must be clean as Da would say, a clean slate, a clean break, you get the idea. It was no clearer to me than when I saw those two boys of yours, Seamus the younger, and Shane. I knew then it would not stop with you, even with Aengus out of the way . . ." Finbar paused and stared at James.

"Ya' think you'll be killin me in this shack, that's your plan? Because I'll kill ya' both, or all three of us will die, and it won't stop here, Finbar. It would just be gettin' started."

"Aengus wasn't clear like the rest of us. We've been given a reputation we don't deserve. Where is the honor in that? Seamus, I don't blame you, I blame Aengus and to an extent my dear ma, but mothers must be mothers, no matter what the son is or becomes. A stubbornness that I don't share. Aengus always favored her, though Da kept us killin' and schemin' against all odds. The difference was, he knew it was a lost cause, but put us through it anyway. Ma, Ma . . . she believed in the cause and in Aengus, cut from the same cloth. Realist run the world, Seamus, and a small group at that. That leaves us here now, boy—you've outdone yourself, exceeded all expectations to the point of extinction, I'm afraid."

"Do it, Finbar, if your balls be as big as your mouth."

"Not balls the size of yours, Seamus, to be sure . . . fearless."
Finbar chuckled. "And you are, I believe that about you. At this
moment, you show not one sign of fear and a man who does not fear
death is a dangerous man. I could use you and your code of conduct,
you wouldn't have to like it, mind you, but family, your family must
be worth that concession. Too many to hide, and an abiding fondness
for all is all the assurance that I need. Something happens to me, well .
. . you know the rest. That telephone there will determine who lives
and dies this night, Seamus. Men have been dispatched to your home,
'The Lehigh House' as it's referred to, to each his own. When your
phone rings there and I hope our Bridget answers it, but I expect she
will in lieu of your profession. One of us will speak to her, Seamus,
either you or me. It's your one chance . . . at least, that's how I see it."
Finbar sat for the first time, reaching into his coat.

In that frame, that photo of Finbar reaching . . .

James pulled the long-barreled Colt and fired between Finbar's
eyes, before shooting each man at the windows. A terrible mistake for
a man so smart as to think he would be the head of anything more than
money whores. That left him and Declan, Seamus knew he had
emptied the barrel. Smoke and the pungent sting of gunpowder stung
the eyes and filled the lungs of James. His counterpart, having
reentered the shack showed no signs of either and spoke.

"I've waited for this moment in time, I imagined it again and again. Let us see what miracles you can perform without a gun, Seamus O'Suilebhain." Declan produced a long blade from workman's trousers.

Instead of pulling the revolver from his ankle holster, James took the serrated knife from the lambskin sheath. He did not employ a blade in his work, except to dismember after the fact.

This, however would be for his father, Padraig, and for Aengus who, for all he knew, was dead. He clutched it first to deliver a combination to Declan that Pug would have been proud of. Declan stayed up, looking more focused than before. The two men now with blades in their hands. Swipes were exchanged as blood poured from the broken nose of Declan O'Boyle. The two grappled in close quarters, blood of both mixed in pools on the wooden floor. James thrust Declan's blade into his own stomach, just below the bullet proof vest, startling Declan, who strengthened his grip and grinned. With eyes, wide, Declan was stabbed through the heart. Death came quick to him.

James knew to act fast without panic while in shock, as he severed the hand of Declan O'Boyle while he sat atop him, before pulling it from his own abdomen.

This tactic was something of a rumor he had heard many times as a boy in Ireland and it did fascinate him. This was done by Aengus

O'Boyle in a close and fierce battle with *'The Lion'* himself. The English Captain often hunted Aengus O'Boyle by night, alone, calling to him in the darkness. One such night, Aengus did appear from the woods, he waited for the Captain Edmund Wainwright to dismount. A fierce battle ensued for minutes that seemed as hours. Blades were drawn at the point of exhaustion, Aengus took the captain's hand and guided the knife into his abdomen. He then cut *'The Lion'* deep about the neck and face, but did choose not to kill him. Instead, he left him scarred and shamed. More tales were spread that the captain had killed Aengus O'Boyle that dark night of the new moon, as it was known, though the captain knew better. Afterwards, young Seamus was told of such a tactic by his father, Padraig and how to employ it when in dire straits, when in close hand to hand action—never thinking it would mean the death of another Irishman. Let alone an O'Boyle.

To his surprise, Declan had a revolver on his person. This gave an air of respect to the man who lay before him, dead without his right hand. James thrust the knife still gripped by the bloody wrist and hand into the bullet hole in Finbar's head. He then emptied the bill fold of Finbar and shoved a fistful of twenty's, fifties and hundred-dollar bills into his mouth. James straightened Declan's body and crossed his arms out of respect.

James had to get back to Lehigh Avenue, he drifted in and out of sanity, shooting each man outside once more into their blurred faces. A small torch burned from the shiplap wall of the shack. The dying man held his knife in the flame, before searing it against the wound in his stomach. Delusion turned to adrenaline and James tossed the torch into the river, that now stirred with excitement, though just a river.

Taking the same route back to his car, men unloaded crates and cargo in the distance. Not a man approached—James poured himself into the ink black truck and drove with caution until away from the docks. He sped possessed with hatred and murder on his mind, keeping him awake. Blood dripped from leather to floorboards, time was nonexistent, shadows in black and white was all. No more colors, was this life through death's eyes?

Police, sirens in front of the house on Lehigh— James eased the truck to the end of the block and passed out, not knowing what awaited him.

CHAPTER 12

James awoke to the stern, somewhat gloating face of Mrs. Byrne. He lifted his head to feel the spinning of his bed and the room itself.

"Don't be movin', James Sullivan Sr. I'm the boss now and it's a good favor you'll owe for baby-sittin' the likes of you for the last two weeks . . ." Tears in her eyes, she leaned down and kissed the sweated brow of a boy her own mother delivered in Ireland years before.

"Where's my Bridget and children, Felicity?" James's deep voice was weak, but invoked a certain kindness in the calling of the name, Felicity.

"All are sleeping sound, sir. I dare say, it's good to have you back, Seamus. I'm sorry . . ."

"Don't be. Where's the doctor that made me whole, Mrs.?"

DP Curran

"Tom Kirkpatrick said no doctor could be called, so they went and got me. I could've been a doctor myself . . . given the chance. I patched you up just as good as any doctor might. The knife that pierced your stomach missed every organ. Made my job easy, was a matter of blood loss and inner strength as far as you were concerned. Prayer what pulled ya' through, if you want the truth, yes sir, Jesus isn't done with the likes of James Sullivan Sr. That's one thing for sure, it is. By the by, Tom sat each night with you and your family the whole time. T'was him who killed them men sent to kill your kin, the whole Clan of Sullivan. Three men in all, dressed like whoremaster's the lot, for what I'm told on good authority. Tom's a *'Firstie'*, but a better man you'd be hard to find these days. In this wild place . . ." Mrs. Byrne sat in the rocker reserved for the baby, off in her own thoughts for a spell.

"Ya' know, James, one of the policemen gave Bridget a bit of advice that night . . ." Felicity went on, "He said, *'Tell James not to worry'*, now . . . why would a policeman say such a thing? Bridget would be the one to worry. A fine Irishman that Officer Dolan, Terrence be his given name, I believe. Handsome devil he is, poor man a widower at such an age. Needs a good woman is all."

"I'm sure you've got one in mind, Felicity . . ." James answered then moaned, "Ooh."

"Serves ya' right, James Sullivan, just when I thought we reached a new beginning in the throes of death. I'll fetch Tom, he drinks coffee in the kitchen, you've fouled a good man with that American mud. Don't move . . ."

Thomas Kirkpatrick entered the darkened room, still holding the machine gun. Confusion, and pride made for a bad case of nausea. "The police seemed almost pleased with the death of the three men. Not much of an inquiry was made, a few questions for your wife and the neighbors, but little mention of you. Two days ago, a note was given to Bridget by the boy who delivers the newspaper. The envelope was sealed, not a name or initial on it, blank. Bridget thought it best to wait for you to open it . . . and James, she knows about her cousins and the scene at the docks."

"How did she respond?"

"Like a rock, not a word from her on the matter. A strong woman . . ."

Tom continued, "I'll sit while you read the note if you like?"

"Suigh." James motioned to the rocking chair.

Tom handed over a pocket knife to open the envelope. A small card read as follows: *'Will be over in two night's time. Have spoken to Bridget. A .'*

"Tom, thank you, my life is tied to yours now. Together we go forward, your problems become mine and together we will find a solution. Anything is possible, but worry is a useless endeavor—put all worry out of your mind. What of the truck?"

"I had it taken to the shop that night under the cover of a thunderstorm. It was dismantled and sits at the bottom of the river. A duplicate is parked out front, identical. I took care of it . . ."

"The other people involved?"

Tom then took to a ramble of sorts.

"Little Emmett, my Uncle. A foreman of the railroad yard, another blacksmith and mechanic by trade. I owe him my life and that of my own family, he kept me from certain death more than once. I'm not so popular with *'The Natives'*, but you know this, James. My uncle, he wasn't born here in this strange place, and they fear him. Emmett was no fan of the brothers O'Boyle, Declan and Finbar, but he feels that he has given his word, and that to him is sacred. Now, his mind has changed, given the open contract out on his life, because of O'Boyle's dealing in Atlantic City, for which Emmett knows inside and out. He would've strangled the O'Boyle brothers with his own hands if you had spoken the word. He would like to pledge his loyalty to you, James, though he speaks for himself, not through me. There is nothing left of the truck, nor was there any conversation concerning its condition. I, we needed help. Uncle Emmett does not ask questions. He prefers not to speak much, though he sure can, when the need

arises. His life and mine I offer you for any dishonor, whatever . . ."
Tom bowed and took the hand of his boss.

"*Dea,* Tom. Little Emmett, humph . . . like a small mountain.
We'll need Emmett, now, he's a good man, from good stock. You
saved the life of my family and you used good judgment where the
truck was concerned. Until then, speak to no one about anything, no
one. There will be more challenging times ahead and we need to be of
one mind about certain things. Your uncle was used by Donnelly,
though never treated with the respect deserving a man such as Emmett
McGowan. Bring me this Little Emmett, Tom. I don't imagine he's
far."

"Behind the house, James. I would have taken my own life had
anything happened to your family . . ." Tom's feet rocked as he spoke.

"I understand, Tom—don't second guess yourself . . . ever."

Tom blossomed like a plant after a storm at James Sullivan's
encouraging words.

I'll want you here tonight for the meeting. Matter of fact, bring
Emmett, for the door. He'll get what he needs, clothes, pistol and let
him carry his prize possession, his garrote. I know of Emmett's work,
clean and quiet for a big man. In the meantime, you will be our guest
here. I want you to bathe, shave with a straight razor and we'll find
you suitable clothes for a man of your position. I'll need you now
more than ever, Tom. Safety is paramount, now eat. Mrs. Byrne has

made plenty of food, I'm sure. Go on, bring me Emmett. When we're through, have my wife come in . . . alone.

James read the note once again, and thought back to his father's insistence on the necessity of reading, the reading of the classics of course, but now he under stood why he was given books on strategy concerning war and conflict. The Art of War is the ancient Chinese war treatise dating from the 5th century BC. Devised by the ancient Chinese Military strategist, Sun Tzu. A genius. It was the one book that Seamus O'Suilebhain, allowed himself for his journey to America. All his sons of the age of knowing, will read and discuss it in depth with their father, as well.

Little Emmett entered the room, he stood as a backdrop for Tom.

"Come forward, Emmett. Wait outside the door, Tom, please."

Emmett began to speak in the Irish. "*Meas* . . ." He was cut off.

"*Meas*, you have my respect, as well, Emmett, but speak American as to get acclimated. That is to say, get used to it. We'll speak in our own tongue when needed. Right now, there is no such need. Please, go on . . ." James made the effort to sit up, though not much more. And the term, "American", filled Emmett with a sense of pride that James thought so much of Ireland and America that he did not use the word English to describe their second tongue.

In the thickest of brogues, Emmett began once more.

"Mr. Sullivan, sir. I pledge my loyalty to you, if you'll have me . . ." Emmett also bowed and reached for James's outstretched hand.

"Your actions over the years have been well noted, Emmett. You stuck your neck out for your nephew in a public manner for all *'The Natives'* to see. Your private work, I've always regarded as professional and worthy of respect. We never spoke, but there are reasons for such silence, reasons that you, of all people, understand. The drawer, the top drawer on the high chest of drawers there. You'll find a Bible . . ." And the men drew blood and a judgment was made.

Emmett closed the door, facing it as if still bowing to his new boss. He nodded to Tom with the glassy eyes of a giant. "Send in the Mrs.," he said, looking down at the twenty-dollar bills that he had spread out as a fan. Tom looked on in disbelief at his uncle, not so much older than he, with a smile about him, speaking in a language he hated. What other wonders would this man, James Sullivan, perform?

The big man squeezed down the stairs and left the house and went straight to Dooley's Barber Shop, then to Kavanagh's Haberdashery to be fitted for five suits and other niceties at the generosity and insistence of James Sullivan.

The sight of Bridget was as medicine to James. She read the note from Aengus and was glad, for she loved Aengus as a brother and a father both. They spoke little of the fate of her two cousins at the hands of her husband. Something for which she forewarned him of in her own way. Instead, she locked the bedroom door and did all she could to pleasure him with a smile befitting a naughty yet loyal friend and wife.

Sleep came again upon James, but not before instructions to be awakened in time to make himself presentable before Aengus. A weak looking man is just that.

Dreams came at once to James as he imagined they did for any man in a world such as his. He accepted the dreams, not as punishment, but as a by-product of circumstance, of the decisions he had made of his own volition. Ireland . . . Ma, Da, Lilly, Mrs. O'Boyle and the brothers he lost all waiting for him to fall to a deep sleep. Each their own troubles they poured out to him, even that of the dead, in the blooded clothes they wore on the night of their murder. And the English Captain, *'The Lion'* sat high in on his speckled white horse in their midst.

"Seamus . . . Seamus." James awoke this time to Bridget, the sight of her was painful at times, her beauty was to him a weight. He would do anything to protect her above all others. He stared at her when she wasn't looking, but she smiled because she knew.

"Had I married a woman with the face of Mrs. Byrne, my life would be care-free. Come here and make me better again."

"You are a burden on my heart, sir. And if you weren't as handsome, I would have stopped at two children at most. A frustrated man you would be." She sat beside him once more, strong and straight.

"I would have taken you then . . ." he said, with a laugh.

"You would have had to." Pain be damned, the two tore at each other's clothes and melted together as one, her long strawberry hair fell with its full weight and texture to her soft, ample bottom, that complemented her long legs and thin ankles.

Putting the final pins in her hair, Bridget smiled through the mirror at James as the children filed in under the command of Mrs. Byrne, who greeted husband and wife with a disapproving glance, each.

"Da," the children clamored, all but Jimmy and Shane who showed all the signs of retaliation. For which the two spoke of without a doubt. James saw this and whispered for both to stay, as he shaved over a boiling bowl of water and a cup of shaving soap. The wound was bandaged, though blood found its way.

"I'll draw a bath, James . . . easy, Seamus," were the words she whispered in his ear, before kissing his cheek.

"What will I do with the likes of you two? They'll be no talking about what you think you know to anyone but me. Understood? I can't have my own flesh and blood acting out behind my back. That's not how we work, we're a family, a real family. One forged out of things either of you know little about. You are my sons and you'll do as I say, as good sons do. As loyal sons do. And that is the most important thing, not saying anything to anyone, but me. Always me, my job is to teach and protect you. Your job is to obey me, James Jr. Do you understand what I tell you?"

"Yes, sir. I do, but there must be something . . ." he was cut off.

"There is nothing, nothing . . . nothing." James's face now inches from his oldest son, blood seeped from the gauze.

"Shane, this violence in your own neighborhood, it stops now. Unless of course, you are provoked and then you have my blessing. Don't overdo it, son. Use just enough energy to disable your advisory. Never expend yourself, without cause. Do not show anyone what your limit is, or they will figure you out and then you will know what it is to lose. We use our heads here in this house . . . and our physical skills to prevail out there. I'm proud of both of you. I want you to know that, each of you. The two of you will dress well this evening, we have a guest coming and I want him to meet you both. Now, go on." James Sr., stopped his sons, "Boys . . . well, thank you, is all." The words he wanted to say above all wouldn't come, and it hurt worse than his wounds.

The hot bath had done James good, but he knew he would need a medical doctor to see to his injuries. That was the least on his mind as he dressed, wrapped in gauze, by a silent and attentive Mrs. Byrne. No words were needed between the two, a deep respect was mutual.

No matter their constant chiding back and forth. Each enjoyed it as much as the other. And the widow Byrne felt safe because of James, a safety that comes from knowing that he would step in at any time, without question, to help or defend, her and her beloved son, Stevie.

CHAPTER 13

Three light taps to a single glass pane of eight at the Sullivan's back door, meant that their guest had arrived. Tom opened the door without showing himself and in the framed opening was Aengus O'Boyle, overshadowed by the sheer width of Emmett behind him.James, dressed as an Irish banker, stood in the middle of the kitchen with hands on each suspender, legs spread in defiance. "Emmett, A shotgun?" James asked, stretching the suspenders.

"I saved a few bucks on the clothes, Mr. Sullivan."

"This is our guest, wielding a firearm is not the behavior of a friend. Though it does show that you are my friend. *'Dea,'* Thank you, Emmett." James gave a nod, as Emmett closed the door from outside.

A heavy pause fell over the room, nor James or Aengus blinked as they stared into one another. The sound of children in the background gave the silence more tension.

"It's a dangerous world we live in, Mr. O'Boyle . . . where a man's own wife and children are not safe in their beds at night. Are there no unspoken rules, even among criminals, for that is all that we have become, no? It no longer stops at our own doorsteps, just tell me now at least if that is true, because many, many people will die. We spoke once about the Bible, sir. I gave you no proper answer then, but I will now. I have always preferred The Old Testament." James did not waiver in his tone. Calm and true was he.

"I'm here alone, Seamus, man to man. If you don't trust me, kill me now, tonight. Most all that I ever lay claim to love is dead, two at your own hand. I've been checked by whatever the hell that is in your back garden, Seamus. I came here to die or do business." Aengus still hadn't blinked. A fact not lost on James.

"You told me to trust no man, to use judgment instead. It is my judgement that we will do business." James walked toward Aengus and the two shook hands, each as stubborn as the other.

"An mhaith," said Aengus. As to say very good."

"Tom Kirkpatrick . . . Mr. O'Boyle." Aengus did not look Tom's way. Tom never moved, body nor eyes.

"Welcome, Aengus, let's take to the study and sit." James turned and walked with a pain that required him to defy the rage it produced in him. Pain was as hate to him, a drug.

Tom opened the pocket doors that exposed a study plied with walls of books and a large oak desk and one long table lined with chairs on two sides. Paintings of Ireland hung with palpable meaning and loyalty associated with each one.

"Sit. Please, sir . . ." James motioned to a large leather chair behind the desk for Mr. O'Boyle to take his place.

Aengus looked surprised, perhaps even with pleasure, at this gesture. This made James glad. His hopes were to move forward with the one man who might still have a sharp vision, for James's vision was blurred by lack of information and violence.

"Thank you, Seamus. Given the recent circumstances, I believe we could call things even and wipe the slate, as it were. It would have to be said now, if it were to be so. Time and doublemindedness renders a man dead long before he dies, Seamus. No good will come from it, I would prefer we settled our hearts and minds this night, without reservation." Aengus settled into the green leather chair as he admired the color. "Not a gaudy green at all now, is it?"

"I agree with what you have said, and I too, want full disclosure and some semblance of loyalty, where men can come together and reason with one another, assuming they are friends. Each of us have been given a job to do, some of us like yourself it was thrust upon, for me, it was my choice, my life. I have no regrets about what you and I agreed to those so many years ago, but I thought, I thought that there would be some structure or some tangible progress to measure my actions. Something, I don't know . . ." James sat in a leather side chair. Blood shone through a cummerbund, which was doubled up to prevent such a thing. Aengus noticed this and looked down in thought.

"You have kept your word, Seamus O'Suilebhain. It is I who owes you a debt. The slate is not clean until I repay that debt. I spoke out of pride, but I can see you are more real than any man I've known, sir. You will never give up this seat again, you will have your rightful place in this world. We have much to do, I'd say we are family, but that is a liability with you, James Sullivan, The King of Swampoodle. I asked you to tell me what Swampoodle was if you ever found out, but there is no need. You are Swampoodle. And Tom, please forgive my slight earlier, but when death is near, I do not turn from its gaze." Tom nodded with all due respect, but said nothing.

"Where do we go from here, Aengus?" James asked, pushing himself up and opening the wooden box of cigars to Aengus.

"The meeting, Seamus, the meeting in Atlantic City is still on. It will be you and I who attend, with sufficient muscle and finance. Finbar made many mistakes, God rest his soul. Money and the storing of it was just one of those mistakes. We are sitting on millions, Seamus. Right now, this night, that money, paper, gold, stocks, bonds, diamonds . . . it goes on and on, has all been transported to a safe house in Center City. An old bank that I bought for scraps years ago, before the Great War. With the refurbishment of the city, all I did was reface it, remodel the interior and wait, wait for greed to do the rest. Not even the mayor knows of the vault, its undetectable. Of course, the unfortunate fall-out was the necessary killing of the men who helped move it and all of Finbar's inside contacts. All scum anyway, no purpose or bigger picture than themselves." Mr. O'Boyle took out a cigar cutter and a lighter.

"This meeting in Atlantic City, what will it involve?" James sat, once more.

"The sea, whiskey, rum, guns and money for starters. It's what we do with the profits that will define us. Prohibition, boy . . . prohibition. America is the land of opportunity, what other country would provide any such opportunity by its own laws? It's set, Seamus, it's ours to fuck up. Three things, Seamus, *'The Trinity'* holds true . . . percentage, political protection and finance. We negotiate the first and make more money off the next two, for which we already have."

James was holding fast, but fever came over him as he lost more blood.

"When is the meeting . . .?" James motioned to Tom for water.

"Fourth of July, two weeks hence. We'll get you a real doctor this night and you will breathe the salt air for a week before the meeting, Seamus. Tom, go and call this number, tell the man that answers to be here right off. No need to worry, he's a good man and a fine doctor. We pay him too much, but the results are worth it. We can't afford to lose Seamus, no disrespect to the widow Byrne." Tom turned to James for approval. James waved him to the phone in the corner of the room. A small table with pencil and paper sat ready if needed. No ink was to be used in matters of business.

"I'll let my cousin and the children in before taking my leave, Seamus." With that he opened the pocket doors and called for his favorite cousin and the children.

Bridget appeared first, kissing Aengus on the cheek, red-faced with happiness. "Aengus, help Seamus, help him to understand what it is he is fighting for, please." Her soft tone meant more than any scream might to Aengus.

"Worry yourself not, woman. We are of one mind this night. I've sent for a doctor—one we can be sure of. One who wants to live and live well . . ." said Aengus, now comfortable again.

As was usual the children were in single file, as Bridget went to James, feeling his forehead. "To bed with you, now, Seamus. The doctor is in route . . ."

"Introduce the children first, I want to see that . . ." James sat straight up to see the visit through. Fading in and out with astounding fortitude.

Aengus handed Tom an envelope and spoke below the voice of Mrs. Byrne, herding the children off to bed, before taking his leave.

James awoke next to the face of a young doctor, who had given James an intravenous solution for dehydration and gave his wife the necessary pills for his recovery. "I've gotten the fever down. The wound has been cleaned, sterilized and re-stitched, it will heal much faster, Mrs." The doctor stopped short of using a last name out of self-preservation, for he knew all too well of James Sullivan and one Aengus Boyle. "I'll be here early tomorrow morning . . . by way of the rear entrance. You have my number should you need it, for anything, anything at all." The doctor took his leave, tired having worked under more pressure than even he was used to.

"Thank you . . . Doctor?" Bridget quizzed.

"Doctor, would be best for all ma'am. Goodnight."

"As you say, Doctor . . ." Bridget uttered without concern.

The trip was set. Bridget held the envelope given to Tom that contained train tickets. The Sullivan family of which included, Tom, Little Emmett, were to board the Crusader Luxury Line for Atlantic City, New Jersey, in two days' time.

The indispensable Mrs. Byrne and her son Stevie would stay at the Sullivan house on Lehigh Avenue. A vacation of their own given all the fine amenities and food that filled the Sullivan's pantry. It would not be odd for Mrs. Byrne to be seen taking in the bread, milk, and newspaper each day at the Sullivan home. She would do the same for her own smaller row home, as if nothing was askew. She was waggle tongued, though she knew the limits placed on her by James Sullivan and did abide his wishes, though never an option. On the day of the Sullivan's departure, Bridget handed Mrs. Byrne a folded wad of money, held secure by two large rubber bands in the shape of a cross. For which Mrs. Byrne replied, "Ooohh, the mans a big teddy bear at heart, Bridget. God Bless him . . ." Bridget smiled, as she grasped the woman's hands, nary a word did she speak.

The children had not traveled so far by train before, and watching the happiness on their faces made James's recovery more than tolerable. James, of all people, decided that the widow Byrne deserved a holiday and to breathe the salt air she so craved from her home by the sea in Ireland. Bridget agreed to take the credit for asking, but in the end, James thought it more important she stay behind and tend to daily tasks. Things would need to seem normal, normal enough for anyone too close or far to ask about.

Emmett shadowed the children and Bridget on the train. Tom stayed in arm's length of James, more a second pair of eyes than protection, though Tom was no joke when it came to the action. Given James's present condition, he allowed it. The two talked for hours about the past and the future. Still, to James at this point, things were as clear as mud.

DP Curran

Across from James and Tom in the next suite entered a rotund, older man. White hair with remnants of its former throughout, with a mustache of the same that covered his upper lip. He wore round glasses and dressed with an aristocratic flair, right down to his shoes. As the gentleman spoke with the porter about refreshment, James noticed an English accent, with a tinge of Scottish that interlaced like so many hairs on the man's head.

"I told ya', Tom. There he is right across from us." James laughed at his immediate discovery of a man who prided himself on stealth and deception in public.

"No," said Tom, staring.

"Tryin' to hide right under my nose again. Almost hate to ruin it for him, Tom. I mean he is the great Aengus O'Boyle, master of death and disguise . . . I can't look, the laughin' goes through me like another knife." James looked away as to not give himself away. He felt himself drifting off with the smell of the sea already in his mind.

James awoke to a small encounter. Tom was speaking with a porter who had opened the glass doors of the suite. "Nothin' needed here, boy, don't come back unless called for. Now, look me in the face and tell me you understand that, boy."

James interrupted, "What has this man done, Tom?"

"He opened the door without being called for. Niggers know better here, James. I straightened him out. No call for your sleep bein' interrupted." Tom spewed his words with venom.

"There's no call to put a man down without cause, Tom. Let's be mindful of who we call Niggers. I once killed a man with a brick that called me the same and I'd do it again. I treasure the idea itself, I do. Take this for your trouble, sir, and heed my friend's advice." James gave the trembling porter a new dollar bill and adjusted himself in his seat.

"That's an undiscerning' strain of hate ya' got there, Tommy Kirkpatrick . . ." James grimaced and was about to close his eyes.

"All respect, Seamus, but your da turns in his grave at your affinity for underdogs"

"Such as yourself, Tom? Be it best not to speculate on the thoughts of dead men." Tom sat, bewildered, as the porter smiled and went on his way.

With that, the man of extended years smiled and pressed his middle finger to the window of his compartment.

"What the feck, James. That man across there is mad, he is," said Tom.

"Keep that little gem to yourself, friend. It's a long walk to hell from a train at full burst. "The old man in the suit across, busied himself with newspapers while licking his thumb and finger to smooth his mustache.

"No, it couldn't be . . .," Tom muttered.

"Oh, it could, Tom, it very well could . . .," James smiled and drifted off to the smell of salt once more.

Tom kept a close eye on the white-haired man in the adjacent suite and each time the old man turned with a quick playful jerk of the head to catch his watchful eye.

Soon the welcome sound of the whistle carried through the slowing train, as James Sullivan took his first full breath of air in weeks.

Emmett led the line of Sullivan's as the made their way to the exit, having arrived in Atlantic City at the strike of the noon hour. To the second by James's watch, he was a stickler for time he was. Before a collection or an execution, he would check his watch first and then again when the job was finished, never quite satisfied. Even a baseball game starting late infuriated the man, though known himself for oft times being late. A ploy, James would call it, but someone else be late and his mood would darken, a sullenness, but the fact that this engineer guided this train to its destination on the dot was rousing to James Sullivan.

"Tom, I want you to find that distinguished white-haired gentleman and apologize for lack of respect, given his years." Tom was last in the procession behind James and could see his shoulders shake with laughter. Tom wondered, in that moment, how these two men of equal destructive natures could also have such sense of humor. To him, O'Boyle and Sullivan were of a different breed and, though Tom be guarding James, he felt safer than he ever had in his life here in America.

Behind the long parade of Sullivan's and company was the man with the white hair and mustache. He carried a leather suitcase and squinted with the face and whiskers of a walrus, as Tom turned to find him following.

The seasoned gentleman exited the train. He never stopped or slowed his pace in any way, as he moved in the opposite direction, sporting a white brimmed hat that matched that of his suit.

Tom watched as he grew smaller with distance, more puzzled than afraid.

"Give this to the engineer, Tom . . . Tom." In his pain, James was losing his patience with his friend.

"Pardon, James . . .?"

"Pass this to the train's engineer, find the words without the use of names, go on." A tip for a man's dedication to his work, something James appreciated, even in enemies or marks.

For the first-time, James had second thoughts about Tom's ability to focus with consistency. James would chalk it up to himself being run down a bit, the effects of the blade. After all, Tom had saved the life of his family, James reproached himself for the thought, a thought that lingered, none the less.

<u>BOOK III</u>

Swampoodle bleeds into Atlantic City, New Jersey. 1919

"We all have to decide how much sin we can live with"

~Patrick Johnston~

DP Curran

CHAPTER 14

A familiar trace of pitch from the famous 1870 Boardwalk of Atlantic City enhanced the smell of salt and sea air for James Sullivan Sr. A scent he hoped to remember for the rest of his life, he stopped against the rail to gaze past the bathers and frolickers in the surf. The wind took him, and he knew then that this was the place, the one place in America that could perhaps ease his mind. A surreal mix of old and new, mammoth hotels growing out of the sand, contrasted by the Atlantic Ocean, a tangible sense of home, of Ireland, his mother and sister. He wanted to go to the water's edge to touch and taste the salt water, to close his eyes and imagine himself . . . in the Bay of Donegal.

"James, are you alright now, dear?" Bridget stepped in between her husband and Tom. Sounds of the Sullivan children's laughter as they frolicked in the water's edge.

"I am at that, Bree . . ." James had not called Bridget by that name in public, ever.

"What is it James? You've spent your childhood in and about the sea, what then?"

"I've not seen it here, not like this, though it be so close the whole time. Why haven't we come sooner, why didn't it register when Donnelly announced it every time he came here?"

"You've been doing other's biding for so long that you were lost in your duties, to the promises that you made. So far, you're the one man who's kept up his end, till' now. Who knows what might lie ahead in this wondrous place called Atlantic City." And the two stood, hand in hand staring out into the sea.

Tom waited then spoke, "James, better we take to the hotel and settle ourselves, rather than having the Mrs. and the children so close . . ." James turned from a distraction he could not afford, hearing Tom's words, but not acknowledging the man himself.

"Emmett, lead the way," said James, as Emmett was familiar with Atlantic City and its layout. He had first worked here on the muscle end of Liam Donnelly's uninvited intrusions into high stakes card games and the likes. The inclusion of Emmett was a gamble to be sure, in all places, but O'Boyle's decision to go in James's favor of using Emmett would not be questioned. It was after all, the accumulative wreckage and debt left by Donnelly that led to his

DP Curran

sanctioned killing at the hands of Finbar O'Boyle. Atlantic City was not the place to wet your beak without an invitation. In an undisclosed meeting, a hefty sum of money was agreed upon to ensure Emmett's involvement going forward in Atlantic City. The trickle down would mean a task of equal measure, to be exacted at a later date.

The Blenheim Hotel loomed against the high blue sky with white clouds as strokes of an artist's brush. An advertisement, a likeness of the hotel on the train didn't compare to what he now saw in person. It made a large man feel small, and what sort of man dreams of such buildings as this and then builds the same?

A diminutive man with a face of freckles appeared beneath the great awning to the hotel's entrance. Red hair darkened with tonic, a meticulous part separated his fine, but full mane. Bellhops moved in unison at the snap of his fingers, as he raised his arms as a conductor of music. Emmett stood between the eager bellhops in full dress and his charges, there was a sudden halt in their movement.

"Emmett McGowan, I see you've found your way to the other side, *failte* . . ." The slight man stepped forward, but not from the shade.

"*Go raibh maith agat*, Cornelius, thank you." Emmett corrected his slip of the tongue and showed it by shifting his weight. Something that was not unnoticed by James.

150

"Mr. Sullivan, if you would allow our staff to take what luggage you choose acceptable to your rooms, it would be a pleasure, sir."

"And who might I be speaking to?" James was again in the game.

"Forgive me, sir. My name is Cornelius McGillicutty, I am manager of the hotel. All of your needs are in my hands, sir. You need only to ring the switchboard and I will make myself available to you and your party. You are a guest here, sir, and you will be treated as such." Mr. McGillicutty produced a thick business card from his person and motioned for a young boy by his side to deliver it to James. The man did not step into the sunlight.

James took the card from the boy, glancing at it before holding it out for his wife.

"And what floor will we be on, Mr. McGillicutty?"

"The top floor, of course, sir."

"How many floors does a fireman's ladder reach, Mr. McGillicutty?"

"Six, so I understand, sir."

"What floor do you stay on?"

"The first floor, sir."

"Smart man, indeed is the manager. Follow the smart man, Emmett, and lead us to the top."

The curt look of revelation and contempt came over one Cornelius McGillicutty, as he was sure that James Sullivan's words were more of a warning than that of a question.

Large ceiling fans hovered in the dim lobby of a king. Opulent statues and ornate moldings with Chinese palms. At the center of it all was a huge fountain, filled with orange fish that caused the children's heads to turn as they gathered round in wonderment. They spoke to each other with their eyes, every eye making contact.

Two sets of elevator doors opened to James and his family and he wondered again if including them was good judgement. He chided himself and vowed that every man, woman and child in the hotel would die at his hands should any harm come to his flesh and blood. He felt a certain warm hatred that strengthened him with that thought.

James paused until the service elevator opened for the bellhops. "Tom, if you would." It was clear James wanted Tom to ride with the luggage and its handlers. Another sharp turn of the knife for Mr. McGillicutty. James smiled and allowed the dismayed manager to enter the elevator first, just as a curious, but familiar man approached in full suited attire. James motioned for the operator to close the doors and tipped his hat to none other than Aengus O'Boyle.

In the next car, Bridget wrapped her arm around her husband's as they moved upward with Little Emmett between her family and the elevator doors.

Three successive blows were delivered to Cornelius McGillicutty in just minutes. A feat that would be relayed to his better. He had seen in short order what kind of man his boss would soon encounter, should he be so inclined.

James slipped a fiver into the hand of the elevator operator without the boy ever moving his hand to receive it. He waited in astonishment, after crackling out a voice changing, "Thank you, sir."

Even in a world of high rollers and gratuitous gangsters, a fiver was rare by any standards. The boy known as Lemons due to the fact that when he was tossed a quarter dollar for his first day's work around the hotels, he handed it back to the hotel manager and asked instead for a lemon. The boy cut and squeezed the lemon into a glass of tap water and drank it with more satisfaction than a well-made man of means. This so impressed his employer, Mr. Johnston, that he gave the boy a small room of his own, and often made the example of the orphan boy who turned misfortune into lemonade. Orphaned at the age of five the boy didn't know any other life than that of service to Mr. Johnston, who treated him as he might his own bastard son, had he one. Not like that of the other orphaned waifs of the Irish persuasion, he took in with impassive sentiment.

These boys grew into men, the smarter one's became lawyers and councilmen, some ascended to the level of federal officials. Anyone not bright enough worked a lifetime in the service industry.

DP Curran

One as loyal as the next, Mr. Johnston was their one priority, and they were paid according to their worth. Forbidden to give out information, the younger boys implied such knowledge and made enormous tips without divulging a word of logic. They did, however, supply Peirce Tracey with any and all information on every guest, without consideration for its importance. Any knowledge learned would be discerned by Mr. Tracey alone, and then passed up the ladder as it were. Peirce Tracey was an outsider, in the fact that he was from Hell's Kitchen in New York, himself a *'Native.'* Vetted and shadowed for years he was recruited for his prowess of deciphering information. At first, he himself thought the inclusion of mere boys in his daily routine an insult, but his mind soon changed, given the ripeness of information laid out in great detail by these same boys. He was impressed and took this as a lesson, a lesson of experience by his new employer. His position covered a wide range of information and threat analysis, but he remained fascinated by the effectiveness of such young charges and their daunting loyalty.

He indulged himself on a humid afternoon in a closed meeting with three of the boys, he would put their loyalty to the test. Without cause, Tracey took a boy, no more than the age of seven by the throat, holding him up for the others to see. He accused the boy of lying and having been given more money than allowed to speak such lies. To his surprise, Lemons, as it just happened to be said, in a calm and parched tone, showing the red telltale finger marks on his throat. "Kill me then, sir, as it would be your duty."

The enraged Tracey slapped the youngster, though he held his ground. The others in attendance sat at a long wooden table, that held the smell of salt that permeated the open room. The sound of switch blades in unison cut through the faint roar of the sea.

"Dismissed" Tracey said, in a tone of misplaced power. He did not consider the matter closed, though he did not speak of it.

That night, Mr. Tracey heard three knocks on the door of his suite. Three, tall V shaped men of the Irish persuasion stood outside his door and in their midst, was Lemons. No words were exchanged, none were needed. A rare warning by Mr. Johnston, was all . . .

Lemons, was a boy not concerned with such thoughts of what the future might hold. He was struck with the timeless, here and now. You could be kind to him, one might even think to understand him, but he was of his own. Loyal, though not clingy, thankful, though never bootlicking. Unafraid of life or death he was, as James Sullivan put it, an entity, that one would do best to treat as a spirit, one to be in the presence of, without malice or fear. Lemons was just that to James, a dead boy, walking amongst those who believed in life, fearful people, all. Lemons knew James was different from the others, from the boisterous men of cowardice beginnings. They were aware of one another, travelers of both dirt and sea, giving nothing of themselves away. Easy, one with the other.

"Johnson's boy's", as they were known, though not called that in the confines of Atlantic City, were an enigma. The further lesser men tried to rattle or find a flaw in their performance, none were successful. As far as the business end went, *'Button Men'* were as high as these boys rose. More than a few inquisitive men met their death by these same *'Button Men'*.

Mr. Johnston believed in Karma, for which he defined as death.

Even the brightest stars in the ranks were relegated to settling matters in a court rooms, board rooms, council meetings and the likes.

Lemons real name was Archibald Black, the son of a prostitute and degenerate gambler of the same name. The father shot dead in the sand, paces from the old Breakers Hotel. The boy's mother, found washed up on the beach, two blocks from her boarding house one day later, by perhaps the one honest cop in Atlantic City.

Officer Pete Carney, stood six foot four inches tall, with the disposition of an unbridled Irish stallion. He was off the boat and meted out justice at the end of a nightstick. That's if you were Irish, from Ireland. *'The Natives'* first-generation Irish got it worse, crippled if they were lucky. All others, the Negroes, Polish and unconnected Italians were arrested after a casual beating to the stomach. Officer Carney's thinking was such that the Irish should know better.

Although not on the sheet, as most of the police force and politicians alike were, Pete Carney liked and admired Mr. Johnston. A smart Irishman, indeed, he would think often to himself, bursting with pride as he did, so many times. No, Officer Carney was not on a sheet that included policeman that were paid each month to subsidize their meager pay. No one begrudged them that, a perk as it were, a given. And earned at that.

Pete Carney walked that beat that included Mr. Johnston's hotel, otherwise known as the famous Marlborough Blenheim Atlantic City. Pete took this personal and kept the area clear of any unknowns or rabble rousers, looking to make a name for themselves. Officer Carney was a family man with a fierce reputation for loyalty and toughness. He often escorted Mr. Johnston without reproach by newspapers nor gangsters alike, because there were no dots to connect the two. Though strange, friends they were, a mutual respect for who each man was in this world.

The Carney family received a fresh turkey for Thanksgiving and Christmas, imported ham for Easter. And of course, a handsome tip of one hundred-dollar bills in a personal Christmas card signed by Mr. Johnston's own hand. The same was provided for his birthday, a day for which Officer Carney did not announce. Yes, they were friends in the only way each man knew how, and it was good. This was part of Patrick "Paddy" Johnston's appeal. He related to the rich, the poor, the strong, and most of all, the defenseless. Oft times the most defenseless of all, children, children beaten and abused. Mr. Johnston took the matter a personal slight, and a crime against humanity. A heavy price was paid for any persons connected in such behavior, this included the prostitution of minors. That was forbidden in his world, and Atlantic City was just that, his world . . .

CHAPTER 15

James Sullivan and Aengus O'Boyle sat alone on the balcony overlooking the Atlantic Ocean and spoke in hushed tones in the shadows of Little Emmett and Aengus's lone bodyguard, seen for the first time this night. One, Kevin O'Hennessey from Ireland born and trained. Elbows to their knees, the two leaned in to one another and whispered. Cigarette smoke provided a thin veil, and their words vanished with each breath expended.

"What we have here, Seamus, is a game—not a game played out on a card table or roulette wheel, no, this is a game of wits. You'll see nothing of Mr. Johnston on this trip, the game has been played and he now tallies your earnings. For you see, Seamus, you've put more than your cards on the table. You've done what's been asked and more, though you, yourself, have not lost yourself in doing so. You're one of the few who has kept his honor, yet showed respect to those that will never demand it, but require it none the less. Let's not forget, your whole family is here. You're all in, as they say, in this wild place, where justice finds its way."

"Then we leave on the first train in the mornin', is that it then, Aengus?"

"*Ifreann ar bith*, that's not it. Don't make me crazy, stop takin' me back to when we first crossed paths, ya feckin' hard head ya'. Soon as Bridget and the children are settled for the night, the four of us here will be meeting some people out at sea, under the pier, there." Aengus lead a line with his eyes to the place.

"As you've said, I've got my family here, Aengus. There's no feckin' way, I'm leavin' em' here in the dark of night." James snubbed out his cigarette with his thumb and index finger.

"It's not that way here, Seamus. Not like it was in Ireland, where your enemies would sneak about and kill your kin under the cover of darkness. It would be too easy to return the favor now. You must understand, here in America there is too much money to be made or lost. They have rules on such behavior, and I should say, Seamus—Mr. Johnston thinks you a winner. You and your family are his guests here in Atlantic City. No man would lift a finger without his say."

"My judgement tells me different, Aengus. That skinny boot licker, McGillicutty needs a long nap."

"Don't, Seamus, just don't . . . your boyhood mate, Brody McFarland . . ."

"What of him?" James sat up in surprise of this name.

A pause fell over the two men suspended one hundred feet above the boardwalk.

"Mo theanga . . ."

"It's not your tongue that worries me, Seamus. It's your own mind, son. It's you and I, to the end. I have somewhat of a surprise for ya'. Brody, he made it away with his life the night ya' left Ireland. Big as a house he is, somethin' in the well water by your houses, I swear by Christ."

"What are ya' sayin', where is he this evenin', Aengus?"

"Right here, in the same hotel." Aengus chuckled in amusement.

"Is he in with us, then?" James asked, somewhat shocked.

"Aye, in deep, he is. Deeper than he knows." Aengus lit a cigarette and handed it to James, though he refused it. "Before we go any further, Seamus—Tom is dead. It's over and done with. It's an old score, Seamus, and now the slate is clean, as far as Mr. Johnston is concerned."

"And Little Emmett?" James asked, in a quiet voice but loud enough for Emmett to hear.

"Little Emmett, he wiped the slate clean, Seamus. It had nothin' at all to do with you or his loyalty toward you or your family. He wouldn't have gotten' anywhere near ya', if that be the case. It had to do with Donnelly and his meddling down here of all places. Tom lived in the middle and that's nowhere for any man to live. He was the key that unlocked this door for us here in Atlantic City, let's remember him that way. He went out without a whimper, eyes open."

"You knew then?"

"Aye"

"Is Brody in danger?"

"That he is, to be sure, but we're all in danger, every one of us. Always have been, people like us, Seamus. We stick with our own for now, and by now, I mean until your sons are of age. If ya' have the mind for it, Seamus." James gave no indication of his intentions concerning his sons. Though James knew what Aengus had meant, they would be dealing with *'The Natives'*, but they would not be in the same circle. As to how long, Aengus made it clear using family to solidify his point.

"What time at the pier?"

"Midnight, you've got a few hours to catch up with McFarland, but Seamus . . . talk without sayin' anything. Converse on what happened, and not what's happening. You'll soon see what I already know of the young McFarland's character. Oh, and Seamus. Your wife's cousin, Owen is with us—we'll need him now." James again showed no sign of emotion, for he knew the bond between Bridget and Owen. For the first time that evening, James was encouraged with certainty.

James and Aengus rose together and walked past Little Emmett and Kevin as it were, and James held no feeling one way or the other for Emmett.

Right now, James was still under the tutelage of his brother-in-law, Aengus O'Boyle. He would wait and sharpen his wits as a butcher might his collection of knives. Trusting no man, save perhaps Brody—he would need to study his childhood friend. That was paramount . . .

CHAPTER 16

The doors of the balcony closed behind James Sullivan and the fresh taste of salt air had left him and for that, he was glad. The stuffiness of the hotel's confines suited the mood all the better. The next time he breathed the clean salt air, would be after reuniting with Brody McFarland. His mind went back to the dark sight of the ship and dead Irish sea captain tied to the ship's wheel, and he did wonder of his friend's escape from the hands of the English patrol. He would need to use his judgement once more.

Two men flanked the door to James's suite, three perfect taps to the door by Aengus and it opened, as if by the three taps themselves. Behind the door, stood Owen Morrison, with a natural grin that had not left him as it had so many other men in his position. He embraced James, unfitting an Irishman, but tonight would be different, tonight there would be the strong sense of familiarity and kinship that James thought no longer existed.

"*Am ar fad, Seamus.* Too long . . ." Owen said, with his words parodying his embrace.

"Owen . . ." was all James could say. The cold steel of their eyes was enough.

James grasped his wife's outstretched hand, as the children gathered in bedclothes. Holding the baby, Michael, with voices of all people known to him, James noticed from the duct of his eye, Brody McFarland. He kissed Michael, unabashed for Brody to see, before giving the boy to his mother.

"Seven English heads I counted as you were pulled to the deck, Brody McFarland. Yet, here you stand more alive than I could keep your memory all these years." James spoke the words, as he approached a boy long dead.

The same embrace was not applied, but a handshake, as the two looked each other over in astonishment. James spoke once more to Brody's appearance.

"Not a scratch on ya', Brody, a few more stones mind ya', but nary a scratch?"

With that, Brody McFarland coaxed James to yet another balcony. Little Emmett followed, unmoved in the strong sea breeze that ten stories provides. Owen took his place behind his beloved cousin, Bridget, making clear his role, as a close relative and personal bodyguard to Bridget.

After pausing at the sight of Emmett, Brody took off his tailored shirt and tie to reveal the most horrific sword scars and braids of skin produced by an English whip. He turned for James to see the fullness of his suffering. Brody motioned to his belt, and James nodded for him to continue with his exhibition, lifting his cock to show that he had been castrated. Emmett looked on all knowing, at that moment the hatred of the English was palpable and not even the pureness of the sea could quell it. James looked on, clearly unmoved by his friend's loss.

Brody dressed himself with his head down, not sure of his old friend, who he had exchanged the oath of blood with as young men, though still boys in any other world perhaps.

"Maith dom." James breathed the words.

"There is nothing to forgive, brother, except our weary minds and the deception that separation brings." Brody sighed and the two did embrace in the sight of Emmett McGowan. In Emmett's mind, despite the fondness for his dead nephew Tom, Little Emmett knew that he left this world without shame. To be born in Ireland was the one, solitary way to ensure loyalty in dealings with all others. The Italians understood this, the Jews understood this, and now for this group of men born on Irish soil, this was how it was to be. The fiercest rival to the Irish were *'The Natives'* or *'The Firsties.'* First generation Irish born in America.

The time was right, better than it would ever be for the Irish, but they now knew above all, that they could not have *'The Natives'* in the inner sanctum. Though by blood and appearance they were indistinguishable.

In less than ten years' time, many an Irishman would have to groom their sons to be the masters of their surroundings in *the business,* as it were known, which included law enforcement, judges and politicians at the local, state and federal level. What the Irish were about to embark on now would ensure this. Not just for their children, but to arm and fund the rebels in Ireland, something for which *'The Natives'* had severed all ties with, save a small percentage and they were not well received by their parent's homeland of Ireland.

Mr. Johnston was born in The United States of America, yet he knew better than anyone the value of the Irish. They were determined, fearless and disciplined in smaller numbers. "Paddy" Johnston knew that extracting any information at all from the Irish factions, as they were known, was next to impossible. They were impervious to the usual forms of torture from rivals, if captured, they would provoke their own death before talking. Even the police and federal agents knew that jail time for the Irish factions was nothing more than an adjustment of sorts. No information elicited and in the end, they ran the prisons and lived in conditions much better than they ever had back in Ireland. Yes, they seemed the perfect match for what lie ahead in the land of opportunity. And in Atlantic City, they would be appreciated for their efforts, without regard for how they spent their money. They were more than fair in negotiations and took out their own trash. Any notion or slightest rumor of self-aggrandizing was met with certain death, and not a disappearance or apparent suicide. Gutted like a fish, as was the custom in Ireland, given the sparseness of guns. The Irish and *'The Natives'* knew this was the way of the old, but they respected it to a man.

A bottle of fine Irish whiskey and two short heavy glasses of cut crystal were placed between two old friends on the balcony. Brody wasted no time in opening the bottle and pouring the glasses to the brink. James watched in amazement as Brody held up his glass without so much as a shudder, the content of the glass did not sway.

"*uisce beatha* . . . water of life," James said.

"*Slainte mhaith* . . ." Brody held up his glass and looked at James to respond.

"How long, Brody?" Taken aback by James's terse question, Brody produced the look of feigned surprise. James had read too many faces to conclude otherwise.

"I don't follow, Seamus." His face now showing a natural contempt, for what was now about to be determined.

"How long did the ship dock in Donegal Bay on the night you were captured, flogged, castrated and then released?"

"That one night, Seamus. It slipped out of the bay before daybreak. I lay in the reeds, bleeding, until I awoke in a hospital. I was released, yes, but as an example to others who might try the same. Nothing new about that, Seamus. Are ya' questionin' my veracity, now are ya'?"

"A good break is all I'm sayin', Brody. The fuckers were fileting boys like mackerels. I watched just to let it burn into my heart, and each boy pulled from the bay unawares, hardened my heart into a brick. You'll have to excuse my bluntness."

"Excuse you, as ya' sat and watched from above . . .?"

"A dead man exacts no revenge, but a live man, now that's another story, altogether."

"You've seen what they've done to me, my balls were cut clean off, as that I might never father a child, and you judge me?"

"Your alive, and that's all that matters, Brody. How many children do the balls of a dead man produce?" James was calm in his words.

"Emmett . . ." James said, just above a whisper.

"Mr. Sullivan, sir?" Emmett had a tragic tongue for the English language.

"Allow Mr. McFarland his glass of whiskey, but take the tray, bottle and my full glass."

Without words, the giant known as Little Emmett squeezed between the two friends and took the tray and its contents. Brody stared in disbelief, he swallowed a full glass of whiskey and placed it on the moving tray.

"Why do you not drink with me, Seamus . . .?"

At that moment, Emmett's presence allowed for the slightest illumination of light onto the balcony. James began to speak in a way not before seen by Brody, though years had passed.

"You know, Brody. The strangest thing happened to me here in America, I've always loved to read as you have, that's a given, but what I've been reading resonates with me more than all the poetry and literature from our own shores. The greatest writers to me are still the Irish, nothing compares, but I'm bias and unapologetic, mind you. There are some fine writers in America, new and fresh, breaking through to a different way of thinking, as some have put it. I believe it's a freedom of thought to paper, not a much different way of thinking, so much as the freedom to write it."

"Literature is it now, Seamus, you've become a dreamer, a philosopher?"

"I've become aware, Brody. Aware of a great weakness about us, the Irish. I've read about the American Indian of all peoples, and there are a few definite parallels."

"They're heathens, Seamus. The lot of them . . ."

"Heathen, now there's an arbitrary word—so, too, once were we considered, don't forget that. That's not the analogy though. It's the drink, the whiskey, in particular. We were denied rights, food, freedom and dignity, but we were plied by the barrel in whiskey. The same was true for the American Indian, it was as a revelation to me."

"You've given up the drink then?"

"No, Brody . . . I've just not given in to it. Rational men, serious men cannot allow for such a luxury. Once a man takes a drink, the drink oft times takes the man. If you are so disposed to the drink as many a fine man is, it will be your death in this place. That is a fact, look around and you'll see the serpents among us. It's not as if we work in the shadows anymore, Brody. I don't know what you've been told or what you know, but take this advice from an old friend, and keep your wits about you."

"You baffle me, Seamus, yet, here we both are."

And so, it was . . . that the two-digressed back to Ireland and to boyhood, and dared whispered of *'The Ghost'* who sat, leg crossed waiting for midnight as the moon aligned itself with the view that shimmered on the expanse of the Atlantic Ocean. An ocean that gave them both a connection to home and to how they once were to one another.

The words were uttered, by Aengus O'Boyle, "It's time, boys."

A slight nod and a blink of their eyes was all James and Owen needed to convey their solidarity and conclusions concerning Brody.

Five men left together, though Brody McFarland walked in the opposite direction to a separate hotel. Turning to look at Seamus for the last time through the fog and smoke of a fresh cigar lit by James own hands. Something which James was taught early on by *The Ghost'* himself, never let another man light so much as a cigarette for you, always refuse such feminine acquiescence.

Men in suits appeared in numbers coming from the opposite direction, though Brody walked without hesitation into their midst. Resigned perhaps, to his fate that had cheated him once before in the Bay of Donegal . . .

CHAPTER 17

The muffled waves of the night played out on the jetty. Unseen by the people of the light and all things normal. Four men cloaked in loose black clothing walked beneath the fishing pier, their soft soled shoes wet with sea water. The smell of the mooring gave each man a different strength, as all were men familiar with the sea and the riggings that led into the deep.

Aengus led the way, followed by his man, Kevin, then Little Emmett in front of James. Aengus broke the tranquility that danger brings to certain men.

"Your thoughts on Brody, what are they?"

"Send him back to the English or the American authorities in pieces, that was my first thought." James spoke no more.

"And your thoughts now, Seamus?"

"The same. He was flogged, gelded, by a surgeon, no doubt. He would have bled out if not, too clean for a man that was to be killed in the end. Then, he conspired, was rewarded, and sent with untold wealth to find us. Never again will you or anyone else bring this thing we have into my home, anywhere near my wife or children. That is a solemn a promise as I can give another man. There will be blood in these waters tonight, Aengus. Right now, I don't much care whose. Ya' with me, Little Emmett?" James stopped.

"To the end, a bloody battle in the sea would be a fitting way for any true Irishman to go out, having no choice in the matter, Seamus." Aengus and Kevin found themselves now ahead of James and Emmett. Aengus turned.

"Brody, poor Brody. He gave us more information than he would ever hope to acquire. He was useless in matters of violence, Seamus. The man would not have been anywhere near our family, given the slightest notion otherwise." Aengus turned, as a man fit for any situation.

"My family, Aengus. Immediate family at that, you have misjudged my respect and loyalty as that of a dog, or some other family pet. Fit for your own usefulness or whims, maybe. I'll not be your means to an end, and the fact is, Aengus, I don't care, not in the slightest. You fuck with my family, my family, Aengus, and one or both of us will be dead, surrounded in Irish blood."

"Careful big man, your spendin' words on somethin' you can't afford."

"You can try to baffle me with your bullshit all ya' want, Aengus, but I'm willin' to spend all that I have right here in this grey shit smellin' water . . ."

"Some men must be told, they can't see far enough ahead. Though it be no fault of their own, Seamus. Once you've been told, yer' no longer livin' in ignorance. Then ya' take what comes with that. I don't doubt your willingness to kill or even be killed, but you've got people countin' on ya'. If you find yourself a friend in a double dick dog, ya' don't cut one of em' off. No offense, to my Kevin and your man Emmett there, but you and I can't afford to be dyin' on people, not just yet, and not by my own hand. I heard your wishes concernin' your wife and children and that will be respected no exceptions, but don't ever force my hand, Seamus, there are some things even a man as myself would find hard to live with." The temperament of the wind itself had shifted with Aengus's words. Lights flicked unanswered at the end of the pier.

"Those words were a long time comin', Aengus, and I meant what I said, and I can't change that. Your words hold their own weight and meaning, not to be taken with a hint of doubt. The words had to be said . . ." James said, as he stood tall in the shifting waters under the pier.

DP Curran

"A long time comin', Seamus . . ."

"Aye" and the two men shook hands in the dark of night where the words of men were settled in an earnestness not found by day.

"Now, then, the boy you once knew as Brody died that night in Donegal Bay as sure as were fuckin' about under this pier, he just still had the misfortune of still roamin' the earth, the poor bastard. He helped us more than all our paid informants combined. Yet we paid him nothing, your assessment was correct, Seamus. We'll not see Brody again, but your method of delivery will not be used, by all accounts he's already dead, and he was shown the mercy of a quick death. You've seen now that being born in Ireland alone means little in of itself. We are liars, thieves, and murderers all, the four of us each, let alone those who now approach us. You must assess every man, woman and child from this point on, Seamus. Not based on their origin alone, but their actions and reputation as well. That is, after all, why I choose you . . ." The four men moved forward together, closer now than before.

Two boats with lanterns extinguished, bobbed in the choppy waters at the end of the pier. A lifeboat bearing the name "Atlantic City" on both sides, appeared and angled toward the four, in slow strokes. The strained baying of intermittent fog horns lessened the sound of the wooden oars in their metal rings.

One man sat with the oarsman, the row boat rollicked in the uneven surf that the pylons of the pier provided. A brogue as thick as any man's cut through the tension and salt air.

The man spoke, "Gentleman, we'll agree on one language during all transactions, be it only fair to our native partners. Sad to say, some don't even understand the Irish tongue, let alone speak it. A casualty of assimilation, I'm afraid. Though we want the same for our children now, don't we? Grandchildren in my case even."

The man not looking the age of a grandfather climbed from the boat. A man of medium height, though stocky in his gait, even amongst the tug of the tide. He reached out his hand bare and rough as the wood above.

"Aengus, you've not changed much since the last we met." And the two shook hands.

"Aye, and you've not changed a bit, granddad is it now?" Aengus smiled with the creases of a serious man about his eyes.

A hush fell over the lot and the sounds of the night were all there was. Aengus then spoke, "What are ya' doin' here, Neil? I wasn't told you'd be part in this."

"The boss thought it be best havin' an Irishman handle our dealings, bein' we've known one another for such a time and we've not had cause to quarrel in any of our dealings. We're straight, you and I, are we not, Aengus?"

"Aye, to this point, I can say that with certainty. Truth be told I'd like to have a bit of catchin' up, but we both know that won't do, don't we, Neil?"

"All that matters is we are square and good, Aengus. *Dea?*"

"*Dea*, good, we are, Corrmack."

"Shall we . . ." Corrmack chided with the dark smile that Aengus knew all too well. He had seen it many times in his youth, as Neil Corrmack was second only to *'The Ghost'* Aengus O'Boyle in English deaths. His forte was somewhat different than that of the boy that admired him so. Corrmack scalped each of his victims. Quite the way with a knife. A warning sure to be passed on to the others, as soon as was possible. Ironic that James spoke of the American Indian that very night, in his comparison with the Irish. Little did he yet know.

"Boys, this is Mr. Corrmack, his reputation and word is unquestioned, both in Ireland and here in America."

Mr. Corrmack shook each man's hand with equal measure, being sure to put the clamp on Little Emmett in a way the big man could not forgive.

The last was James, the wake of the sea at knees height. Eyes squinted in the moving darkness, as James pushed against sea and sand toward his elder. Hands clasped, and the squinted stare continued for each man.

"I knew yer' father, Padraig, Seamus. Can't say as ya' favor him, more that of your mother's clan, MacBranain or as the English dogs would have it, Brannon. A clan of giants from the beginning, I suppose. Brannon is used here in America now just the same, but at least we have the pleasure of being in a land that sent the bastards back to England in disgrace. The English wept as babies at the notion of guerrilla tactics. That was a valuable lesson for us, the Irish. We've put it to good use. Strange lot here in America, Seamus, but not a lot of fuckin' about when it comes to makin' money. That's why we're here this evenin'. Do as you have been and whatever plans you have concernin' the territory of Swampoodle or anywhere else on the Eastern seaboard will be left for you to discern. You've got everything it takes, and you'll need all of it. Stay close with Aengus, as close as any man might, *'The Ghost'* . . ." James stood, hand still locked with Mr. Corrmack, until his grip subsided. The black smile returned, and the men climbed into the boat.

Out of the grey, Corrmack spoke again. "I know your heart and mind hold an unknown date back to Ireland, Seamus O'Suilebhain. Necessity may it be—make that your own concern, your mind and body are in the here and now, always. Behave that way, I ask but that much of ya', lad."

"How do you suppose to know so much, sir?" James was dry in his words.

"We've all been looked up and down here, Seamus, be it James here in America, dependin' on who it be." The men's words passed over Emmett, who sat in the middle of the boat as a ballast, as Aengus shook his head to signal the end of any further questions by James.

Two larger wooden sailing boats, sat beyond the pier, lanterns out. The metal rings that held the oars of the lifeboat mixed with the slapping of sea water and the hollow sound of boat to boat docking.

Short ladders secured to the wooden sailing vessels made the traverse onto the closest ship all the easier. The crew of Irish origin did not speak, but shifted as Little Emmett took to the ladder with all of himself.

"What you hear from these men is all that you will ever hear, nothing. The two boats are identical, gentleman. Familiarize yourselves with this one and you'll know the other as the same. The same short wide girth of a man stood next to Mr. Corrmack after the others were dismissed. It was clear that this was Neil Corrmack's bodyguard. James thought what an adventurous life Corrmack and O'Boyle must have led before responsibility to others created the need for the help of another man to keep each alive. One more person to worry about, James thought. His own days as a freelancer were also gone, he thought. Gone for good.

"Finn and I will show ya' around. Ain't that right, Finn?" His man nodded, his thumb and index finger grasping his tweed cap. Short mechanical fingers, stained with oil or blood, had a reddish hue, by the trickery the moon plays on a man's eyes.

"Quiet unto death that one, but you know that without bein' told, Aengus. Most of the old crew be dead now, though young they were when the *reaper* came for them. Death comes for some men many times, but only once for some. We don't try to figure such things out, you and I, Aengus. We just keep usin' our judgement until the time comes, be it day or night, no man knows. Myself, better that it be at night, we live in the dark, all of us here. Better for us to die in it, I've always thought." The old man talked in a way that made James think he was talking to him, personal like, and he hated it. James fumed at the thought of having his thinking done for him, and to satisfy himself he vowed that he would not die at night, but in the light of day surrounded by his family. "Grandad" would be Neil Corrmack's moniker from this night forward as far as James would see things. James's musings were cut short by more talk from the old man.

"If ever there is a time I am not here when a transaction is to take place, kill every man you see, whether or not you see that man this night. It will be a set-up, as sure as a mother's love. Take to your territory and wait a messenger, one that will already be considered a dead man and of no consequence if he be killed delivering such a message, but hear him first. Now, with that unlikelihood out of the way, these same boats will be three miles from the shore, use the pier as your bearing for now. You'll need your own boats, that we will square at the marina tomorrow at noon sharp. Sharp being the key word, the boss is a unique man of Irish decent. First generation here in America, mind ya', but Irish in the most important ways. His fascination with his partners being punctual is by all accounts a matter of life and death." The absence of words fell over the men once more, a gust of salt air and spray filled each with strength. James filled his lungs and spoke in a respectful manner that eased Aengus's mind.

"Why the three miles when these boats are so close to shore now, sir?"

"The boats are empty lad, and more to your point, the limit of United States maritime jurisdiction is three miles out. A fair question, Seamus, for I asked it myself. The old eighteenth century smooth bore cannons reached all of three miles. They've not changed the law of yet, but given the concerted effort of smart men, we can count on that changing. We've made our own plans in lieu of such changes, but for now . . . three miles out."

"We'll talk percentages tomorrow, and gentleman, the percentage of a lot of money is a lot of money. They'll be another man with us at the marina, second but to Mr. Johnston, as far as any of us are ever to be concerned . . ." A lantern was lit and waved to the open sea, another lantern shone back from a ship painted as dark as the sea at night, it's sail's the same.

"Ah, there we have it, my shanty Irishmen—three miles to fortune . . ."

James and Aengus sat together and talked well into the wee hours, staring out at the sea. They were nearer in thought than ever before, and it was certain by both that they were in the company of cunning, dangerous men, in both mind and actions.

CHAPTER 18

The morning sun rose upon the sea in a radiant ball of orange. The suites that faced the Atlantic had the luxury of viewing both the sun and moon rises. The quiet tones of children with the deepened sounds of sleep, played in James's mind, as he sat on the edge of the large bed. He lit a cigarette from a full pack, no longer in the habit of buying *loosies* from the dime store. He kept the lighter recovered from Tom's body, as was his last request before giving up his life, that James be given the lighter as a sign of respect.

"Breakfast, James Sullivan, but first I want ya' to try what they call a shower. Nothing can replace a tub of hot water, mind ya', though the shower was exhilarating and a bit decadent. Fancy soaps, creams and towels to die for, Seamus. In ya' go now, go on, I'll have your breakfast waiting right here in the bedroom for ya'." Bridget fussed with the clothes that James had on the night before, and she put his shirt to her face to capture the lingering smell of the sea.

From a fog of thought, James focused on the words of his wife, as if he had been listening in earnest. He pushed his hands through his coarse blonde hair and turned to her.

"You spoil me woman, but a shower you had whilst I slept. That will be the last one of those you'll be takin' without me . . . come ere', girl and sit with me."

"Oh, no, ya' wicked thing, ya'. Your children and my cousin are right beyond the door, and I'm not so gullible as I once was— Seamus O'Suilebhain."

"You were never gullible, Bree. You were a wild mare with a golden mane that touched your perfect bum, and nothin' has changed, nothin' at all."

"Seamus, quick and quiet. Don't think I believe a word more than my hair hasn't changed either. I've got a few stretch marks from passin' those behemoths of yours. I like the way ya' tell a story is all." Bridget locked the door and pulled the pin from her hair, and she was more beautiful to James in every way.

"Stretch marks are the badge of a real woman, Bree." The two fought what clothes they had to the floor and coupled as wild animals might.

"Men are full of such shite." Bridget whispered, as they fell to the bed in a fury.

The shower turned James's skin to red, as he stood still full in his girth. He leaned his hands against the tiled wall and waited for the blood to return to his head, though his side did ache still.

Over breakfast, James read the police blotter section of the Atlantic City Press. He was amazed at such petty crimes being reported, given the fact of what went on in what was to be called, "The World's Playground." He took from it the difference that the power of one man could have. At this moment, James Sullivan's thinking was to change. He would observe and put to memory all that he could from this day forth. Instincts and sheer brute force would no longer be enough. He thought that he had never learned so much in so few words on paper. He closed his eyes with his back to the cushioned headboard and drifted into a state of realization and sleep. He was restful, but at the same time conscious to where he was and the voices around him. Hours past, as he found himself stiffened still by the wound in his side. Bridget had tended to it after his shower, and it showed all the signs of mending, though sore. James did not mention pain of any kind, not even to his wife. That he could not do.

Three short knocks at the door of the suite, and James knew it was time. He took a crisp white shirt from the wardrobe and had it on before Bridget came into the bedroom.

"You've taped over the peephole, so I've not answered the door." Bridget finished with the buttons on her husband's shirt, before pushing up on her toes to be lifted.

"I'm under your spell, witch. What'll it be, woman."

"A hug, Seamus. You will never leave me without one . . ."

"Aye, never, Bree."

Three more identical knocks, as the two embraced, understanding one another as no one else ever would understand either. Be it, they lived one hundred years.

The children were quiet from the first knock and remained so, as they hugged their da in front of the door.

"Never look through a peephole in a door and just as important never open it, without permission. Better yet, don't open any doors here in this place. The lot of ya' . . ." And James left through that same door, nodding to Owen, making sure to make eye contact. That was more than enough, for Owen loved his Cousin Bridget and her children more than life itself. No one would survive a man such as Owen, even if it was just business and not the last shred of goodness in his life.

James shook his head at Aengus, with a smile and the two walked with their bodyguards out into the bright sunshine of Atlantic City.

DP Curran

Aengus quietly said, "This was delivered by Lemons himself this mornin', Seamus. Sealed in wax, I had to cut it open. The boy had white gloves on—I uncovered the envelope on a small tray, under its own silver lid, along with a breakfast fit for an English king, for feck's sake. Here, read it."

The note was put back in the wax covered envelope itself, it read, *'Forty percent'*. Two words, was all. Two words that James read back to himself once more—James struck a match that filled the hallway with the smell of the sulfur, a stringent, powerful stench that reeked.

"What is it you're doin', man? Don't be burnin' that . . ." Aengus snapped his head to James, as was now somewhat of a habit.

"We've both handled this without the benefit of gloves, Aengus. This wax may serve more than one purpose. Keeping, young Lemons from opening it and perhaps to make our fingerprints more viable than ever. Fuck it, not a chance . . ." James lit the envelope and a Mexican standoff ensued just steps from the elevator. James pushed open the door to the steps and dropped the contents to the floor as it melted into a waxy buildup on the tiled landing.

"Great, genius. Now what about this mess?" Aengus kept the appearance of the upper hand with his tone, though in the process he conceded the necessity of destroying the elaborate message from Mr. Johnston himself.

"As soon as it dries, we scrape it up and count the numerous ways of disposing of what's left, as we wait." James smiled and looked to Little Emmett who smiled as well.

"We . . .? No, no. You and your large friend there can see to that. Why I let the two of you team up has left me, we're on a time table here, son. Do ya' get me?" Aengus looked through the small glass in the metal door into the hallway, as the elevator door opened and closed, empty.

"Plenty of time now, Aengus. It's damn near dry already, a tiny parcel of ash and wax. That bein' said, that match was the devil's match of the pack, it was . . ." The men all nodded in agreement, as James took the lid from the trash receptacle in the corner. He tore the lid from a small pastry box and scooped the mangled sculpture from the floor. Little Emmett kept his eyes on both Aengus and Kevin, feeling somewhat awkward at the sight of James Sullivan performing such a menial task. Still he waited for the slightest notion of foul play.

"Little Emmett, under this suit is a working man. Ease your mind, sir . . ." and Emmett felt the better for it, for his loyalty to a righteous man if he had ever known one.

Pastry box in hand, the men made their way straight to the elevator, the lighted numerals moving without a single stoppage, until the doors opened, to none other than Lemons.

"Good morning, gentlemen. What floor . . .?"

DP Curran

James cut the young man off. "Main lobby."

"Yes, sir . . ."

Lemons caught his tongue, as the four men awaited the last name Sullivan, but he did well to hold his tongue. It wasn't the sheer size of Little Emmett or the reputation of Aengus O'Boyle that gave the young man in waiting the most pause. It was the overwhelming presence of James Sullivan, not for fear of death, for Lemons lived in and around death itself. He was unafraid of death; it was to him an escape hatch from all that surrounded him, something, the one thing he himself had control over if he sought to take his own life. No, this was different, much different, even from that of Patrick Lewis Johnston, who Lemons feared, but admired as no other. A strange affection from that of a son, perhaps. For all the boy knew of such things.

In James Sullivan, he felt the overpowering need to not disappoint the man. He suffered at the thought of a judgement against himself for disappointing him, though just meeting James informally just one day before. Such was his impression of one, Seamus O'Suilebhain of County Donegal, Ireland. This too was the exact same feeling of Little Emmett McGowan. A person so large and fierce that one would never think that he and such a skinny man to be would have this in common with the cold-blooded killer of the highest degree. It had begun . . .

CHAPTER 19

The Marina District was a bit of a distance, and they had chosen to walk there, as James lowered his hat to shield his face from throngs of beachgoers and onlookers. The smells and sounds of the Boardwalk heightened his senses and relieved the pain of his wound. All that was left was the adhesive tape, pulled too tight by the one person who he would endure any unpleasantness with a certain pleasure.

"What untruths are more discernable, Aengus? Those told by day or night?" James exhaling his words with a smooth stream of cigarette smoke.

"Those told by day, and then discerned by night, Seamus. We see who we are dealing with better by day, though we know better for what we deal with in darkness." Aengus wiped the sweat from his nose without removing his hat.

He went further, "This feckin' sun will melt an Irishman like so much wax, lest he keep movin' . . . give me the light that the moon and stars provide this mutt filled country." His ears of red showed his true feelings.

The men left the boards and made their way down a path of sand and stones that the beach gives birth to, beaten by thousands of people before them, and headed for the Marina District of Atlantic City. A safe path that Little Emmett suggested, and knew all too well.

The wanton shade of the marina held Aengus without any further talk of the sun, as James pocketed the charred lump of wax and pushed the pastry box into a large cage like trash can that stood at just above the steps of each beach entrance.

Fifty yards from the dock, two men made their way to James and Aengus, strangers both. Slicked back greased hair, was unbefitting any fair-haired Irishman.

"*Natives*, Seamus. Sullied by gilded possessions and no real purpose in life, Irish in name and lineage, not born into or bound by true commitment. Consider them as nothing more, ever. Lest it be your own sons, ah, but they will know how to deal with the likes of these geldings."

"Gentleman, we approach with the honor of showing you to the parties concerned here today." Both men stood at a safe, but unenviable distance, given the reputation of the men they came to greet.

The imposing height and girth of Little Emmett, combined with the face of the man every bit as foreboding as his violent exploits in Atlantic City alone. A man deemed impossible to kill, given the numerous attempts on his life, by way of open contracts. He was now connected and any further attempts on his life would have to be approved.

This was not the time for such dangerous actions, given the money at stake and the need for seamless cooperation by all parties involved in what was to unfold. They had their chance and now Little Emmett would prove to be more dangerous than ever. A fact that "Paddy" Johnston was resigned to, with his usual confidence. He respected a man who eluded death in plain sight, more so a man of Emmett McGowan's strengths and unwavering commitment to his fellow Irishmen doing business here in America.

A large decorative canvas covered a secluded section of The Maritime Marina's outside eating area. Blocks of Ice and low fashioned fans blew cold air against the ankles and knees of the diners. A cool respite for the disagreeable Irishman, Aengus O'Boyle. One of the greeters spoke as if a master of ceremonies.

"Gentleman, I give you your captain . . ." 5A tall man with faded red hair, streaked with the blonde of the sun approached, he looked with distain at his undue introduction. Just then a smile appeared, as he reached out his hand to James, which embarrassed James, being all things respectful to Mr. O'Boyle.

"Bill McCann . . . please, James, Aengus, take a seat." James shook the strangers hand with a strange ease about him, though his name being spoken first was no doubt discussed beforehand by those in wooden rooms of fine cigar smoke.

This was the moment, a sublime moment of freedom for James. Without the need for explanations or musings. He would listen, focusing on the moment and the task at hand. Gone now was the second voice of a man that hesitates out of abundant caution, not the calm discernment that experience brings to a man. James never looked to Aengus, he shook the hand of a man who spoke unabashed American English with an air of confidence and wit about him.

The sky seemed more blue, a cerulean blue. the sun brighter and more tolerable. Even the ice in his tumbler of water was colder than he had ever remembered, as he watched the beads of water sweat from a translucent glass. His vision had improved, he looked to his tie in amazement, the green and white so vibrant and true.

"We'll keep this as short or as long as you like, gents. I'll have my say on behalf of myself, it's cut and dry. You can ask me anything, as long as it's fishing, mind you. Do you men enjoy fishing, I mean real fishing, big game fish . . . well, sure you do, you were born on an island, for cripes sake . . ."

"The purpose of this visit then, sir?" Aengus asked.

"Simple, now I know you, you know me, that sort of thing, come on fellas', you're in or you're out, this is how I do things. Me, I don't fret over what I can't control, do what you have to do, and I'll do mine. No need for animosity, I'm consistent, time will prove us all out . . . let's eat. Freddy, bring us some menus." And the man with red hair under a tilted straw fedora, wearing a bright tropical button-down shirt exuded happy prosperity and a zest for life itself. Not the pious, bitter mind set of a man born and raised in Ireland under British rule, no, this was a man of a revolutionary spirit. A spirit that James wished for his children, the thought rippled down his spine in the way splendid destiny came to a man for the first time.

Without pause, James raised his glass. "To America . . ."

"Now, we're cookin' with gas. Grab a menu, boys, everything is on me."

The ire of Aengus O'Boyle was palpable, though he spoke not of it. The men ate the finest lobster and steak whilst talk of fishing ensued. The host's name was Bill McCann and he spoke in detail of his favorite fishing routes, which happen to lead from places such as the Bahamas and Florida, straight down the coast to New Jersey. All the while leaning in to make a miniscule point about a trivial matter, and speaking aloud things about the size of his boats and their capacity, in terms of cargo weight. He was a breath of fresh air to James, though to Aengus it was a different matter of its own.

The meal was concluded, over ice cream, for which Mr. McCann had an obvious affection for. He spoke these, at first curious words. "I'm an avid reader fellas', but I don't like every book that I read, and the thing about me that's rather funny, I have to tell you . . . I do judge books by their cover, all the time. Never understood the old saying myself, just the opposite . . . ah, but maybe I'm just contrary, Irish blood and all."

"Thank you for the meal and genuine American hospitality, Mr. McCann. Your reputation proceeds you. And, if I may, the percentage is more than generous. Please, thank your boss, sir." Aengus said, now standing.

"Few things there, Aengus. I don't know anything about percentages, and ah, I'm my own boss. Oh, and one other thing, don't expect this kind of hospitality from all Americans, Aengus. Some are like the flu; you could catch your death from one . . ." McCann ended with an infectious laugh.

All were now standing, including the tall, lanky Irish-American who left an impression on both James and Aengus, howbeit somewhat different for each.

"*Saol Fada,* Seamus . . ." Bill McCann said, shaking James's hand with direct eye contact, an Irish touch of sincerity.

"A long life for us all, Bill. Thank you . . ."

After shaking hands with nothing more than a nod for Aengus, William "Bill" McCann disappeared into the side entrance of the tackle shop with the same robustness for which he appeared.

Aengus wiped his hands clean, spilling water from a glass and drying between each finger with the heavy napkins provided. Any conversation about the meeting that just took place would have to wait, wait until the moon was in its place.

James reached into his pocket and tossed the remnants of both wax and percentage into the flat bay next to the table, under the shade that the canopy provided, and the cool sensation of ice enveloping his knees.

The two men who greeted Aengus and James reappeared, with the same impassive looks on their faces. James feeling the tension as many others might, but he, he was a man to effect change. He always had been, even as a small boy, he could change the temperature in the air with a mere word or two. Notwithstanding his early talent for fisticuffs to effect change on boys twice his age. James waved the two men of definite skill and purpose closer, though their skill was not in the muscle end of things, to be sure.

"Yes, sir?" The elder of the two spoke, perhaps he provided the tutelage for his younger. A greeter, so to speak, or as James would understand it.

"Bring me two cars, of different makes. Sixty seconds, lads, fifty-eight—make the best of your time, for it well may be your time, fifty-two . . ." The men ran, revealing their comprehension of the man who gave the command. James lit his own cigarette, something for which Aengus taught him years ago, on a steamer bound for America. He did remember it so, as he looked to Aengus.

"What in the bloody hell are ya' doin', Seamus? For the love of Christ Himself, tell me." Aengus sat once more, breathing in the cool salt air that leveled the large ice block with each passing moment.

"Let's drive back, Aengus. Fuck the walk, one way I'll do, but not both ways. I won't have you do it. It's beneath ya', Aengus. I don't like it, not one bit. They'll take what they can get and give as little as they can on what they consider petty things. Sure, they'll pay top dollar for the best, for what they care about, take care of every creature comfort for themselves. I say, fuck em', we're here to stay anyway, as far as I'm concerned." The men each driving a car squealed around the tight corner to a stop.

"Big balls, this one, Kevin. Why did ya' give them but sixty seconds, Seamus?"

"I figured they couldn't wire two cars with explosives in less than a minute. It makes sense that they already have one ready to go at their disposal. Plus, they had to start them for us, we'll take the nicest one of the two . . ." James laughed.

"My fuckin' pride and joy, this man is the genuine article. I want you men to know that." Aengus rose, seeming a younger man, as the last of the ice trickled between the long boards of the marina cafe.

The long black convertible went against all conventional wisdom—riding open air for anyone to see but, it would be a short ride. After all, this was becoming known as "The World's Playground."

The ride back to the hotel was refreshing to James, though he knew there would be heated conversation that night. James looked to Little Emmett and smiled for the first time since the news of Tom's death. Emmett nodded, and an unbreakable bond was renewed without a word having been spoken.

James was grateful for many things, not least of which was the confidence he felt in Emmett. There were other things though, things that were put into place by the solitary mind of James Sullivan Sr. Business was a means to an end, his family was the equation that all of his decisions and planning hinged upon. Each meticulous step taken without knowledge or premonition of those around him. He forged personal alliances only with those he trusted and that benchmark for trust was family. How did men such as he see family, what was its priority? Any man in his inner sanctum had to be on the right side of this fundamental question. Jonathan Hirsch was one such man that met that standard, and the house on Taylor Street well, pure genius.

CHAPTER 20

The house on Taylor Street was a lifeline for James in more than a few ways. All of the mail concerning his mother and sister was sent there. The mail was put into the mail slot, which slid down into a safe, concealed in the walls below, in the cellar. Undetectable, even the mailman had no idea, all the better.

It was a sad day indeed, when James got word of Orla O'Boyle's death, it was said that she had died in her sleep, though James was at first skeptical, he thought perhaps that was the only way death could take her, unawares. In that letter, it was said that Sinead and Lilly were moved by *'The Ghost'* himself to a secluded farm near the sea in County Cork. A move from north to south would be the safest bet, so wrote a proxy of Aengus. This however made James more determined than before to get back to Ireland and reunite what was left of his family.

DP Curran

James had long since set his wife Bridget up with her own bank account, along with gold coins, and bonds to last her a lifetime. She had her own key and access to the safety deposit box in a controlled bank in Center City, Philadelphia.

The contents of which was that of a man of his lot in life, a construction foreman. The real security, enormous amounts of cash, gold coin, and the bonds were in a concealed vault in the cellar of the house on Taylor Street in Swampoodle. Designed, constructed, and built by the expertise of Jonathan Hirsch, a German immigrant, whose family was famous for their craftsmanship and ingenuity. The Hirsch Safe Company, Philadelphia, Pennsylvania. USA. A brand synonymous for quality and discretion. The family had amassed a fortune designing and crafting vaults for the most prestigious banks, up and down the Eastern seaboard.

Jonathan Hirsch was more infamous than famous, to certain clients, he ran the most secure and trusted private vault and safe operations in the country. All private work was performed by Jonathan alone, and all records were destroyed upon final payment. He had been used in many of the building contracts that James ran throughout the city. All of this done away from prying eyes of even the most influential people in public office. Jonathan Hirsch could be counted on, and was paid well for his skill and judgement. He and James bonded in such a natural way, as their mindsets were forged of the strongest of metal found in any vault ever constructed. A trust built on mutual respect for life and death. Few other men's word was so true in both life and death, better death than dishonor. It was an unspoken bond that both men felt for one another, it gave them both a sense of themselves as who they were, and they thought themselves honorable men in a world full of betrayal born out of fear and weakness.

The importance of family and the unwavering sanctity of marriage, a rare a thing as there was in the circles they traveled in. Each man was beholden to their wives and no other. Powerful, wealthy, educated men were unfaithful and boastful for it. This was not an option for such men as Hirsch and Sullivan. Loyalty was everything to both, and they conducted themselves as to be known that way at all times, though seldom seen together.

In Germany, the Hirsch's were known as machinists, metal workers, masters of the lathe dating back centuries. True as this was, they made a reliable name for themselves as gunsmiths of the highest quality. Handguns, for concealment, made for aristocrats and the like. That like other lucrative enterprises in Germany, they prepared for passage to America. Production had dropped as the economy worsened. The Hirsch family had no quarrel with the German government, for they had always been loyal Germans. The stability and limitless prospects for the future led to their liquidation and preparations were made for the move to America. Something for which was little known to all save a few influential men of means who sponsored their arrival to America. New, advanced factories were constructed where access to freight cars and shipping by way of the rivers and ocean was plentiful. Any risks taken, though calculated, reaped the rewards of the Hirsch's unparalleled skill and forward thinking.

The Irish maintained control over the loading docks of Philadelphia and were steeped with influence within The Pennsylvania Railroad. Much was to be gained for all involved, from upstate coal country to the entire Eastern seaboard. The Hirsch's had several subsidiary companies that dealt in everything from iron, steel and every other metal of profit to the construction industry. They were backed by Irish muscle and influence, after all, anyone of German decent were considered Irish by the Italian's and Jewish factions, and not to be trusted. They made no distinction between the two . . . an odd fact that suited both the Irish and Germans in matters of business. This was believed in large part due the undeniable resemblance of both ethnicities. Once a first generation of both were born in America, a common language made it futile to try and distinguish the two. Names were altered, aliases used, they were a perfect fit at the perfect time in history. Now, in World War I, known as the Great War, the Germans and Irish were enemies of England and British rule. In Ireland, German submarines were refueled along the Irish coast. Lookouts and

German spies slipped in and out of Ireland, without designs of conquest or contempt. A mutual enemy had made this so. Pro-Irish Nationalists were in favor of Britain's demise due to mass genocide and other atrocities by the English.

In Jonathan Hirsch, James not only had a trusted ally, but a man of unknown knowledge and expertise for which he shared with James alone. This was the relationship the two men had cultivated that would span years.

Personal, customized handguns were a favorite of James. He took pleasure in providing his wife Bridget with various handcrafted models as for her own protection, should she find herself in any precarious scenarios of personal danger. Bridget was more than capable with a firearm, and kept several with her always. Her quality as a person was formed from the inside out. A hardened interior with a mind for handling trouble covered with the disguise of beauty. The deadliest type of all women, so some would say . . .

James returned to the hotel, to find Bridget and the children readying themselves for the beach, thoughts of shallow ocean waves and salt water taffy in their little minds. Owen would accompany Bridget and the children now. This was appreciated and mentioned often by James for several reasons. The main reason was not to ever let it out of Owen's mind the importance of his duty, howbeit he was as solid as they came. That being as solid a man might ever be. Owen was leery of James, but not to the point of resentment. To the contrary, he admired James, though he felt best not in his presence, for the two were similar of their worst traits.

James was a danger to any man, whether it be an unconscionable beating doled out by him, or be it the unemotional way in which he administered death to a man. Owen had seen James carry out the most bizarre orders concerning retribution at the behest of his superiors. Afterwards, often eating a large breakfast at the all-night diner on Lehigh Avenue. Owen knew what carnage would ensure if anything were to happen to his wife or young children. The thought never left Owen, who he himself was renowned for his merciless ways in all matters of business. Owen did feel at ease when James was surrounded by Bridget and the children, or even when Bridget was with James and Owen. She diffused what was indeed a short fuse that could be sparked over the slightest of misspoken words where his wife, his Bree was concerned.

As it was now, Little Emmett had become much more of a visible presence, never leaving his boss's side with anyone other than Owen present. Even then, he lurked on the balcony or in an adjoining room, seconds away.

After seeing his family off, Emmett sat vigilant in the suite as James slept on and off, with the nagging wound still fresh with fire.

CHAPTER 21

Three familiar knocks at the door of the luxury suite of James and Bridget Sullivan meant the arrival of Aengus O'Boyle and his bodyguard, Kevin. James made it a point not to speak to Kevin, an unnerving fact not lost on the young man who made his bones a decade before.

"Seamus . . . you promised supper, seafood no less for the children and myself this evening, now you'll be running off with the likes of Aengus, and returning at dawn. I won't have it, you promised, I'll hold ya' to this and only this during our stay here. Seamus . . ." Bridget sang his name at the end and he made eye contact with her and did smile.

"Just so happens that your Uncle Aengus came here to take us all out for fresh seafood, let's get a move on, now." Bridget kissed her husband and whispered promises that the pre-dawn would provide, should he return and wake her. The thought of more seafood gave James pause, but he knew he'd have plenty of options.

"I'll be a son of a bitch, a one-time matchmaker who pays for life, I am." Aengus forgot his fury over earlier events and grappled with the boys, before relenting to his sister Bridget's chidings otherwise. Aengus pushed back his thick hair and sighed, as if to gather himself.

"This hotel has the finest seafood in all of Atlantic City, right in its own kitchen below us, Seamus. I'd feel better for all involved if we took advantage of that fact." Aengus seemed to look for an answer rather than an acquiescence.

James looked to Emmett and then to Aengus. "Mr. Johnston guarantees all of our safety, here at his hotel, that is what I was told, I believe . . ."

"Aye, Seamus, that is the man's word. Anything else on your mind, concerning what you've been told, Seamus?" Aengus's concern was now directed at James, and he alone. Unlike the meeting with Mr. McCann.

"Nothing we can't straighten out later this evenin', Aengus. We've had our say, I have a few questions of my own is all. You'd agree I'm at a disadvantage with my wife and children here to think of as well, no?" James looked as a man ready take action by people who knew him best.

"After dinner then, Seamus, no more of this. Here they come, dressed proper down to their shoes, a beautiful sight . . ." Aengus took on his former demeanor, only then did Emmett and Owen part to allow the children and Bridget through.

Kevin O'Hennessey realized that he too was at a definite disadvantage should things sour between Aengus and James. A quiet man, he did not fear or hesitate in matters of conflict, though in this situation he was an outsider. Whatever measures Kevin would take in order to protect Aengus would prove to be his own death, whether it be in Atlantic City or Philadelphia. Kevin was satisfied with Aengus's judgement this night, howbeit, because of the children and his sister, Bridget.

Aengus took Kevin aside and had him call down to the main lobby. Preparations would have to be made in the dining room given the company involved.

Four men of the first generation stood on either side of the dining entrance. A polite nod by the oldest of the men was given to Aengus O'Boyle. Aengus nodded in return, without rancor or disregard of any kind. The scent of cooked seafood wafted through the room and descended on the children and their mother. It was an experience that stays with a child into adulthood, never quite fading, the particulars came back in moments of reflection, no matter the years between.

DP Curran

With a slight smirk on his lips, Angeus was greeted, "Mr. Greene. Welcome. Your table is ready, and all precautions have been taken to ensure you and your family's enjoyment for the evening." A mustached man of middle age, with the utmost skill and talent for his position stood firm, as he snapped his fingers in the direction of four wait staff, dressed in perfect unison. A fifth followed soon behind, a girl no older than eleven or twelve, reasoned Bridget. The girl of obvious Irish blood smiled at Bridget and bent to chide the youngest of the Sullivan clan.

"Your accent is ripe with the sweet nectar of Ireland, dear. What county do you reside?" Bridget asked, with a certain kindness reserved for the innocent.

"County Derry, ma'am. My parents and . . ." The girl was cut short by the manager of the restaurant.

"Lory, know your place—pardon the girl's infectious tongue, madam. She has not been here so long and tends to ramble without cause. I will have her replaced immediately . . ." The man was polite, yet stern in his speech.

"You'll do nothing of the sort, sir. I don't know where you were born, but I do know where this fine young lady was. She'll not be turned away . . ." Bridget surprised no one but the manager and perhaps, the young Irish girl with her words.

Five men of ill-repute stared at the manager in what was perhaps his closest to dying he had ever come, should he say the wrong thing, but he did not.

"Your every wish shall be honored here, always, madam. My apologies are offered, without excuse." The man bowed his head.

Aengus stuffed a fifty-dollar bill into the man's cummerbund. "Even closer than you think, my friend, but if I find out you have the tiniest amount of English blood running though those veins of yours, give it to your wife, good tonight." Aengus stayed with Kevin for the perfect amount of time for a response, should the man have one, a good response or none would do.

"County Cork, Mr. Greene . . . my parents that is, County Cork. I was born in America, in New York, it is well documented should you require it, sir." He spoke with a clear voice.

"Not necessary, but see that you don't cut the lady off again while she speaks or is being spoken to, or it won't much matter where you're from." This time a twenty-dollar bill found its way into the stoic, but helpless man's cummerbund.

The manager looked on as James's only daughter, Deirdre and the girl known as Lory spoke as friends, as the family was seated.

"An bhfuil Gaeilge agat?" asked Lory.

"Is ea! That is to say, yes, but we are forbidden to speak Irish in a public setting, such as this. We must speak American . . ." Deirdre

looked at her father with a slight grimace, for which he smiled back with no anger in his blue eyes. Deirdre knew all too well the Irish squint, but there would be none of that this evening.

Bridget patted the hand of her daughter and held it in a gentle manner that quelled any doubt of Deirdre's loving nature and that it was accepted by her father, without condition.

The girls being near the same age in responsibility at least, made both comfortable acquaintances, if not fast friends and chatted most of the dinner hours.

The wheels were turning for Bridget Sullivan, she had already resigned herself that God, Himself, would help her in her next idea and maneuver. For she was a woman with no shortage of either, to the contrary. James looked across the table in the full knowledge of her certainty, without yet being privy to her plans. He was filled with a gratitude for which he felt he did not deserve; in the eyes of a God he knew to be real. James would not allow himself to think the words that he knew were true. He would go to this God once more to say his peace with respect.

This was as definite as the sun and moon, there was no reservation about it. These moments of certainty come to a man in such a way that there is no doubt or second guessing of the slightest order. In the morning, he would go to church and kneel, with Little Emmett by his side. A man who, he himself, found the one respite amidst the violence, death and upheaval that was his life from that from that of a child in Ireland.

No talk of business, as dinner was served. Laughter prevailed, and Aengus and James locked eyes in obvious remorse for their earlier lack of discipline and respect for themselves and their family. Smoke rose from both men, as if letting it all go.

Two hours past, and to a person this was the best time spent as a family in any of their lives, Kevin and Emmett included. When Aengus called for the check, the manager emerged once more. Aengus looked around the table, putting his cigar out in the remaining spoils of a teacup.

"What the feck is it with this guy, now what? We used to play a little game called brave or crazy. As kids, we'd watch men fall out of the pub, swingin' and kickin'. It was like clockwork; one would always be a little guy. We'd all put up what we had in our pockets, no matter what it might be, a rock, money, it didn't matter. Then we'd say brave or crazy. We all knew that crazy was bound to beat brave, but there were always exceptions. Someone had to win, whoever picked the winner split the pot. Whoever lost got nothing—you, sir have got me wonderin' for the first time in all of these years, brave or crazy?" Aengus looked on in anticipation, an obvious dislike for this man stuck with him, to the point of the poor bastards' certain death.

"Neither, Mr. Greene. I was sent to tell you that your dinner has been taken care of, compliments of the owner of The Blenheim. There is also a case of our finest wines, as well as mementos for the children. At your convenience, sir." The manager did not look down, but away out of respect.

"Braveness has prevailed this evenin', my new friend. Solid, ya' are, there can be no mistake of that . . ." Aengus again reached into his pocket, and this time handed the manager a one-hundred-dollar bill. "You earned it. Tell the owner it is much appreciated on my behalf."

"Back to the top, Sullivan's. Come on, you're fallin' asleep from all of the food and laughter this evenin', get up now." James spoke with a gentle, but clear tone, there would be no mutiny, even Shane Sullivan, the bull of the bunch raised no objection.

Slumber soon followed tired murmurings of the Sullivan children. Bridget looked to James with her hands behind the back of her head, releasing the strawberry blonde hair that caused the blood to drain from James's head and engorge his groin and parts thereof. Bridget's smile was a coy one.

"I'd like to talk as soon as you finish your business tonight. Before dawn, Seamus." She reached up and hugged her husband around his thick neck. "Something is pushing me away, let's see what that might be . . ." Bridget grabbed James's cock with the unbridled freeness of a wild woman, untamed by conventional ways concerning marital sex. She saw it as a freedom that no one could take away from her or her husband. Bridget Sullivan was as straight laced in public as any lady of royalty might be, save a sharp tongue and wicked smile. In the bedroom, she was uninhibited in every way.

"You're killin' woman, tell me now what's on your mind. You already know the answer is yes or no, as you please." James sighed, his whole body radiating the musk of a wolf. His chest expanded, as the veins in his massive forearms pulsed.

"The girl, Lory, from the restaurant earlier, Seamus. She's no more than twelve, if she' a day. This is no place for her, I feel nothing, but harm will come to her . . . She could come home with us, stay and learn from Mrs. Byrne, she's always wanted to pass along her knowledge of being a mid-wife. Surely, you could help the girl . . ." Bridget paused.

"Bree, the girl has an obligation here. Mrs. Byrne, Bree, come on. To meddle would be foolish, foolish for us, all of us." James turned from his wife.

Her hand was on his shoulders now. "We have to give back Seamus—this girl will die here. She is one of us, here out of servitude, not choice. Servitude is slavery, the two of us know it to be so, and we can change things for this girl, this Irish girl. Send her to school, a boarding school, so long as she does not stay here, Seamus." James turned, the blood had returned to his brain and he was deliberate.

"Aye, Bree. The girl was bought; she will be bought again, but not as a slave this time. She'll not know of the details. We will give back . . . I'll see to it, she will attend a fine boarding school and marry well when the time comes. You are the only one to make my weaknesses feel like strength, Bree . . ." James put his arm around his wife and they stared out at the sea, the moon aligned with the two as one.

"You have no weakness, Seamus, for you do what you must concerning good and evil. A good man does bad things to defeat evil, but a bad man is given redemption . . ."

"Redeem me then, Bree."

"That is blasphemy, Seamus, but I can love you as I do, forever. That has already been written in the Book of Life—make your peace with God, no man is given eternal life on account of his good deeds, the belief in Jesus and God's Grace saves a man. Share your heart with Him, that is true courage, not weakness . . ." And the two stood silent in the sight of the moon. And then whispers. "We are not meant to be perfect, I much prefer a man with the scars of a real life . . ."

"And so, you will have it, woman . . ."

CHAPTER 22

The men sat in an informal fashion around the plush velvet curved couches of the large sitting area. All but Owen, who stood closest to the hallway leading to the bedrooms. Emmett opened the French doors that let in the sea breeze that engulfed each man in a way of its own, a way the salt air might affect a man of the sea raised on an island.

Aengus spoke first. "We cannot allow ourselves to appear divided, whether or not we are family. If for no other reason, your son, Shane scares the shite out of me when he looks at me, Seamus. I think the boy has plans for me that don't include me for long, if ya' know what I mean . . . a little scary, that one. If ya' might have named him Aengus, I'd be feelin' a bit better about my chances, but no. Well, fuck you, Seamus, ya' prick ya' . . ." With tears in his eyes from laughing, James looked to the one other person but himself with just a faint smile. Little Emmett shared a glance that overshadowed the laughter of the most dangerous of men, of family.

"The percentage is sound; I don't have to like our captain to get along. Provided my interaction with him is limited. I'll go up the chain to see to that, myself. Aengus wiped the salt from his hands after assaulting the round crystal bowl of mixed nuts on the ornately carved wooden table in the middle of the men. He sat back and waited to hear from James.

"At some point, we'll have to train other men—I don't plan on wading in the darkened water off the coast of a foreign land once the routine is set."

"Fair point, Seamus. Other men you shall have, then. They will expect that from a man like yourself."

"A man like myself, Aengus?"

"You didn't think I'd be sticking around here for too long now, did ya', Seamus?"

"Long enough to get into some detail on what my ultimate role is . . ."

"Your ultimate roll is whatever your doin' at the time. The men in Center City, Philadelphia are happy with the way things are, I'll not be fuckin' about with that. Besides, we have our own country to think of, Seamus. I'm sure ya' didn't forget about that now, did ya'?"

The room grew warm again, as Seamus stood, prompting Emmett to do the same, and then Kevin. Aengus remained seated, returning to the bowl of nuts once more, unaffected.

"Always more questions than answers, you would think after so much time, more might be revealed to me is all."

"More is being revealed, Seamus. Who else has gotten' this far?"

"This far? This deep, maybe, but those fat cats in Center City are getting' rich off you and me, yeah, me. You know more than I do about everything, I don't begrudge you that, I owe my life to you, but I thought that you might confide in me more. I won't be made a fool of, Aengus. Is that sayin' too much?"

"Not to me, no. There are other people, powerful people, Seamus, that don't give a fuck how far you've made it or what you think. One wrong move and it's all a waste. Remember why we got into this in the first place, Seamus? That first night on the ship, we talked of our own country. I haven't forgotten that, and I never will. This is a means to an end, for Ireland, not me, that's all. I don't give a fuck about Center City or Atlantic City. Ireland, Seamus, your Ireland. You're free to find out whatever you need to concern yourself, I'll not begrudge you that, you've earned that much, at least. Just don't confuse me with these people, Seamus. I'm asking you, as an Irishman and a member of my family. Don't fuck this up with your pride, I've swallowed mine more times in this country that I yearn for death, but for Ireland. Do what I ask you to do, and you will be free to do what you need to do. There is no two of me, Seamus, just the one you've always known."

"Fair enough, Aengus, but I haven't forgotten. I haven't forgotten, just waiting to hear the words, the words of when I can return to Ireland and take care of what's left of my family and an old friend—'The Lion', I believe he named himself, an asshole gives himself his own nickname. He should be killed for that alone." James smiled, for the first time in years concerning Ireland, and his family there.

"Take the lead here, Seamus, and you'll have your passage by year's end."

"When are ya' leavin', Aengus?"

"I don't know myself oft times, it's my way is all . . ."

"You'll not leave without us bein' squared now, will ya', Aengus?"

"We are squared, we always have been, it's you that didn't know it."

"Aye, but I know it now, Aengus. You'll always be *'The Ghost.'* The heart of Ireland."

"Anything else, son?"

"I ask for your forgiveness . . ."

"Forgiveness is for those who require it. You, Seamus, have my thanks, and my admiration. Consider your passage back to Ireland a gift from me and take care of Bree, our most precious export, no? Be well and you'll see that everything has been put in place. Owen here, will be takin' the drops for Ireland. You let him worry about that. He knows all of the particulars concerning the allocation of funds, percentages or points, as they call it here." The two men did embrace, both thinking it would be the last. Aengus spoke as if forgetting something, Seamus knew better. "You'll be gettin' another note, wax, the whole fuckin' thing, you handled the last one, do the same. A meeting, Seamus, where more will be revealed, as you've already put it. Oh, and the wine is for guests, but the mementos are from me to the kids. I'll be seein' ya' when ya' need seein', Seamus O'Suilebhain." Aengus smiled and turned hugging his cousin, Owen, as James shook the hand of Kevin, pulling him closer.

"Take care of him, Mr. O'Hennessey . . . *Meas.*"

"Aye. All of my respect to you, as well, sir . . . *Meas.*"

James sighed, as was his custom. "It's late, I'll need you more than ever now, Owen. Until tomorrow."

"Nothing has changed, Seamus. Rest well, we both believe in Aengus. Game of cards, Emmett?" Owen chided. Emmett sat in an oversized pillowed chair, with two sawed off shotguns on each thigh.

"Play cards, with a Morrison? No thanks, just the same. Too dangerous."

Owen retired to his room, as Emmett watched him.

"Too, dangerous indeed . . ." Owen said, as he closed the door on another long day.

"G'night, Emmett . . . One eye open?"

"One eye open . . . sleep without worry, Seamus."

James had other plans for the next hour or so. It was still dark, though the sun would soon be up. He loosened his tie, as he opened their bedroom door. Before he could say a word, the white cotton sheet was pulled back to reveal the naked silhouette of his wife. Her strawberry blond hair unfurled with its matching hair below glistening as the tip of the sun met the ocean.

CHAPTER 23

Alone in bed, James listened with eyes closed at the faint sounds of the ocean, whistles and the ever-present sound of children in the salt air that blew through the open widows of his room. Three knocks broke the peace.

"Come . . ." James held a revolver tight, beneath sheets of cotton, knowing his wife would not bother to knock.

Little Emmett blocked the door way. "Another letter, sir. The same as before."

"Let's have it . . ." James sat up, noticing there was no pain whatever in his side.

The letter was cut open and its content pulled from the waxed envelope. It read: *'12:00 Noon. Main Lobby.'*

"Wear your new suit, Emmett. We have a meeting at noon, two hours from now, send in my wife, please . . ."

"As you say, sir."

"We'll have to come up with a different name for you to call me, Emmett. It's been this name, that name . . ."

Emmett spoke, "Mr. Sullivan, in all things business . . . and maybe, boss, when we are amongst our own?" Little Emmett was emotionless, no expression registered.

"I see you've given this some thought, Emmett. So, it is then . . ." James looked on shrugging.

Emmett backed out of the room, head up, eyes down.

Bridget entered the room, with the smile that told the story of that morning.

"A meeting at noon, Bree. See that you follow Owen's instructions without question. Are you all packed?"

"Aye, Seamus, as you so commanded, so it was done . . ." Bridget stuck her tongue out, which was seen as more than an invitation for James Sullivan.

"If you could take this bandage off me, I think I'd be on the other side of this whole thing now. You could look for yourself, if you would?" James took off a white under shirt and boxers, as he headed for the bathroom. "I figure it'll come off a lot easier in the shower, we'd better hurry, now." James started the water.

"You know, Seamus, it's a wonder we don't have a dozen children and all live in a giant shoe, you know like the fairy tale.

Almost as good as the one you're tellin' right now." With that, Bridget ripped the adhesive from James's side, without warning or the softening of the shower to loosen its grip. James dropped to one knee in laughter and pain . . .

"You are a wicked girl—you are, Bridget O'Boyle." James continued to laugh calling his love in her maiden name, as he grabbed his wife and took her into the shower fully clothed. They both laughed and embraced until the laughter subsided and he was again inside her. Bridget's hands clutched his blonde hair and a full release filled her. They stayed interlocked under the hot water, one naked, the other clothed. There was nothing to say, they had it all.

James had given up on reading the Atlantic City Press, that read more as a brochure than a newspaper. Everything was under control, a huge contrast to the nasty print that awaited him back in Philadelphia, in Swampoodle. Murders, rape, burglaries, stick-ups. There was no limit to what you might read. This was strong on the mind of James Sullivan—he would go about putting a stop to what was, for the most part, sensationalized reporting about crimes for readership. This was bad for business, what was good for Patrick Johnston in Atlantic City would be good for North Philadelphia, for Swampoodle. James put a copy of each edition away to study further, as a model upon his return to Philadelphia. He had a plan to contact his friend and trusted associate, Jonathan Hirsch. A man that would know those in a position to help James, if Jon thought the idea out of reach, he would say so without the need to repeat himself or make equerries involving the slightest of risk. These two men, two minds, thought in those terms. Everything calculated, they considered others fools by nature. This was the land of opportunity, but it was also filled with careless opportunists. They were not of the latter.

"Coffee, Seamus. More and more . . . American's and their coffee, it's a drug, I tell ya'." Bridget fixed her husband's tie and collar, up on her toes.

"Mrs. Sullivan, why is your hair still wet, you've been up for hours now?" Bridget looked around and found no one listening before putting both hands on his face and kissing him hard.

"Come home to me, Seamus, that's all I pray for the two of us. The children are another hour of prayer unto themselves. And Seamus, that talk with Shane cannot wait until we return to Swampoodle. The two of you, my biggest worries. You're both so much alike, though that is what keeps you at a distance from him. He needs you, Seamus, humble yourself. I know it's hard for you both, but you and only you can get through to him, you already know what he's feeling. He feels the weight of protecting those around him and he will never ask for help. Go to him as few men have come to you in a way you understood. Please . . . for Shane and myself, we both need you to do it." Bridget showed a small, rare crack in her brick exterior.

"Tonight, we'll walk amongst the pine trees and talk, Bree— he'll be fine, look at me." And she did wiping her eyes, with a laugh and a tear. "I'll take care of it, Shane is blessed with intelligence as well, Bree. Intelligent men have an edge, they are teachable. He is no exception, worry no more, Dove . . ." James lifted her from the couch and all of the children saw the two embrace under control. An example was being set, that love and loyalty with family was to be expected and not to be regarded as weak, though hard for James at times, he made it a point to been seen as such.

Fifteen minutes till the noon hour, James and Emmett, waited in separate corners of the reception area. Affluent people came and went. Five minutes till the clock struck, and of all people, Mr. McGillicutty knocked on the marble counter at the reception desk, his shoulders even. He was questioning a clueless man in charge behind the counter, with vigor tapping a pocket watch with equal vigor.

James nodded to Little Emmett and they approached the desk.

"Mr. McGillicutty, will you be our escort, sir?" James asked.

Surprised, the diminutive man of fine clothing and jewelry answered in kind.

"Yes, I'm afraid the pleasure is all mine, sir. If you would follow me . . ."

There was no short walk to the elevators, no this little journey took the men through the bowels of the hotel. Passing the back of the kitchen, mechanical rooms and then, just then a small set of doors. Not decorative by any stretch, industrial if anything. The small hand of their escort moved aside a large red light that looked to be part of the industrial nature of their surroundings. Mr. McGillicutty used a small key that opened the metal doors, revealing an ornate elevator car. The men entered without talking, within less than a minute the men had ascended at a rapid clip to an unknown floor of the hotel. There were no numbers or a single clue of what floor they were on.

"This way, gentlemen." McGillicutty looked again to his pocket watch, this time with obvious pleasure. Two men with grease in their hair, stood with smirks of achievement on their faces. No way of realizing what was right in front of both. Not just men, Irishmen, but death itself, in the flesh.

"A mere precaution, gentlemen." The small man of precision waved the two men to search James and Emmett. Thanks to Jonathan Hirsch, only handguns that were obvious were confiscated. After being searched, James and Emmett were still in possession of one small, but high caliber handgun each. All but undetectable, these men at the door were no match for the likes of Little Emmett or James Sullivan.

A quick, but sharp, knock at the thick oak door, was followed by the door being opened all of the way.

An expansive office with shutters drawn in such a way that you knew it was daytime, but not the location or proximity of the office.

"Greetings, gentlemen. I hope your stay here has been more than pleasant." A tall man with eyeglasses came around a huge desk, not before signing some paperwork for a man of numbers and words. A lawyer perhaps, though James dismissed that thought due to the man's clothing. He resembled more of an office mole, whose sole job was to crunch numbers while eating and sleeping those numbers just the same.

CHAPTER 24

The tall man straightened himself, while a stout gentleman helped him on with his suit coat. The man approached in an amazing stride. His large hand out to shake that of James Sullivan. "Patrick Johnston, I appreciate the pleasure of your company."

"James Sullivan, sir. The pleasure is all mine—I can assure you."

"Fine, fine . . . have a seat, please. Refreshment for you and your man, Mr. Sullivan?"

"Seltzer water, bottled, if at all possible, sir."

Mr. Johnston let out a laugh that spread to his unnerved underlings for which there were but a few in sight.

"Willie, draw Mr. Sullivan seltzer from the bar tap, but let him see you drink a full glass first. Would that be suitable, Mr. Sullivan?"

"Yes, sir, it would."

"Trust is earned after all, isn't it Mr. Sullivan? I must admit two things straight off. I admire your candor—it does not have the ring of disrespect as so many others that surround me at times. And if I might, you strike me as a man with the reliability of a man known as Jimmy, not James, or even Seamus. That could be the American in me talking, however. Moreover, you have an impeccable record, regardless of your moniker. Being that we are business men, I'd prefer to call you by your given name of Seamus, without objection of course."

"That would be an honor, sir."

"Good, good, now let's relax and talk about what the hell we're both doing here."

James had one last glance at Emmett before sitting down with a glass of seltzer, a side of fresh sliced lemon and lime on a silver tray. Emmett declined any drink at all should, something go awry by the hands of the man behind the bar concerning his boss's drink. This, too, was appreciated by Mr. Johnston and not questioned, for it was sound reasoning.

"This meeting was out of respect, respect for your professionalism and the way in which you conduct your private life. By that, I mean that your private life is your own, add that to your reputation as family man in the traditional sense. All that I have said is to be commended, your conduct is most decent, except in but a few matters out of your control. Other men have paid the price for that. Your tactics are to the letter, Seamus. No matter what the order, you do, however, have one exception. I'd prefer to here that exception in your own words, if you don't mind."

"Children, sir, I have an aversion to harming or otherwise killing children. I believe children should handle their own problems among themselves, sir," James answered.

"Admirable, indeed. Let put a hypothetical to you, Seamus. What if a child were employed to kill someone in your family, God forbid, mind you, but you must consider the question, no?"

"I said that I had an aversion to it, sir. Some things are unavoidable, I'm not a man set in stone. I'm much more fluid than that, but it would be unwise for any man to give such an order. A weak man, who would pay a high price himself."

"My last question on this matter, Seamus. You have refused this order twice before, why was that?"

"The children in question were family members of another faction. It was to be done to avenge an outstanding debt. I felt it cowardice, the children were innocents, sir. What kind of man does this to an innocent child, and what kind of precedent might it set, for any of our own children to be killed?"

"You discerned this and made the decision not to follow orders, on your own behalf, Seamus, without fear of reprisal?"

"On my own life, sir. I was a single man at the time, as well."

"Good point, excellent point. None the less . . ." Patrick Johnston cocked his head.

"Again, sir . . . circumstances would dictate that outcome, if one were to leave me no choice, well—my family comes first, above all else."

"And if the situation was similar to the one you refused . . .?"

"I would, again, refuse. There is already that understanding by anyone requiring my services, anyone who has my ear."

"And if the matter was pressed, by those above you? You are now a married man with children of your own, after all."

"Then there would be blood in the streets, the likes that no man in this room has ever seen, sir. Starting with the one who pressed the matter." James leaned in.

"Interesting . . ." Mr. Johnston sat back.

"Perhaps, I am not your man, sir. It might be best if I take my leave, and we have no further dealings." Emmett's eyes scanned the room for reinforcements, as James spoke.

"How would you go about leaving, you are unarmed, and you don't have a clue where you are in this hotel, am I right?" Mr. Johnston extinguished a cigarette with the calmness of a man discussing baseball.

DP Curran

"Unarmed, sir? The respect that I have for you is not mutual, that is apparent. As far as where I am. I am on the fifth floor, a glimmer of light shone as we past each floor to this one, sir. You might want to have that looked into. Perhaps, McGillicutty, here, is not as efficient as you might think, all due respect. So, you know, too, Mr. Johnston, or is it Patrick or Paddy? You strike me as a man with the humble roots to be known as Paddy to some, but being this business, I'll call you Patrick, better yet, Mr. Johnston. Given your superiority, it would only be right, without objection, of course . . ." Mr. Johnston waved back the eight men that entered through several side doors, guns drawn.

"As I was about to say . . . that first day here upon my arrival, I asked Mr. McGillicutty how high the fireman's ladders might reach, being this such a tall building. He told me six floors, I then asked what floor I'd be on with my family, my family, Mr. Johnston. He told me second in height to your own private penthouse. When I asked him what floor he was staying on, he without hesitation replied, the first floor. Now, why would a man as brilliant as Mr. Johnston take such a risk as to stay on the top floor, when the fireman's ladder reached but six floors. Just didn't add up. If we're going shed blood here today, let's do it now, Mr. Johnston, because if I'm dead, I've got nothing to do today, but if I'm alive, I've got plenty to keep me busy."

"You think I want to get rid of you, Seamus? A foolish man would do that, you are without a doubt one of the most remarkable men I have ever met. I could never expect to find a better man than you, Seamus. I would have never believed that you would be so forthright. You are a man of character and shall be paid according to that character. My apologies for my unorthodox vetting process, but it has served me well to this point, Seamus. It is Seamus, you'd prefer, no . . .?" Johnston laughed, holding out his hands in jest.

"Yes, Mr. Johnston . . ."

The two men smiled as only the Irish might and laughed a solid yet tenuous laugh together, for the first time that day.

"McGillicutty, bring me my maps, and the name of the special contractor, Otis, who designed this fucking elevator. Oh, and our other friends, as well" Johnston sighed.

The grandfather clock in the corner was audible now, it was good to hear the ticking of time, of life for James.

"Are you armed, as well, both of you?" Johnston sat back, resigned to his decision and the man of character that he had become allies with this day.

"Aye, sir. Right as rain ya' are . . ."

"I'll be a son of a bitch, I've searched far and wide for a man of your talents. I've tried to train, and educate many boys into men more than I'd care to admit. And in the end, he was born in Ireland, brought to our shores by *'The Ghost'* himself. I'll be damned . . ."

"It seems inevitable that you will be, Mr. Johnston . . ."

What no one knew but James and Bridget, was that James had instructed Owen to take Bridget and the children to New York, where the O'Boyle's owned a string of lodges in the Catskills Mountains, by way of a straw purchase years before.

"You'll be compensated upfront, Seamus. A signing bonus of sorts, free and clear. Today, we'll go over your contacts. O'Boyle said you'd want to know what involved you alone, and your men, of course. He said the fewer the better, I like that and so does the captain, he spoke well of you, Seamus. You need to hear that, you're the second man to get such a nod from him, it speaks volumes of you, believe me."

McGillicutty brought in, tubes of maps and two manila files with the names, addresses, and pictures of two men, quite different in appearance, as both folders lay open in front of James.

"Enough for today, McGillicutty . . ." A pause ensued, until the door was shut. Then, one of the files was slid in front of James "A hardhead this one, to be sure, would you do me the honor?"

"This man, this Italian of the first generation, a big talker, with plans of his own. We can't have it, Seamus, not here, not anywhere. Here, we provide what the people want, but this, this is the by-product of the evil that often pervades fun and frivolity. You'll find him in Philadelphia, James, he has an interest in a pool hall there. I'll handle any fallout, the way must be paved, and no better man than you in your adopted city of Philadelphia." James nodded his acceptance.

"Done . . ." And it meant just that.

"Now, this one, this one here is a special case. One of a personal nature, not one of business, the first one was a man, a business man. I hold no animosity toward a man with ambition, though it leads often times to his own death.

He continued, "This one here, Seamus is not a man, he was born out of Hell and must be returned to Hell. His heart cut out, while he's alive—burning while it still beats. Mutilate the body, but leave his face recognizable. I want others to see it, and to talk about it, here . . . here in Atlantic City." James looked again to Little Emmett, both men had a seriousness about themselves that Mr. Johnston knew full well. He spoke once more . . .

"This man has a penchant for little children, both boys and girls, the younger the better. Babies, weeks old up to the age of ten. Here, look at these . . ." Johnston reached into a separate folder and produced photos of some children that had died.

James looked with the emotion of a shark. Cold eyes, attached to a killing machine.

DP Curran

"I'd like to do him, first, if it makes any difference to you, Mr. Johnston." James slid the photos back across the desk, after letting, Little Emmett take a glance at one of the victims, the youngest, an infant.

"Not just yet, the next time we meet, it'll be all set."

"Indulge me, sir, please . . ."

"We believe he's close, here in Jersey, or New York. I have private detectives working on this, the best there is, trying to find a more secluded place he might be hold up at, even living at, most of the time. The police want him just as bad, they won't back off, but they won't interfere either. I don't want him arrested and sent to prison. He'd be killed by other inmates within a day, but I need to leave an example, an example for the demons like him who walk this earth, and breathe our air. I know a dozen policemen that will kill him themselves, they all have children, they're good decent men, police in this country. Did you know that, Seamus? Good decent men, save a few hard-ons who don't live in the real world. I want you to tend to this fucker, no one else. We can't have this, not in Atlantic City, not anywhere. My own father beat the living shite out of me my whole childhood, now that, that can strengthen or break a person, but this, this takes a child's soul. Give me any figure on this one, Seamus, any figure. Just do what I ask you to do, when the time comes . . ."

"I have a specialty for men such as he, sir. Notwithstanding, your own wishes, of course."

"I'll triple your usual amount—need be . . ."

"They'll be no payment to discuss. You see, Mr. Johnston, I have a weakness, you smile, but, I do. The slaughter of innocence, those unable to make their own decisions. As they say in America, "underdogs" I have a weakness for underdogs. Now you know . . ."

"You'll handle it then, free of charge, is that what you're telling me?"

"Were these children, these babies free, Mr. Johnston?"

James's face hardened as he looked at the photo of the mark. "Consider it taken care of, as soon as you're ready . . ., just as soon. What of the "elevator expert?" Paddy shook his head in a candid moment of astonishment, that such a man as Seamus O'Suilebhain even existed, let alone sat before him in total agreement.

"Construction accidents happen every day in this country, Seamus. So much construction, these things are bound to happen. Imagine a man falling one hundred stories to his death, down an empty elevator shaft during a routine inspection, right here at The Blenheim Hotel in Atlantic City. Nowhere to go, but down. I wouldn't waste your time on something so trivial, this is my mistake. I mean, the man professes to be an expert, so he gets paid for being an expert, and then this. I say this out of respect, Seamus, but after all, its people like you that make people like me have these types of things installed. Am I right . . .?"

"That's not for me to judge, Mr. Johnston. Any requests for your Italian friend here, sir?"

"None, your work speaks for itself. You know, you are seen in certain circles as an artist, each piece of work with a meaning when given the choice."

"As you say, sir."

"Hmm, well yes . . ." Mr. Johnston paused in a moment of thought before speaking again.

"You have to keep an eye on everything, ya' know the greatest lesson I've learned is finding the right people, but still keeping your circle small."

"Sound advice . . ." James said, in the tone of a true compliment, and perhaps the first of many lessons to be learned by him.

"If I can be of any help . . . oh, and from your end you'll need trucks, a lot of trucks, different types and signage on them. Manpower, too, reliable men, I'd prefer you stuck with the Irish, they're Marines, solid and tough as they come. You'll have to use your own judgement as you go forward, mind you. You know as well as I, that we're all accountable for ourselves, no matter who doles out any free advice. We'll give you a man who knows the routes for each truck until you're up to speed. Who would have thought the American government would have given us the gift of Prohibition . . .?" He stood as a man pleased, yet not so used to looking a man in the eye whilst standing, given his uncommon height.

"Thank you, Mr. Johnston. You have of my respect, sir."

"We agreed on the name Patrick, did we not?"

"In matters, such as these, I think the proper amount of respect is due, not just for you, but we spoke of innocent children as well. If you would indulge me that, this day, sir?"

"That sounds fitting, you have all of my respect as well."

"If there's nothing else . . .?"

"I wasn't going to mention it, but after your showing here today, I think it the honorable thing to do. It came to my attention during our meeting, that your family has already left the hotel, undetected, I might add. Every trace of them, gone. Before you speak to that fact, I just want to tell you that I don't blame you in the least, nor does it offend or lessen my respect for you. On the contrary, it bolsters my opinion of you, sir, a family man will always protect his family. I admire that, I will say that you and your family will always be my welcomed guests here in Atlantic City, Seamus. With all of the security and kindness due a friend of mine. Contact your wife, let her know you are alright, and please, give her my regards and apology for not having allowed ourselves to meet as civilized people might. A dinner of spouses I hope, is in the near future, Seamus. I would like that very much . . ." Mr. Johnston stood, hand extended.

James nodded in approval, before glancing at Little Emmett, who stood without emotion.

"Again, thank you for your confidence, Mr. Johnston, sir."

"Oh, and it is the fifth floor"

"Pardon, sir?"

"My living space is the fifth floor. This whole floor, we do have plans in place should such catastrophe as a fire break out. One of the perks of having friends in the fire department, Seamus. Your thinking is sound, analytical, and constant, Seamus O'Suilebhain, *Meas . . .*"

James nodded once more, intrigued, "As far as further contact?"

"I like a man to know when and where . . . a message from Center City one week from today, and another meeting here in one month. Rumor has it Donnelly's brother decided to get out of construction all together, strange I was told he had a real passion for it. A change of heart, I'm told. A brother's death will do that to some folks though. In the meantime, you'll be set up in Donnelly's old office in Swampoodle. Shibe Park, Seamus, now that's a ball park." Mr. Patrick Johnston laughed, in earnest and shook James's hand once more, as he pushed a button on a desktop machine. "Send in McGillicutty."

Patrick Johnston put his hand on James's shoulder, but removed it feeling for himself the solidness of the man and the energy that came with it. "Donnelly's office is just temporary—a new much larger building and warehouse is being built right next door. Expansion is the name of the game in Philadelphia, it's all those people understand. Power through, expansion and monopoly, a full-blown state of the art construction company, Seamus. Everything from custom homes to skyscrapers, I'm told, and they want your name on it, not an order, just an option. Think it over, you'll have a month to think about it. Meanwhile, relax and know that you have a friend here in Atlantic City. Time will prove that . . ."

Owen approached Bridget, "No word from Seamus yet, Lassie. No worries, I'll wake ya' when I hear anything, anything at all." Owen followed everything to a tee, now all he could do was sit and wait for word from Atlantic City.

"I'm not worried, Owen. Seamus promised me he'd come home to me, and he will, he will. No matter where home might be . . ."

Little Emmett sat nearest the doors of the express train to New York with James. He had decided to wire Owen from the city, still a bit uneasy, though glad he had found common ground in Mr. Johnston. He remembered what Johnston had said, about time proving things out, and he was happy in his decision to wait until New York to make the call, the call his Bree was waiting for.

James rested, but didn't sleep after the meeting with Johnston. Aengus expected a lot, more than James had bargained for, but if it kept his family safe and he was able to return to Ireland and destroy *'The Lion'* it would all be worth it.

He tried to imagine his mother, much older now, be it from worry if not years. Most of all he thought of Lilly and how he would shower her with the finer things in life for the rest for her days. After all, Swampoodle wasn't such a bad place. In fact, in that moment Seamus O'Suilebhain thought it to be the best place in the world for his family, ma and Lilly included.

BOOK IV

The King of Swampoodle.

Pigs get fat, hogs get slaughtered.

~Anonymous~

CHAPTER 25

James and Little Emmett shook their heads when they saw that construction had already started on the new building next to Donnelly Roofing & Masonry. The remnants of a dead man still remained, for now . . .

Pug sat in the shadows of the old warehouse on a backwards, high-backed wooden chair, his face swollen, the whites of his eyes still red with the blood of broken vessels. His right hand reaching in and out of a bucket of ice with a silver dollar in it, pressing it to both cheeks in intervals. It was the first-time James ever saw Pug sit, save between rounds during his last fight at the Cambria Athletic Club, on Frankford & Cambria Street, North Philadelphia. Swampoodle.

"I've dealt with brutal people all my life, Jimmy. Beat the will out of more men than I'll ever know, with gloves on and off, but the boys that came around here last Friday, well . . ., they were some rudderless motherfuckers. Born right here in America, but they're not like us, Jimmy—no, they're foreign trash, no fuckin' respect, fer' nothin'. They got the safe, Jimmy."

"Fuck the safe—their names, Pug. I want even one name, one name . . ."

"No matter their names, Jimmy. It's not who they are, but what they are. All of em', Jimmy. Kill one, another takes his place. By the way, a couple of those fella's left here with liver damage, some solid shots, Jimmy. Found the sweet spot on a few, and one with his jaw hangin' as if it were in a sack of skin on his chin, ahh, ya' should have seen me, Jimmy . . ." James put his palm up, as Pug acted out each swing, leaning into the back of the chair with his chest. The wooden chair scraped on the concrete floor.

"Take it easy now, Pug, try to keep your mind from racin' on ya'. Did they say if they were comin' back anytime soon?" James knew the accumulative affect that boxing took on a prize fighter. One with as many fights as Pug in the ring, not including the streets, was incalculable. James knew too many "stumble bums", taken for drunks, when the problem was blows to the head. The drink proved nothing more than a useless friend to a fighter.

"Not that I recall, was a bit busy, though. Could be . . ." Pug drifted for a moment, before his eyes lit once more.

"Three out of eight, Jimmy, I'll need to start trainin' again if I'm to be any use around here when you're away."

"You're sixty-one years old, Pug. You've kept your reputation and honor intact, for fuck sake. I'll still be needed one name . . ."

"I may not have as much coal in the furnace as I did as a younger man, but I'm no snitch, Seamus O'Suilebhain. You know that to be true, I'll not live with that shame hangin' over me."

"Fair enough, but these men could be out to hurt one of my own, one of my own, Pug. My fuckin' family, do ya' understand the ramifications of that?"

The large mallet of a fist submerged into the bucket of ice water and a silver dollar.

"I'll find out myself, today, not tomorrow or next week, today. Many people could be hurt in getting' this information. We'll not stop, Little Emmett and me. No, this is of a personal nature, I do it not for money so that my family might eat, as even the humblest of men do each day. This is retribution . . . pure and simple. Answer this, what did they really want?" James knew full well, that taking the safe was just a power play. They did it because they could. A more than sizable sum though it were, an entire week's payroll, including the men constructing the new building just outside.

"They wanted you, Jimmy, they wanted you."

"You were told that by one of these men, these brave men in suits . . .?"

"Aye, Jimmy. The one that did what little talkin' that took place."

James sighed and put his head to Pug's, out of the gratitude and respect that had no room in him, whilst filled with anger. The old boxer's wet frozen hand came up from the bucket and squeezed James's shoulder, the affection abounds.

"It's me they shall get, then, Pug." James raised himself up until his lower back let out a cracking sound. "Lock up and go home, Pug. Don't feed that Irish Wolfhound of yours this night—and Pug, have the shotgun at the ready."

Little Emmett put on the hat of an American, tilting it. The two men started from the darkened building once occupied by one Liam Donnelly.

The foreign voice said quietly, "A certain man, of Moorish blood—black suit and red tie, did mention a new office at Broad & Lehigh . . ." James and Emmett stopped without turning for a moment. An acknowledgement to an old friend was all . . .

The sun was bright, and the smell of Philadelphia sickened James at times. Construction continued without one sighting of a man wearing a suit.

DP Curran

James knew the office at Broad and Lehigh, not yet even furnished, was to be the new headquarters for operations, emerging out of Atlantic City. A proxy office for the site of the warehouse and factory being built on the lot of what was already known as the old Donnelly shop. No one but legit bean counters and low-level accountants for appearance sake would work there. Whoever came to call on James Sullivan would have known this, if they were part of what was to come. This went through James's mind in seconds, something that would take some time to explain in words.

"Swing by *'The Lehigh House'*, Emmett. If things are as they should be, we'll be headed for Taylor Street." Emmett knew whatever happened in the next twenty-four hours would be excessive, for James was determined in his craft. Pug had taught James what it was to be tough, but fair to those deserving fairness in life. Pug owed a small gym above Keenen's Shoemaker Shop on Haggart Street. Just about all of the money he had earned as a prize fighter was in this gym. Many penniless boys, now successful men, owed their lives to Pug, for givin' each a place to learn what it was to be somebody. They learned how to fight, be on time, discipline, and self-respect. James Sullivan's sons, Jimmy and Shane trained there three days a week.

Emmett spoke, "Boss, I don't know the big picture here, and I don't want to know, but if I might, I'd feel good about you and your family if we took care of this thing at night. I know of your work, you know of mine, daylight is dangerous, a time for men such as ourselves to give the appearance of thoughtful men, men of patience . . ." Emmett was uncomfortable, but glad in the fact he had said his peace.

"You have all the wisdom of a quiet man, Emmett. Owen will need to know, but not a word to anyone else. We'll have other things to do before the sun sets behind the smokestacks in Swampoodle. Emmett . . ., for the sake of my own mind, don't look at me when you're drivin', for fuck sake, these are real streets with trucks and phone poles, and the likes. There is no horse in front pullin' us along with eyes of his own to keep us straight . . ." And James did laugh, and Emmett was better for it.

"Da, Da, Da. Double header tomorrow, don't forget. The Red Socks . . ." James Jr. was on the running board of the car as it eased down 22nd Street. Across from Shibe Park, *'The Lehigh House'*, as it was referred to, wasn't on Lehigh Avenue, of course, but for the sake of a dream as a young man, James Sr., gave it that moniker which stuck with the house for as long as there was a memory of the Sullivan family.

James had forgotten the double header—his life was changing and his mind with it.

"Forget? Come on, boy. Jimmy, was there anyone out of the ordinary about the house today, son?"

DP Curran

"No, sir. Ma had us stay within yelling distance today. Cousin Owen's been home all day. Is he gonna' live with us, Pop? Mrs. Byrne says . . ."

"Please, son, leave Mrs. Byrne out of my mind until the time comes to see her face once more, she's yammerin' on at a rapid clip, I'm sure."

Owen met James at the door. Motioning for him to stay on the porch.

"What of it, Owen?"

"A telegram from New Jersey, it came this mornin', just after you'd gone. Didn't dare leave on account of it, but I damn near opened it." Owen's auburn hair seemed to turn red when he felt the rage, as the Irish called it.

"From now on, open anything that comes to this house while I'm not here. Nothing should be sent here, nothing. Not one fuckin' telegram with my name on it, not for any reason. This is my home, that lesson must be taught again. What do ya' think, Emmett?" James turned to the big man.

"Perhaps, you could leave someone alive this time, so they might teach the lesson to others . . ." Emmett shrugged at his own reasonable statement.

252

James smiled before looking around, as if realizing that the three were easy targets standing on the front porch. Not knowing yet what they were dealing with.

"Jimmy, son, have Mrs. Byrne call everyone home, by way of the back alley. Stay in the house with Cousin Owen, no exceptions."

James Jr. ran past the men in a sharp-witted manner that pleased his father.

In the side study, James opened the telegram. *'Matter now urgent.'*

"Match, Emmett . . ." James held the telegram beneath the flame of the stick match, and made his plans. Mr. Johnston had sent word, the mark of a friend or a confident enemy. Seamus O'Suilebhain had been told years ago, on the ship that would carry him here to America, that judgement meant more than trust.

In that moment, the moment it took some men to light a cigarette, James had made his decision. It was not just the impression of Mr. Johnston in Atlantic City after their most interesting of first meetings that convinced James, it was as much his consciousness of all that Aengus O'Boyle had prepared him for, and led him to.

James had no advisor in Emmett, the comfort of a valued friend and bodyguard to be sure, but not an advisor, or consigliere, as the Italian's would have it. James would have to make his mind up concerning Owen, who was more than qualified with the interworking's of the underworld, both in Ireland and here in America.

A list, a list of Irishmen. No one of the first generation in America, not yet, not until the children of *"Fir na emerald."* Meaning the men of emerald. This was the term given to the *'one-hundred percenters'* by Aengus O'Boyle himself. Given to a man, born, raised and having died a thousand times in Ireland. A man willing his life be taken, without remorse if he should shame his brothers or himself. This included all that was theirs. Family, property, disputes of any kind. To take a life and give his own with equal measure.

And so, it was, in the side study of the *'The Lehigh House'* that Owen O'Boyle would become the Chief Advisor to James Sullivan, as witnessed by Emmett McGowan. A knife, the Holy Bible, and their native tongues would make it legitimate, for no man to question unto death.

CHAPTER 26

Emmett opened the pocket doors to the study to find Bridget Sullivan standing erect with fists on hips. Not a good sign for even the likes of James Sullivan.

"Prisoner of war in me own home now, is it, Seamus O'Suilebhain?

Little Emmett, looked down and to the right, to catch the accepting sigh of Bridget's cousin, Owen Morrison. Owen had long since witnessed the ire of his little cousin, even in the presence of his da, Uncle Laughlin Morrison. A man with little tolerance for any woman's opinion, much less his niece's long dissertations, beatings that continued whilst taking the brutality at her uncle's hands. A man feared by all of his son's, given his size and hateful demeanor. Bridget never relented, suffering for it, though she did.

"A moment, Bridget . . ." The pocket doors closed with James and Bridget alone in the study that let in enough light to soften words that are meant to leave indelible impressions.

"I wouldn't say or ask anything of you, that bore no meaning. Your safety, the children's safety, is my reasonability."

"Yet, my cousin, Owen is charged with our safety, no?" Bridget said.

"The decisions that I make for us all hold more weight that any one man's duty. This includes your cousin. Do you doubt my judgement, Bree? Is there anything you want to share with me that gives you any reservations at all about any of this?" James tilted his head back, leaving no question about what the words, "Any of this" meant.

"Oh, there most certainly are, Seamus. Your decisions have a way of scaring the shite out of some, but not me, you thick headed bastard. You can't have it both ways, my mouth open to please ya' when the sun is risin', but shut tight as a clam when it comes to my own opinion . . ."

James knew this was not the way, not the way for his, Bree. She deserved better, leeway as no other. She would have it, so James promised to the deepest part of himself. The place within himself, where his most sacred attachments resided. If anyone should have it, be it Bree.

"Since when have you been denied your opinion, Bridget O'Suilebhain, I've spoiled ya', I have. Livin' here in the lap of luxury, passin' gas through silk, as some high society dame from Center City . . ." James's slight smile infuriated Bridget.

"Bridget O'Suilebhain, is it? You . . . jackass, you wait until now to call me by that name. O'Suilebhain, indeed. Monsignor Ryan knows of ya'—even Father Maguire knows of the name you've meant to keep a secret in this this country. No one dare mentions the name— it's not that people don't know it. I'll not say it, but nor has anyone ever asked. All but one, Seamus."

"And who would that be, temptress . . .?" James pulled Bridget close and she went of her own. Her husband's large hands, cupping her soft ass that shone through in the bawdy light that the study took on, the sun now an interloper.

"How ya' manage anything else, you're a man possessed with one thing . . ." They locked mouths and the notion of time was now of no importance. The familiar position of Bridget's leg lifted up, as to allow James full entrance past the loose-fitting undergarments of Bridget O'Suilebhain was complete. The two thrusted with the sound of papers and objects of no meaning being wiped to the floor by Bridget's own hand. Saliva and nectar circulated through their mouth and nostrils, until heavy breaths brought back the small dagger that life keeps lodged in a person's neck, just below the base of the skull.

DP Curran

They held each other as to never lose one another, their hearts and breathing in unison. Die they someday would, but the loss they would not tempt was one that would drive each apart whilst still alive. Eyes closed without words they married their souls.

"Again, Seamus. We've done it again." Bridget whispered.

"It sounded as if two people discussing family matters, Bree. Plus, they've gone to the kitchen to see what Mrs. Byrne left us to eat, as if we were poor." James snapped his suspenders and grinned at his wife.

"Don't you do it, Seamus, I haven't the strength to fight ya' off and I have to pee. You've driven the anger from me, sir. And, as far as Mrs. Byrne is concerned, she does what she can, because she thinks the world of ya', James, all of us. Her and her Stevie, we're their family here in America. Let her be as she is . . . now, no more." Bridget reached up and kissed James on the bottom lip and put her hand to her face and laughed. "We've got a problem, Seamus. The two of us . . . wild animals is all." Bridget shook off another attack of lust, as she called it, that she claimed she suffered in the presence of one Seamus O'Suilebhain.

"I'll have to buy ya' some proper underclothes befitting a woman with such lofty aspirations of moderation."

"Like hell ya' will, I'd fix your hair, but a certain two people can't be trusted by such a simple task . . ."

Bridget opened the windows releasing the odorous scent of desire. She breathed in as deep as she might, the fresh air tangled in the thickness of the room.

"Bree . . . who summoned the name of O'Suilebhain?"

"Your son . . ."

"Jimmy was bound to inquire, he's gettin' older and listens with the ear of a trained spy. Speaking the language makes it all the easier for him. Due to circumstances, I've put off a needed talk with Shane, as well. I plan to remedy that before the ballgame tomorrow, though, Bree. Leave it all to me . . ."

"Twasn't Jimmy, it was Shane who brought up the subject, Seamus. I told him that any such question as foolish as he might perceive one, he must go to you with it. These matters are between father and son. That's what I told him."

"When did he ask . . .?"

"In New York, in the Catskills. He came to me as a man might, though still a boy, Seamus. His grasp and directness on matters of men is unnerving at times, though he means well. Earlier, you asked about my having any reservations or concerns. It's not you, Seamus, it's Shane. Seamus, three weeks ago, outside the market a man looked down from a ladder, a stranger, an American, no less. The man was painting window trim above us when he whistled, the whistle meant for me but the man never uttering a word. With that, Shane shook the man's ladder and waved him down, as God is my witness, your son, Shane, beat the man senseless, Seamus. A man not in his prime, but a man, none the less. A policeman, Officer Williams drug the man to his feet and had the bloodied man apologize to the both of us, without ever asking what took place . . ."

"What was the man's name, the man responsible for the problem your son took care of?"

"Oh, no, Seamus. Shane needs you, he needs your guidance. He would do well to be near you, may God help me for that thought, but he has to learn the rules of the game if this is the game he is destined for. Forgive me, I know . . ."

"He's a good kid, Bree. He loves his ma . . . be glad. I'll handle things from here, I promise." James held his hand up with a smile in his eyes that was more powerful than words.

James kissed Bridget, this time on the forehead. "Your warm . . ."

"Get out—you and that son of yours, I don't want to think about what thoughts are runnin' through his mind concernin' girls or women, for that matter . . ." Bridget tried not to smile, but instead laughed, covering her face as she did when she thought aloud.

"That ends tomorrow, Bree, that ends tomorrow . . . I have to go, be as one with me and we'll be fine, if we have to leave this country, for good and all to make that happen, so be it, Bree. There is work yet to be done and commitments kept still . . ."

"You'll keep your commitments, Seamus O'Suilebhain, that's what we, O'Suilebhain's do. Is it not?" Bridget's hair was back up, the last of the pins being pulled from her full pink lips, as James opened the pocket doors to an empty foyer.

CHAPTER 27

James and Little Emmett pulled from 22nd Street, and headed for the house on Taylor Street. With reluctance, James looked away from the oncoming traffic, which included horse drawn carts . . .

"Oh, Emmett, stop by Ward's Market at 22nd & Somerset and keep an eye out for a man on a ladder next building over, he'll be paintin'. I'll be needin' ya' to make him for me. I'm afraid his paintin' days are over." James found the name he was looking for and committed the number to memory.

Emmett put weight to the pedal and shifted gears, as he navigated the streets better with each excursion behind the wheel.

The car slowed to a creep, just as the painter was wrapping up for the afternoon, a hot and humid day it was in Philadelphia. In summer, men of the trades would start at dawn and end a bit early to escape the cruelest hours of the day when the heat and humidity built to a crescendo of oppression on any man, least a man getting on.

"He'll be hard to recognize in a few weeks' time, boss. The man has one eye swollen shut and one ear bigger than the other . . ." Little Emmett's face was rough to be sure, but it had a natural roundness to it that gave him the distinctness of an Irish ogre with a definite purpose. Emmett's mind bounced to the memory of taking up residence in the apartment above Ward's.

"Aye, me son, Shane, gave it to em' for whistling, says his mother, whilst they were leavin' Ward's place. Not bad work for a boy his age, but no work for a boy his age to be havin' to undertake. We'll be groomin' Shane, sooner than not. Two days a week to start, Emmett, he does well for himself in school, so he'll be stayin' on there." The car went past, with an unknowing glance by the painter. "There's no denyin' the boy's talent for pugilism . . ."

"Boxin', pugilism, is it now? A penchant for violence, that's a grown man there, boss. A tradesman, not so willin' to let a beatin' by the hands of a boy go unanswered. There's no doubt, the man knows not who the Mrs. and the boy are." Emmett's bluntness could be taken as disrespect by anyone else but those closest to him. James was one of a handful of people still alive at this juncture that knew it was nothing more than honesty.

"Stop the car, Emmett . . ."

"The apartment, boss . . ." Emmett's hopes of living above the market diminished.

James exited the car before it jerked backwards in Emmett's sudden stop. Double parked, Emmett stood behind the car as to be visible, though not encroaching without cause.

"Excuse me, I'd like a word, sir . . ." James grabbed the other end of the painters drop cloth, bringing the end to him until the men were face to face.

The painter shook his head, as James spoke. To Emmett the conversation seemed long, too long for the light of day. When, in reality it took no more than a minute or so before it concluded. The tarp was taken by James, as the two walked to the narrow passage way that led between the long row of storefronts at the end of the block. A way for police to better pursue a person on foot. Emmett shifted positions, becoming aware that things were being settled in one manner or another. Even Officer Leary would have to take this into account, so thought Little Emmett, not knowing that Leary, an Irish immigrant himself was on a sheet. He was a buffer for Swampoodle, and paid well for his duties by the boys in Center City.

The thick cloth was laid down, its ends wrapped up the brick on either side. With his back to the street, James motioned for the painter to step on.

"Which leg, Mr. Basil Thorne? Makes no difference to me, the sooner it's broken, the sooner you'll be paintin' again . . . come on, don't make me decide for ya'."

"I've apologized sir, for whistling, no less, and I'm more than willing to make a monetary gesture as well . . ."

"Would ya' rather it yer' right arm, man . . .?"

The man could feel the breath of James Sullivan, and he then said without expression. "The left leg."

"Ah, good. A decision has been made. Open your mouth, come on, you're doin' so well, Basil. No doubt your entire family would be proud of ya'." The reference to family was not lost on Mr. Thorne. His mouth opened, exposing the brown crooked teeth of a most unfortunate man, indeed. He took all of his own painter's rag that his mouth would allow.

James in one violent motion, back kicked the painter's leg against the brick façade, just below the knee. A small bone protruded below the kneecap which was now situated to the side. Tears of pain streamed down the man's face, before he stiffened in shock, now hearing the words that James spoke. "I say, you'll lay on the fuckin' sidewalk, the ladder having' fallen in the midst of yer' work. You'll do well to say the same, Basil Thorne of Oakdale Street."

"When I've' pulled way, you can scream like the bitch that ya' are, ya' English fuck ya', and if I ever hear your name but whispered to me concerning this, be it in a dream, you'll not see me comin' the next time. Understood, sir?" The man now knew the full extent of his unfortunate encounter with his wife and son, nodded his head in the affirmative—in total submission and wary eyed disappointment in himself.

With just his head emerging, James looked both ways, before taking the painter's rag from Mr. Thorne's mouth, and helping him to the sidewalk, laying the man on the now blood-soaked drop cloth. James knocked over what was left in the paint bucket, toppled the ladder and strode to the car with Emmett already at the wheel. "Drive away slow now, and don't give thought to such things, it taxes the mind and body, Emmett."

"In the middle of the day, boss? I've not seen nor heard of this by you before, ever."

"We've not worked together so long, Emmett. There is much ya' don't know about me yet. I've done some of my finest work durin' the day. You got me to thinkin'. A man such as Mr. Thorne may have gotten to my son, Shane, or my Bridget before nightfall, that was the picture that ya' painted, a different kind of paintin' than our friend here. Somethings can't wait, Little Emmett."

"Ya' let him live, I take it a moment of mercy?"

"Nah, a livin' example, I've left more than a few over the years. He'll be paintin' baseboards for the rest of his life. Your place above the market is secured, in response to your previous inquiry. One last thing before we end this, that was not mercy, but never confuse mercy for weakness, Emmett . . . ever."

No answer or words of any kind were required, Emmett was beginning to understand the true nature of James Sullivan. Disappointing him would be worse than death, so thought Emmett McGowan.

"Taylor Street, nothing has changed . . ." One thing had changed that afternoon—Little Emmett would never again question or give unsolicited advice to James Sullivan Sr. Not in matters of business or any other matter concerning his boss.

Neighbor's took turns moving the jet-black truck, given to James during the Donnelly era in front of the house on Taylor Street. This gave other factions the uneasiness of not knowing who might be in the house at any given time.

The Reilly brothers, Larry, Kevin and Mike kept an eye on the house. They were neighborhood kids with more experience and balls than hoods twice their age. The Reilly parents, a mother with a heart of gold and a knowing father who left each morning to work the rails. The family had one invaluable quality—they kept their mouths shut. Uncle Ricky, Mrs. Reilly's brother lived with the family, a veteran of the Great War, World War I, Uncle Ricky had the fortune of being born with the perfect stature of a professional jockey, but the misfortune of having a head twice the circumference of a much larger man. He worked mornings at the newsstand on Lehigh Avenue. He took in a few bets on baseball, but other than that he didn't involve himself—didn't know anything of any use and didn't want to.

Larry, the oldest was smaller than his younger brothers, and would stay that way by all projections. Whatever he lacked in size, he doubled it in fearlessness. He would fight anybody, anywhere, anytime. He earned his reputation and made his bones, by the age of thirteen. All three were loyal unto one another and to the people they knew to be friends, and one of those friends was Timmy Ward, whose family owned the market that Swampoodle counted on as part of their regular lives. By the end of that day, Timmy Ward, if needed, would swear to Mr. Thorne's unfortunate accident by an overreaching painter. Timmy had his own crew that knew the score in Swampoodle.

The Reilly's ran Taylor Street, taking care of their own and answering to one man alone, James Sullivan. He appreciated "The Brothers Reilly", as they were known, and paid each well. Larry, kept away any pains in the asses, with his drop of a hat, natural disposition to fighting. Kevin, the red head, hair thick as wool was a multi tasker, he knew everyone within ten blocks. He was one of the best freelance "Second story men" in the business before he was a teenager—always more than happy to put up his hands. Donned in an Irish cap, he'd sit on the stoop at Taylor Street with a short bottle of rot gut, just waiting.

Mike, on the other hand, the youngest was an observer, noticed things, specific things. Anything out of place, if the milkman was late, if the mailman should happen to skip the house, he'd follow him to be sure that no one else was being given Sullivan's mail. He went about his business, but Mike had another trait, as did Kevin. Their sense of humor was as sharp as any other skill that they possessed. Larry, not so much . . .

As if on cue, the Reilly's milled about as the black Model T passed the house and pulled into the gravel next to the last house on the street.

No conversation was made with the boys; it was as natural as any neighbor might be to another's children. Respect was shown through silence, except when spoken to. James Sullivan would have gotten the word if there was a need for it, through a simple, yet far reaching network of Irish boys of the first generation, being groomed for the future.

James had started this process without consulting or informing anyone, before he moved his growing family from Taylor street to 22nd Street. He knew all too well of *'The Firsties'*, but realized that his own sons would someday be part of, if not running the lot of boys born here in America. There were caveats, however, if a boy becoming a man had kept his honor above all else, that man would be considered, *'Fir na emerald'*, the men of Ireland.

DP Curran

The front door creaked open. James made it so and kept it as such. The light of a row house could not be appreciated by someone having not lived in one. The angle of the sun could change a mood in the slightest of ways. It had a quiet comfort about it, resonating with the remnants of words long since spoken, yet stayed on as faithful stewards.

The cellar door looked to the naked eye as any other wooden door, except for a ticker that counted and recorded the amount of times the door was opened from upstairs. James took a mental note, before recording the number in a separate pad, kept in one of the vaults below, that made no reference or sense to anyone else. All, but for Jon Hirsch, who was given the unlimited satisfaction of developing and testing all manner of cutting edge advantages to a man as open to fresh ideas as he was to covertness, and loyalty. He and James were formidable in both their thinking and willingness to act.

"Keep the door, Emmett."

"Is ea." Meaning, yes in the Irish. Emmett spoke his native language, without knowing at times, though James had made it clear otherwise, save when occasion called for it. James did not mention any such mandate to Little Emmett again, as the sound of Irish being spoken, if just in short bursts was a source of strength to him.

One stone was removed from the wall of the cellar. The combination spun without hesitation. A small section of stone façade swung open with the soundless ease that came from a master craftsman and genius. Jon Hirsch was both of these things, and James's appreciation of such talent grew with each project and idea of Jon's.

In a pristine cavity fitted with a gun safe, James stared with satisfaction, before reaching for two Tommy guns, and ammunition for both.

CHAPTER 28

Emmett sat at the side end of the Sullivan's long dining table, and cajoled with the children, as if a child himself. Howbeit, not Sunday, Bridget prepared a sizable meal. Two large prized chickens had weighed on her mind long enough in the coup out back. Today, she would have her way with both— Emmett and Owen would share in the feast.

Fresh chicken, mashed potatoes, corn on the cob, homemade dinner breads with butter and for dessert, homemade Irish scones.

"Beautiful it was, Bree . . . simply delicious," James said, taking his wife's arm, as to pull her closer, adding more meaning.

"Aye, Bridget, you've outdone yourself once more, ya' have . . ." Owen being the next to spout praise. Then it was Little Emmett's turn, of course.

"Mrs., not in many an evenin' have I eatin' such a fine meal, perhaps not since . . ." He was, however, halted by the Mrs.

"Deirdre, go and fetch your mother's boots, the manure is gettin' deep in here. If the three of ya' have business that needs tendin' to, go and do it then, there's fresh cigars in the study . . . and ya' should be thankin' your own daughter, who plucked the nameless ones clean."

"Thank ya', daughter. You're a thin slice of heaven, as your ma, Dove . . ." James laughed, kissing Deirdre atop her head, for James knew that his daughter had not the temperament of her mother, though she shared her looks. Deirdre would not think of speaking up the way her mother did, and at times, she was embarrassed by it. Not by her mother, but by imagining the same words flowing from her own mouth. The girl was peace at all costs, and may God help the young man that came for her hand one day. Let alone the fool that might hurt her in any way.

"We'll have no need for the study until later tonight, Bree. Emmett and I'll do my best to be back before the kids are in bed, but if not, don't wait up for me . . ." Bridget stood fists on hips.

"That'll be the day or night that I don't wait up for you, Seamus." Just then Mrs. Byrne pushed through the front door, using the key she had been given, just that morning at James's behest. The door was to remain locked until James said otherwise, that included the back door, as well. Judgement over trust . . .

A light rain was falling and that was perfect. James and Little Emmett put on thin black long coats. Each tailored to size for big men such as they, but they left room to conceal the Tommy guns, that James procured from Taylor Street.

The black Model T headed for Broad Street, to a billiard hall being renovated for use as a speakeasy in anticipation of the U.S government's Volstead Act going into effect that October prohibiting the sale of alcohol. Johnny Patrone out of New York owned the property, though it was run by *'The Firsties'* and financed by Patrone himself, including the renovations. The subsequent purchase of liquor, would depend in large part on operations out of Atlantic City. Word had it that Patrone was in town to oversee his investment under the protection of the boys in Center City, men that did not share the interests of an Irishman named Sullivan. There were chasms with the politicians in Philadelphia, assimilation in a meaningful way would take another generation. To keep the peace, whoever had the best hand was the one that ruled the day. What no one in Philadelphia or out of New York had counted on was a contract on Patrone. That became a necessity, given that territory would be more important now. Expansion of territory was the order of the day, not subtraction. James had no qualms about taking out Patrone for Paddy, it was a personal favor that James would see to himself.

The rain had stayed light but steady, as James and Emmett watched a side entrance where lumber was being loaded into the addition that would form the walls of the speakeasy. The workers were oblivious to anything but their work.

There was a heavy presence of muscle surrounding the building, it would be tough to manage a hit under these conditions.

"Pull up two blocks, Emmett, we'll walk down and see what gives."

The rain heavier now, made the two men even less conspicuous—hats pulled down low. A half a block from Murphy's Billiard Hall, Emmett stopped with James on his heels.

"Fan . . ." Emmett whispered.

"Wait? Wait for what?" James looked around.

"Listen, Boss . . . over there." Emmett pointed to a car rocking under a canopy of trees in an empty street vendors lot.

The men crept toward the car loud with the sound of a woman's voice. Emmett peeked in.

"It's him, Patrone . . ." Emmett went back for another look, but was stopped by James.

DP Curran

"Garrote the woman and we're taking Mr. Patrone." James took out a long rag that he kept on him always, as much a tool of his trade as the gun or a knife.

James pointed with both hands how they would proceed. A brief thunder clap and the woman fell victim to the garrote through the open aired car with just the roof up.

"Evenin', Mr. Patrone. You've made my job here tonight too easy. Thinkin' with the wrong head again, are we Johnny?" The wet end of a Tommy gun pressed against his head kept Johnny silent. Emmett, free now, stood watch.

A long fine scarf was placed between Patrone's teeth, pulled back tight, and tied behind his fray of black hair. It was like placing a bit in a broken horse's mouth. There was no fight, no hesitation, the prospect of reasoning or coming to some sort of a deal seemed plausible to Johnny Patrone, in fact, he was sure of it.

All of this flying in the face of reality, and that reality was James Sullivan Sr., a man who was not once sent out to negotiate or bargain. His reputation was legendary, but some, even the toughest go into shock when the final bell has rung. Johnny went without a struggle into the rain, and into a black Model T that rode in the opposite direction of "Murphy's Billiard Hall".

Back in Swampoodle, Johnny Patrone was led to the blacksmith's shop behind the railyard where Little Emmett had worked for ten years, until Mr. Sullivan lured him into retirement as a blacksmith. The night watchman was an old Irishman, by the name of Lonnie McClure. Half blind from booze and age, twenty dollars a week was paid to Lonnie on top of his shit salary as a watchman, for which he was paid in booze. Any real watchmen were *"Fin na emerald"*. No one questioned or doubted that, no one in Swampoodle . . .

James was always happy to give Lonnie the twenty dollars himself. It was never discussed why, and Lonnie didn't ask. It did James well to hear the old man say, "Bless your heart," upon receiving the twenty.

This night, Lonnie was fast asleep in the watchtower, how the old man made his way up there each night gave Lonnie the respect due from better men than him. He'd wrap a coat around a five-foot coatrack and place his hat that resembled that of a policeman's above the coat. From a distance, it looked as though all was well, and it was . . .

Johnny was led to an outbuilding in the field where extra train rails were laid in stacks on railroad ties. This was no ordinary shack, mind you, it had all of the tools to make a man talk or be killed without a question asked. A chair was pulled up for their guest, as the gag was removed.

DP Curran

"Was this necessary? We could have met, we could have talked as human beings. I'm willing to negotiate, come on, fellas, for cripes sake." Johnny yammered with a thick New York accent, as a first-generation New York Italian might.

"What happened to your face, John? We didn't rough you up or even hit you once, there was no need for it, so tell me, what happened to your face now?" James was doing the arithmetic in his head and it was all adding up. The swollen face, the red tie and suit, described to a tee, earlier that day by Pug.

"I had a little argument with some punks outside a diner, what difference does it make?"

"It makes the difference in how you die, John. Period."

"You fuckin' Micks, how fuckin' stupid are you? Unless you have some bargain, you best take me back to where you found me . . ." Johnny went to stand up, but was slammed back down so hard by Little Emmett that the chair smashed to the floor. Now, sitting on the floor, Johnny looked up.

"I spare that old punch-drunk hero of yours today and this is what you do? I came to reason with Donnelly or whoever the fuck is in charge down here in this sinkhole, and now I know who it is. What the fuck are you thinkin' . . .?"

"I'm thinkin', if ya' fought Pug every day of the week, he'd kick yer' arse each time, John. That's what I think. How bout' you, Little Emmett?"

"Me money would be on Pug . . ." His voice sounding all the more final, standing above Patrone from behind, holding a swatch of sailcloth.

"Goodbye, John . . ." With that Emmett shrouded Johnny Patrone from head to waist in the heavy cloth, as James Sullivan Sr. swung a full handled sledgehammer to the top of Johnny's head. One shot and the hammer was through his skull so far that James let go of the handle that rested there just as a ladle would in a stew pot. James locked eyes with Emmett who held their prey tight while on one knee. Blue eyed killers at that moment, in direct contrast to the men who sat and ate food at the Sullivan family table just hours before.

"Cut him up, boss?"

"No, wrap him up tight, and weight him. We'll let the river have him, the river, Little Emmett, it doesn't care who it takes . . ." And so, it went. Mr. Johnston knew the whole program—the players, their numbers, and positions.

In the morning, James would send word to Atlantic City, but for now all that was needed was the short drive to a dense tree line on the banks of the Delaware River, and a rowboat that sat tied off and camouflaged.

DP Curran

A rowboat known but to James as, "Rita." The name of the raucous whore that took the virginity of Seamus O'Suilebhain at the age of twelve in Donegal County, Ireland. A gift from his brothers on his birthday . . .

CHAPTER 29

A light was lit on Taylor Street, as James dried and returned the unused Tommy guns to the most ingenious of all safes. He did marvel at the precision and a certain cleanness that Jonathan Hirsch brought to each project. James eased the door of the safe back and forth, once more—not a sound did it make.

Emmett sat in the small kitchen drinking a glass of milk, sawed off shotgun on his thigh.

Bridget Sullivan used to leave a light lit in the second-floor hall window, that faced the street. She did it to let James know all was well, should he drive by or come in late, as he oft times did nowadays. At first, James thought the gesture one of kindness, he however had known that kindness had no place in his world, not for his sake. He instructed Bridget not to do anything out of habit, or predictability. Light the lamp if she liked, but never as a signal, she and the children should have nothing at all to do with James Sullivan's occupation in any way.

Seamus O'Suilebhain feared one thing. Love. The thought of losing it, losing Bridget weighed on him at times. A heavy load that even when carried for a moment felt unbearable. He wondered how a man, a real man could let his love of a woman, but not his children take him to one knee. With his children, James felt the love that protection could cover, he felt no such cover with Bridget. He took it as his burden in life, a trade off with God, Himself, he thought.

There had to be a price to pay while still alive, given their arrangement that James had forged with God in the quiet vastness of Saint Columba Church. James would kneel for up to an hour in the front pew facing the host, the bread used in the ritual of the Eucharist, in a meditation that all but The Almighty and James himself knew of. Diehard daily parishioners were sprinkled about, under a similar period of Grace, given to all who sought it. Emmett McGowan sat in the last pew, shot gun at the ready.

Emmett had an agreement of his own, of sorts. He would wait until the end was near, to ask forgiveness. He thought it a sin to do otherwise, knowing all the while he may be killed or die unawares. In that case, he surrendered that God would deal with him as he would come to him in death, a sinner.

The entire Sullivan house seemed to have every lamp lit, as the abundance of life that was his family was heard from the street.

The black Model T pulled in front of the house that always promised the space of two cars or hose drawn carts. The men checked their hands and suits in the dim light of a streetlamp for any signs of blood, though their hats and long coats were consumed in the constant fire that burned in the blacksmith's section of the railyard.

The turn of the key and James and Emmett entered into a different world, one of life and not death. The children smiled at the sight of their father, the younger ones clinging to him, while Jimmy and Shane came to stand with him, to be in his presence—they felt something that neither yet understood, call it power or strength, but it was all encompassing for the two brothers. There would be no turning back for either . . .

"Home just in time, husband Sullivan. Say goodnight to your da, come on then . . ." James smiled at Bridget, knowing.

"A half an hour more says your father with his eyes—no more than that, lest the lot of ya' become night owls . . ." Bridget stopped short, as to not disrespect or otherwise offend her husband, for he worked so hard day and night to provide. If he now spent the night hours in his work, and awoke a bit later than he had in past years, so be it. She was more than all of that, Bridget Sullivan was loyal and knew first-hand the illusion of a puppet show.

DP Curran

At times, whilst alone, Bridget would think of her Seamus's death at the hands of those he was now obliged to bare his life for. His back turned to the closest of men, that would be his executioner. She thought well of Little Emmett, though she trusted no one, save Seamus himself.

Bridget saw in full color her husband's wake, adorned in flowers that she could herself smell as the play went on in her mind. She would have him buried in a grey suit, she thought, yes, a grey suit—for that's where Bridget and James had lived their whole lives, in the grey.

The pocket doors of the study closed, James, Owen, and Emmett sat with the windows open. The smell of fresh fallen rain, and Shibe Park's wet grass and wood gave the room the aroma that was Swampoodle.

"Jameson Irish whiskey and cigars, Owen. Bree, for some reason unbeknownst to me until now, has been keeping me in Cuban's." James lit a cigarette and sat, pushing his hands through his woolen blonde hair. Owen, ran the full cigar under his nose, before biting the tip and using a lighter to ignite his favorite brand, Cuban Reina Cigars.

"Another mystery solved . . ."

"A fine cousin she is . . ."

"An American born luxury, Owen?"

"That, I cannot deny, Seamus."

Little Emmett took up a chair facing the window, with a view of the front door.

"We'll need to put this to pencil and paper, note the good and bad in each name, code the ones we keep. Burn the original . . ." James rolled up his sleeves, and looked more the boxer than the boss.

Owen spoke, "What will we do concernin' *'The Firsties'*, Seamus? Your own boys are too young, and the sentiment of any others is frowned upon, if not somethin' to kill over. All due respect, Emmett." Little Emmett didn't move or speak, though he heard alright.

"I've taken this matter into consideration for years now, Owen. My job in this country was to get things done, things that no other man might be associated with. What I've done might have been messy, but I always cleaned up after myself. Men have begged, even bargained the most precious things in life, to have their own life spared. It's those that haven't done that that I respected, great respect for the man who looked me in the eye and took what was comin', and comin' it was. Make no mistake . . ." With that came a low voice from the chair facing the window.

"Aye . . ."

"Follow me, Owen. I've made it a point, observing people in various conditions, from the simplest task to the most extreme. It's just my way is all—in the past ten years, I've compiled a list of lads, now men, who were born in Ireland, but came, some as young as infants. There are, of course, some names of those born in America, right here in Swampoodle that come no lesser men than we here. Loyal, all . . . bringin' up their boys to be American, though still sendin' money back to Ireland for the cause. These are the ones we want, they are few, but must be included, many are now. Think for a moment, the Reilly brothers, Timothy Ward and the like. Are they not workin' for us already, with no one battin' an eye? Not here, not in Center City, not even Aengus, and let's face it, if it were wrong all together, he would say it. I've been taught to use me judgement and that's what I aim to do." James having committed the names to memory, save Owen's input, gave Owen the pencil and paper.

"I've not the knowledge of such people as you have, Seamus. I thought we'd talk about rightful prospects and put it to a vote. I know the names you've mentioned, but outside of those fellas, I don't know, myself." Owen was taken back, not by James's attention to detail, but by his own ineptitude.

"It's settled then, I'll contact the necessary people and we'll interview each at the docks, should anything go wrong. I just don't know if we'll have what we need, regardless of their willingness. My father's thinkin' was, any real father that knew his son would have to kill a man someday should see it first as a boy. I believe there's somethin' to that. Owen, your expertise is with the big boys in Center

City, from the mayor's office down to the dogcatcher, you're invaluable to me, as is Little Emmett. Look at em'. Any man brave or crazy enough to turn his back to a Morrison and an O'Suilebhain must be shown the proper respect . . ." James smiled, as Little Emmett turned and laughed.

"Fact is, boss, if it's comin' from you, I don't want to see it. A decision long since made, mind ya', long since made." And all three men laughed with the sweet smell of Swampoodle giving way to a Cuban cigar.

DP Curran

CHAPTER 30

'*The Tinkers*' worked in the back of the old Donnelly shop, as if nothing had changed. Their foreman remained the same. All foremen were handpicked by one man, Brandon Hale.

A man seldom heard from, outside of an office high above the streets of Center City, Philadelphia. None the less, he knew more about the entire scope of operations than the most seasoned of all executives or politicians of the day. Mr. Hale traveled, with a full detail, to and from and while at home, or work. James Sullivan Sr., held a job as foreman, two years prior to Mr. Hale's appointment, and had not yet spoken to Mr. Hale, as it wasn't necessary to do so, thus far.

James knew the one thing that mattered about Brandon Hale, and that was that he was a man that knew his business well. He was paid well enough that taking a bribe would be a death sentence. In his case, he could be killed, but not bought. This ensured that business would go on as usual until retirement or death, more or less. His predecessor, Mr. Jacob Ross was not paid so well, nor of the same mindset, and eventually vanished as it were into the New Jersey Pine Barrens.

James visited *'The Tinkers'* midday on their lunchbreak with Little Emmett. The little men scrambled to their feet at the sight of the two big men.

'The Tinkers' were wary about the flare up with Pug and the olive-skinned intruders, unaware that James had received word from Atlantic City that morning concerning the matter. A situation that would have cost more lives, now was settled in percentages after the disappearance of one Johnny Patrone. A man so out of touch with the future, he could not be constrained, even after a final warning by his own capo. Patrone went ahead with his plans to take over the remodel and control of Murphy's Billiard Hall as a speakeasy in Philadelphia. Although outside of New York, it was not sanctioned. The power had shifted into Atlantic City, and Philadelphia being just fifty miles away, now had a tinge of salt in the air.

"Suigh . . ." James had told the men to sit, in a reassuring tone. Adin McCray was the foreman of the shop, James motioned for him. For the next hour, in the field behind the shop, James explained in his native tongue the modifications that he needed for the fleet of new

trucks Donnelly had ordered, just before his execution. McCray was a diminutive man in stature, though his reputation in Ireland led to his escape. His knowledge and use of explosives made him all the more useful to James, not disregarding his overall skills in all mechanical trades.

After finishing his lunch at James's insistence, McCray tapped out a corncob pipe and continued to listen to every detail, as he filled the pipe with the cheapest tobacco available. The smoke swirled into a clear blue sky, and looked as clouds in a painting. James wrapped things up with a shake of the hand. McCray knew what that meant, more profound than words and more respectful. James turned and then stopped, collapsing back to the English language . . .

"My father had one of those . . ."

"Logh . . .?" Pardon, in the Irish, and James spoke over him.

"The corncob pipe, Adin. Da slept with it, clenched in his teeth . . ." James smiled out of reflection.

"Aye, Padraig O'Suilebhain did at that, now. Never saw him without . . ."

"He was shot in the head, with it clenched in his teeth, just the same, Adin."

"Aye." Nary a story told without a message . . .

James and Emmett took their leave, as an unmarked furniture truck was due to arrive that afternoon, filled with the amenities befitting such a large man as Emmett McGowan.

Emmett, as planned months before, rented the second-floor apartment above Ward's Market on 22nd & Somerset. The apartment already with a fresh coat of paint and buffed hardwood floors, courtesy of one Basil Thorne just two weeks prior. James Sullivan spoke to Mr. Ward in person, guaranteeing three months' rent in advance and, of course, protection, should anyone present an honest man such as Mr. Ward with any problems concerning his plans to open another store uptown. James was well known as the man that collected or settled all bad debts in Swampoodle and beyond. He often let Mr. Ward slide on bets made from a pure heart on his beloved A's. Meager bets that James took care of himself, forming a bond for the future, knowing full well his son, Tim, and his invaluable importance going forward.

The large apartment was being used for storage and the occasional guest. To rent it out to a stranger when it was not necessary due to finance, left it a concern for burglary by an unmindful tenant. The Ward's had moved two houses from the store now, having made a fine living as a true man of kindness and goodwill, save his occasional gambling. One vice that Mr. Brian Ward allowed himself, be it the ponies, or baseball. Whiskey in Swampoodle, was not considered a vice, lest it consume you, and the word consume had a wide berth.

A young man, now stood atop a twenty-four-foot wooden ladder in front of the last business façade with bucket and brush. He dared not look behind himself in the still of the shade, just before the residential row lined the rest of the block.

"A terrible accident for a man of such experience, Seamus. The old boy came down in a heap, ladder, paint, brushes, the works. An amazing thing it was though, all of the paint and the blood that gushed from him, were confined to the cloth tarp that he laid out beneath him. Twenty years a painter, and the thought of the inevitable must've showed him right were to lay his cloth . . ." said Brian Ward, referring to the most unfortunate Mr. Basil Thorne.

"It's my hope that no impressionable minds, say that of a woman or child saw so horrible a thing, Brian."

"Me son, Timothy, witnessed the entire thing, as if it were in slow motion, the boy said."

"Your Timmy's of a different mind than most, Brian. Tough as boot leather, your boy."

"Aye, he is at that, Seamus. He's a good lad though, good to his mother to the last he is—the sun sets and rises by that son of hers alone, Seamus."

"Tis' a good thing, Brian, and no one may say it isn't . . ."

"You'll be keepin' an eye out for the boy now, won't ya' now, Mr. Sullivan?" Brian Ward could not help but to utter the words.

"We all look out for each other, Brian. Keep it tight, friend, lest your mind gets to wanderin'. What's gotten into ya'?" The sun had made its way from behind the rooftops, and gave James Sullivan the golden glow of a Viking warrior, though dressed in a suit, minus the jacket. His blonde hair and eyebrows framed a chiseled face and jaw.

"Tim is getting' older, is all. His ma, she worries at times. You and I, we weren't born here, we can't know what to expect—a lot of us look to you, though, James. You've taken this strange place head on, riding it and breaking it, as a man might a wild horse. We look to you for strength, at the same time fearing that our own sons will be, well . . ." Brian hesitated, staring up at James, as if willing him to understand, without insult or distain.

A large hand reached into the sunlight, and the two men shook as James spoke, "As my own, Brian Ward, as my own . . ." And so, it was.

CHAPTER 31

The sound of the oscillating fan in the middle of the second-floor hall gave the Sullivan boys the illusion of secrecy, as they planned their escape into the summer night with whispered enthusiasm . . .

"Da won't be back until dawn. You heard em' yourself, talkin' to Ma, Jimmy," Shane stood, dressed in shorts cut to his knee, and worn brown shoes with no socks or shirt. He pulsed with the conviction of ten boys his age.

"If the old man catches us, we'll disappoint him. That's worse than any beatin', Shane, just remember that . . ." Jimmy spoke the words as he slid from the top bunk that he was now relegated to. Shane was prone to sleep walking and other nocturnal anomalies. He split his head open rolling from the top bunk, a year before. Fighting in his sleep, his mother called it.

"I know where he's gonna' be tonight, Jim. Taylor Street, meetin' with Uncle Aengus. I keep the registers in the study and their bedroom open, so I can hear what's goin' on. Two days ago, he told Little Emmett that Uncle Aengus would be at Taylor Street tonight, at midnight."

"That's just a flat out beatin', forget about disappointment. You know he always beats you harder on account you don't cry, well you might be cryin' if we get caught this time."

"We ain't gettin' caught . . ."

The other side of the narrow room had another bunk bed. Rory, was asleep in the top bed, with Padraig below, reading in the shallow light of the moon. Not the types of books that his big brothers read, but books on actual history and religion. Padraig was the tallest, and smartest of the boys, he excelled in all things academic. He had little mind for violence, but did not shy from a fight. Rory was weak, with the curse of the polio, but made up for it with determination and loyalty. Neither Padraig, or Rory feared anyone, in large part due to their older brothers, and of course, James Sullivan Sr. Their natures alone led each into many a skirmish, for which they handled by themselves, as well.

Padraig however was quite different in one respect, his fearlessness was not attributed to any one person, or his own nature per se, but to God, Himself. It was something his family did not

DP Curran

understand, nor perhaps wish to, thinking themselves too far from the mark. Padraig prayed in the open for all to see, should they come across him unawares. He spoke in quite conversations with his mother about college and the seminary. Bridget was able to connect with her sons, all of her sons, although this idea, this vocation of Padraig's was taken with a sense of pride and guilt by Bridget. Though she would not show any signs of the latter while conversing with Padraig, even in the presence of Monsignor Ryan at Saint Columba. A half dozen meetings were conducted with the monsignor, concerning the best course for Padraig, all with the blessing of his father, James Sullivan Sr. With Padraig's grades and his realization of a higher calling, the future was all but set for Padraig Sullivan.

"This week, Da has come home no later than four in the morning. Don't go too far, we'll all take a beating, and Rory . . ." Padraig knew just how to talk, to reason with his all of his siblings, Jimmy and Shane in particular.

"Be back in a few, Ricky . . ." Jimmy made his brother Padraig smile before he set out with Shane to the house on Taylor Street.

Down the wide railing to the banister slid each. A final pause and off into the night they went. The feel of being out when they should have been home was the same as any book that Jimmy, or Shane had ever read about adventure, for there was real danger—the kind of danger that the pages of any pirate book could not produce.

"Remember, Shane, if we smell bread, we're dead . . ." The neighborhood bakery's aroma filled Swampoodle each morning, long before dawn.

The two boys traversed the alleys that separated the backs of rowhomes, to the errant barks of dogs all the wiser than their owners. Cats fought in the distance in the warm summer night, oblivious to dog, man, or boy . . .

A steady pace was set by Jimmy, a cadence set as a clock that ticked in the boys' head. A ticking that had neither a beginning or end. A constant awareness of time and place, something so strong, so omnipresent, that it was as involuntary. Jimmy kept an eye on Shane, maneuvering his brother with a single word or gesture. Tired eyes, heavy with a weight he didn't understand, but knew he had to go, go to Taylor Street, where his father and uncle would be, a place where he wanted to be. The thought of being caught there felt right now, and he was no longer frightened nor worried. Their gate now turned to an all-out footrace, with Shane just over his shoulder, his shadow wide and steady.

A dim light gave life to their old house, a yellow haze that cast a beam down one half of the steps leading to the door of the flat brick exterior. Brick as far down the block as they could see, on both sides of the street. The smell was different here, the wind was more constant. The smell of the incinerator was fresh in Jimmy's mind, as he recalled a place that Shane may not remember so well.

The boys went down the alley behind the row of homes.

"Shane, do you remember living here, I mean, really remember, Christmas, birthdays, and shit like that . . .?" Jimmy took in a deep breath, that turned the air in his lungs cool from running.

"Yeah, I mean sort of, but not so much those things . . ." Shane shifted in the gravel, with hands on hips, more winded, but somehow larger in size from physical exertion. The same way he would get bigger and stronger as he boxed and worked out with Pug in the gym.

"What then, what else is there?"

"I'd follow Da, at night when he went out on foot. If I got caught coming back in, I'd act like I wasn't awake, ya' know, sleepwalkin'."

"You were bullshitin' about sleepwalkin' the whole time?" Jimmy was crouched down as a catcher might now.

"Naw, I heard Ma say she found me sleepwalkin' plenty of times that I don't remember. I followed him just the same though. I saw him do things, things to other men, big men. Bad things, Jimmy, real bad." Shane was looking at the back of the house, as he spoke beneath a maple tree that grew at an angel toward the sun, it's trunk made a hump in the chain-link fence.

"Maybe you shouldn't say those things, Shane, on account of Da wouldn't do anything without good reason . . ."

"He did em', just the same, Jim."

"There's bad men in the world, Shane, sometimes good men have to do bad things to stop em', to keep others safe. That's what Da told me, Shane, that's what he told me, for sure he did."

"He stopped em' alright, Jim—he killed men, Jimmy, he killed em' with his hands, some with an axe. I wanted to look away, but I wanted to help him, too. To help him, Jimmy. Is that wrong, is that bad?" Shane never took his eyes from the back of the house, as he spoke the words that Jimmy already knew.

"Ya' shouldn't have followed him, Shane, you were too young, you just shouldn't have, is all. You can't be afraid of it—you can't ever be afraid of it. Da had to do what he done . . ."

"You seen it too, Jim. I know ya' did. Ya' followed him just the same, and I'm glad we both saw it. I'm glad we both know . . ."

"But, we don't know, Shane, we don't know shit, just what we saw, and that don't tell the whole story, not about Da . . ."

"Ya' think Deirdre knows, or Rory and Padraig?"

"No, and that's how we gotta' keep it too. That's our Da, Shane, we can't ever tell no one. Not about you know . . ."

"Never, Jim. I swear."

The two sat for a while under the tree's canopy, and they could smell the leaves.

"Ya wanna' go check it out, Jim? Look in the windows, at least ...?"

"No, let's go home, Shane. I don't want to see no more, not tonight." With that, the rattling of a trucks motor and the low shine of its lights turned the corner. The lights traced past the tree and the shoes of the brothers as they lay flat to their backs.

James Sr., and Little Emmett, emerged from the truck, their weight had its own sound. They each carried long wooden crates filled with rows of gold coin, no more than a few inches high. Shoes, big shoes walked to the back of the house. The men whispered, then Little Emmett went in alone, taking both crates. James Sr., stood behind the house, his face illuminated by a stick match, showing the healthy vines, straining with red and green tomatoes.

The boys lay frozen, just their eyes reach out to one another. The back door opened, and the low voice of their Uncle Aengus was heard. In their native language, the men spoke in tones meant for themselves alone, but in the mind of the two brothers, they knew they were seen.

The ticking drowned out any talk around him, Jimmy felt it all now. The fear was back, fear of his father and his Uncle Aengus. He knew who they were and what they had done, the two of em' both. The red butts of two cigarettes tumbled in the air and landed not more than a foot from the brothers. Jimmy was back, back under the tree, he lifted his head to watch as his father let Aengus pass into the house. James Sr., paused and looked out into the darkness, as the leaves of the maple tree gusted, connecting the boys and their father. A feeling so authoritative, that it would be that night, each would later claim to one another, that they were a part of this life. A life that could not be avoided or it's coarse changed in any way.

It was Seamus O'Suilebhain, who stood that night as their father, and they were indeed his sons. O'Suilebhain's . . .

The boys waited for a minute or perhaps five. They turned their heads to one another, before sitting up. No words were spoken, as they rose to their feet and picked up the remains of two lit cigarettes and walked down the alley, glancing behind one another, smoking.

They didn't run or even hurry, they walked, just walked alley after alley toward 22nd Street, and their beds.

"Smell that, Shane?"

"Smell what?"

"Bread . . ."

The boys didn't sleep that night, but they heard their father come into the house. They waited in the dark room. The moon was of no help, shoes took to the wooden stairs, the creaks softened, by the oriental runner that provide the comfort of as an old friend might to the boys. Things that mean nothing under normal conditions, stand out under pressure, they always do. They could see the shadow of their father's shoes beneath the door, his hand grasped the handle . . ., but then there was nothing. The squeaking of their parent's bed and the muffled sounds of groans as the bed rocked against the wall and then stopped, to the smell of tobacco.

"He'll be in here soon, ya' know . . ." Jimmy whispered in confidence.

"Who, Jim, the old man?"

"No, Michael."

The two rested now in silence, safe silence.

At breakfast, James Sr., sat at the head of the table in a fresh suit, jacket hanging in the pantry, moving with the warm morning air through the open window and back door. The aroma of ham, was bested by the smell of starch that graced the crisp white shirt of their father.

"Your Da will be away for a few days, and they'll be no funny business goin' on whist's he's gone. It'll be the strap for sure this time, know that you two groggy eyed monsters." Bridget looked straight at Jimmy and Shane, as they did their best to not understand.

With the table cleared, James Sr., called from his study.

"James, Shane, be quick . . ."

The two looked to each other and made it down the hall.

"Yes, Da?" Jimmy asked. The two stood as guilty soldiers, straight as rods, but guilty.

"I'll be givin' ya' both some money, more than usual. Take Rory and Padraig to the ballgames, sit in our usual seats. No extra help for Rory, mind him though, and no trouble for your Ma. Mind your Uncle Owen at all times. Understand?"

"Aye, Da." Jimmy said, still at attention.

"Unless there's somethin' else, lads? If you've got the mindset to entertain a dangerous notion, then you must speak of it with your father. Otherwise, put it from your minds, the time will come sooner than best for ya' both. Howbeit, if there's questions concernin' the business of men, we can resolve it now." James now stood over his sons, left hand on the buckle of his belt.

"No, Da, there's nothing . . ." The boys said, in imperfect unison.

"What you two thinks, keep it between yourselves. That'll keep ya' until your need to know certain truths arises."

"Yes, sir." Jimmy said, feeling the weight once more, he paused for a moment.

"*Teaghlaigh*, boys. Family, there's nothing more important. Go on . . ."

The boys felt the depths of the word *'family'*, and it was not the normal meaning, they know that both in their own different way. They spent the morning in the shade of the porch, after biting off more than either might chew the night before. Checkers, with just the sound of the chips on the board.

James and Little Emmett stood together inside the Pennsylvania Railroad Ferry Station, where a ferry would cross the river and take the electric train to Atlantic City.

"I've decided it's time to sit down with my boys, James Jr., and Shane when we return, Emmett. I've underestimated the two, I'm afraid . . ."

"The sooner the better, given they've got their own thoughts already about their da. Better to hear it from you, a right smart thing to do, though it not my place to say." Emmett looked side to side, as was his protective nature.

"That's not stopped ya' thus far, Little Emmett McGowan. I'll tell each enough to ease their minds for now. For the things they do know, nothin' more. They just put things together, sooner than I had hoped is all . . ."

"The offspring of the Wolfhound, is a Wolfhound, sir."

"Aye . . ."

<u>BOOK V</u>

The Last Train

"Nobody will laugh long who deals with opium . . ."

~Chinese Proverb~

CHAPTER 32

James ran his hand through his hair while in his train compartment, and caught the readied stare of a delicate woman from the Far East.

"That tiny thing has her eye on you, boss."

"She is either bewildered by blonde hair and blue eyes or has a nose for death."

"Maybe both, she's switched to the opposite seat to get a better look. Helpless flowers, those oriental girls . . ." Little Emmett was certain.

"In captivity, perhaps, you speak of brothels and the like. That's no whore house flower there, Little Emmett, she's of her own, or treated as such. By someone powerful, I'm sure. If not, she's a woman fraught with designs that are hers and hers alone." James surmised this in a single glance that held neither malice nor condemnation.

"You think she knows who you are?"

"I'm sure we'll find out, watch the aisle and glass, Emmett." The train moved with Emmett, as he stood and sat close to the glass panels and door. Shotgun on his thigh.

James spun the barrel of a colt revolver, given him by Jonathan Hirsch, hand-picked from his own personal collection. A canvas sack filled with loose bullets, left uncinched lay at his feet. The floor would be the place to reload should things get out of hand. Death would come to James, just as he had brought it to others, but not without the blood of those who would seek to carry out such a task. That was his one real concern when traveling alone or even with the most competent, Emmett McGowan. The thought of bein' takin' unawares was hateful to him.

A half an hour went by, with Emmett making full eye contact with the tiniest of marks, or so they entertained.

Two men, one of slight build, the other, wide and thick in a black suit that did not conceal his muscular build. On the contrary, it gave the man a most formidable appearance. Both of oriental bloodlines, Chinese, to be sure.

The larger man stared back at Emmett, whilst the slender man kissed the hand of the woman and bowed to her.

"Should we light em' up, light em' up to play it safe, boss?" Emmett was cool, but ready to engage the man who dared lock eyes with him. A slight of disrespect for any man of Ireland, except in matters of discussion amongst friends or associates. The rotund Chinese man went so far as to smile, revealing a silver tooth in a row of otherwise perfect teeth.

"Take the big suitcase down, Emmett. If we do get into it, it'll be with Tommy guns. More people than those three may need to be killed if we mean to exit this train alive."

There was a calmness about both men, James and Emmett. Not until this episode in their lives did James realize that if he were to go out, it would be an honor to do so with Emmett McGowan at his side. A large leather case, rigid enough to carry two machine guns with a full complement of ammunition was lowered to the seat, with the care of an experienced man.

"Ring for the porter, Emmett." James said quietly, as Emmett pulled the line designated for service in the first-class carriages.

"Shotgun back in the long coat, Emmett. Conceal the Tommy's by our sides."

The black porter appeared within a minute, looking unamused at the two compartments facing one another. "Yes, sir?" The porter asked head moving to and fro.

"Who is it that travels beside us?"

"Don't know, sir. The manifest has a German name, but them folks don't look the slightest bit German to me, sir. No, they sho' don't, sir . . ." The porter was asking with his eyes to be dismissed or let into the Irishmen's compartment. Neither happened.

"The manifest. Whose name is on it?"

"The names assigned to the compartment behind me, the one you asked about, the one with two Chinese fellas with guns against the glass, sir?

"That'd be the one . . ."

"Let's see, bear with me now, the train is rockin' and I'm shakin a bit, sir. I don't mind sayin'. Says here, Wentz, sir. Would you like the individual names, sir? It was to be an entire family . . ."

"No, that won't be necessary. Is the train full, otherwise, is the manifest full?

"From storage to ceilin', sir." It was then that James knew the fate of the family whose compartment was taken from them.

"What's your name?

"My name, sir?"

"Aye, your name, your first name . . ."

"Ezekiel, sir . . ."

"Well, Ezekiel, looks like we got ourselves a situation here."

"Not much fond of situations involvin' me, sir. Never seems to work out in my favor."

"This one will, if you keep yourself together, you can do that. That I'm sure of. American's treatin' worse than they would their own dogs. No need for that here now, we're all men, just the same. Nothin' makes that more clear than the genuine presence of death itself bein' so near a man.

"I appreciate that, I do, sir. The part about bein' just the same..."

"I don't speak for my friend here—he's not so fond of the colored. For reasons of his own, mind ya'. Myself, I don't give a fuck."

"I can see that, sir . . ."

"Ezekiel, now there's a fine Biblical name, one me own ma would be proud of. You don't hear of any Irish with those most beautiful of all Biblical names, do ya', Little Emmett?"

"No, you don't boss, not that I've ever heard, nor hope to hear..."

"It's rather hopeless, as ya' can see."

"I do, sir . . ." James having mentioned his friend by name made the porter more uneasy.

"Of course, you have your Daniel's and Padraig's, but Ezekiel, now that's a name ya' won't find in Ireland.

"You gentlemen sure are casual about what looks to be a right bad situation."

"Well, we have you in front of us, Ezekiel, I figure you'll take the first of it, that should give my friend and I time to end it." The man froze against the glass of the now closed door.

"That ain't right, mister. Please, now . . ."

"How many stops to Atlantic City?"

"Just about all, sir, all but two. Dinner is almost ready in the dining cars—I'll be expected back there. If it bein' all the same to ya', sir, I'd like ta' make it alive, sir . . ."

"I'll not be keepin' ya' any longer, Ezekiel. A little dry humor is all—move away slow like, and unlock the rear door to the train, then you go to work. You'll get paid for your help here, a handsome sum at that. Where not so tight with our money, even less so with that of others. Your decision . . ."

With that, the door to the adjacent cabin opened with the sweet aroma of exotic perfume. The Chinese woman of natural beauty and courage stood next to the porter with her hands up revealing the longest fingernails James had ever seen, painted, with a decorative metal ornament on each thumb.

James motioned to the porter to take his leave.

"Ezekiel." The porter came to a full stop.

"Sir?"

"Life needn't be so hard . . ."

DP Curran

"I'd like that, sir." The porter moved down the aisle, repeating himself, while speaking aloud about dry humor and the like.

"Gentleman, why the hostility? You have friends here, friends . . ." The woman said, vexed with a mysterious voice and attire, the very thing that killed many a man before in the mind of James.

"What's your business here, woman? That compartment was reserved for others, others not of your kind. Let me assure ya', I'm not castin' aspersions on your race, just statin' fact. I ask for the last time, What's your business here?"

"Same as you, mista'. You are bad man with good idea, I am the same, but a woman. This is strange to you, I know this, but we could work together. Prohibition come, people want to relax, escape, you know . . ."

"What makes you think I could help you?"

"Finbar, he tells me so. He not waste time on bullshit, mista'"

"He's an important man, did he mention me by name?"

"He call you James Sullivan."

"What of your two friends, there?"

"My brothers, a small circle is a strong circle, no?"

"The strongest, what is your business, exactly?"

"Opium, Mr. James, the finest. We could share the same market, and split profit. Mr. Finbar want too much, but maybe you not so greedy."

312

"Finbar if nothing else, is greedy, perhaps we can do business. What did you and Finbar have in mind?" James realized right away the woman wasn't aware of Finbar's death.

"I tell you same arrangement. Your trucks, your daily routes, you know piece of the action, territory. Not everyone, we not interested in your children or poor, just the rich. We do business then, Mr. James . . ."

"I'm at a disadvantage, you know my name, yet I don't know yours. That's no way to do business. You'd allow me that much, for the sake of my own peace of mind?"

"You sound spiritual, Mr. James. You speak about peace of mind when you kill with ease and precision, but there is a certain spirituality in your calmness. I like that very much."

"Your name then, madam . . ."

"Lijuan, Mr. James. It means, beautiful and soft, perhaps you will find that out for yourself in future." James looked through her, she was transparent to him. A strong woman kept herself, save the whore who feigned affection for her mark. This oft times out of painful dutifulness reserved for a child. Or of no other option than starvation, degradation, and shame that awaits anyone of true poverty. A concession of one's self either way, James had always thought. This woman before him had no such conviction.

"Anything is possible. If you would indulge me, there is a more public car reserved for dining, I'd feel more comfortable, as I'm sure you and your brothers would in such an environment. Please, if you'd accompany me. Don't be afraid, the train is moving at an alarming rate. We're all in the same boat, as they say here in America."

In a language, unknown to the Irishmen, the woman spoke in a loud voice, unlike the tone she had employed earlier with James.

"English, as much as it pains me, please . . ."

"They do not understand English."

"Then, have them follow, you'll translate over dinner. Move, now." Both Tommy guns were raised as the two inexperienced Chinamen had relaxed their weapons.

"You not play fair now, do you, Mista' James? Do you not think we have others aboard this train?"

"You've already answered that question to my satisfaction."

"You trusted me, you are not so smart as your brother-in-law has said."

"I trust no one, I rely on judgement, besides, Finbar has been wrong in the past. Be so kind as to ask your brothers, as you say they are, to surrender all of their weapons, however primitive some might be. Tell both to take off their jackets."

A scorned yet still hopeful woman relayed James's orders, as if she, alone, was the boss.

The combination of handguns, Chinese nunchakus and pointed stars filled one of the jackets that James carried as a sack. The odd mixture of foreigners traversed the train's aisle. With James leading the way, his female counterpart by his side, that left Little Emmett last, nudging the men forward.

Cool air blew through the woman's hair in one last act of beauty. The exit was just ahead—the door was unlocked. Ezekiel had done his part.

The interlopers were now seeing the train rails and fields of fruited trees in a setting sun. The sound of the open air at high speed was deafening, the train's long whistle gave the proceedings an air of unintentional dignity. Each accepted a single bullet to the head, as they were thrown from the back of the train, with their nefarious belongings, including two large packets containing the finest of opium. Not one of their names on the manifest, the three would be found and connected to the murders of the Wentz family. A quiet family of German decent, who wanted nothing more than a vacation perhaps, a trip to 'The World's Playground, Atlantic City.'

James and Little Emmett gathered themselves, before heading to the dining car.

"The steak is excellent—may I start you gentlemen off with a drink while you decide for yourselves?" Ezekiel stood straight, as if nothing had happened, something for which he was accustomed to doing. However, tonight, for the first time in his life, he had made a decision that benefited him, and he was treated as a man, by men who lived not in terms of black and white, but in the grey areas of life. This did not diminish his Christian faith, it served to bolster it, for Jesus had come for people such as these men before him, which now included Ezekiel himself.

"We'll take your suggestion, sir. Who better to know what is best, other than yourself, Mr. Ezekiel? said James Sullivan, a dangerous man of definite character.

"Again, I say, sir, that's a fine Biblical name it is, one to be proud of." James locked eyes with the server as he spoke.

"Thank you, sir."

"My pleasure, friend." James and Emmett both stood. The pocket of Ezekiel's white jacket was filled with a large sum of bills by the two. More money than he could have ever imagined. At the end of the meal, a gold coin was presented to him by James. A keepsake given a deserving man of his own decision, and for that he would not soon, if ever feel the same. Ezekiel would tell the story of the Irishman who was different than any white man he might ever know. In his older years, the mere mention of an Irish surname set his story in motion with great tack and respect for each character, as though they might still hear him.

CHAPTER 33

An adjoining luxury suite on the fifth floor of The Blenheim Hotel was adorned with all the amenities befitting a friend of its most infamous occupants.

James sat soaking in a tub of scalding water, remembering the first encounter with *'The Ghost',* Aengus O'Boyle. Until this day, he didn't understand the incredible joy brought by the pain of hot water in the extreme. Certain pain relieved other pains, deep abiding aches of mind and body erased with each bit of skin submerged.

Emmett hovered in the bathroom doorway, as James lay back, though aware.

"Another card under the door, boss. Same as before, the wax is a bit over the top given the heat associated with this place. Don't know as I'll ever adjust to the weather in these parts. They say there's a place above Northern California, where the climate is that of Ireland.

Another ocean all together, the Pacific Ocean. Can't say I like the sound of that either. The Atlantic is our ocean, this place will have to do until my retirement. My retirement and return to Ireland, boss, that sounds like something that might hold a man tight lessen it happens . . ." Emmett looked about, realizing the heat and cold of Southeastern Pennsylvania and the Atlantic Ocean would be his place till the end.

"It's a nice thought, Emmett, a thought that could hold a man tight for a time. Emmett, I promise ya' this much—when our time is not so long, you will go home for all time. Me, I've started something in America that a man, a real man of any substance, can't walk away from. My wife and children and, perhaps, I'll live to see grandchildren. You though, Emmett, I want you to cling to the promise of going home to Ireland. You'll have enough money to live like a free man, take in a woman, not like you've been doin' here, tasting each little sweetheart with a small bite, as some might a box of chocolates. Sure ya' find a few ya' like and leave the rest, but like the chocolates, they don't last long. Be it as ya' will, Emmett, though back in Ireland, you'll find one compatible to your own ways and you to hers. Leave this shite behind with the satisfaction and pride of a job well done. I'd be honored to make that happen for ya', I would. No, Emmett, you hold on to that and let it keep ya', dreams come true for those who keep dreamin' big. It keeps hope in a person, and hope is as powerful a thing. There is as hate or love to those who can tell the difference, I imagine." James lifted his hand from the steaming tub, water shedding from the golden wet hair of his reddened forearm.

Without the ceremonial opening of the previous cards, James ripped this one open without regard for it elaborate exterior. After all, he was not a subject, and Mr. Johnston was no king, regardless of any notions on his part to the contrary.

'Tomorrow for breakfast—in Mr. Johnston's private residence, Emmett. Fifth floor, nine o'clock.' James studied the note once more before condemning it to the match stick.

"Late riser, that man is . . ."

"We'll have eaten long before that ourselves, Little Emmett. I can't have ya' goin' about hungry, those days are gone, for now at least.

"It's poison that troubles me at times, boss. The English . . . they gave us a meal in the square one evenin', not much, but more than we'd had as children in memory. It was a meal presented out of a gesture of goodwill and cooperation, they said. The adults, woman most, were so wrought with guilt, and hunger on account of the starving children that they had to believe the food to be just as the English had said. Some of the elders, men no longer of fighting age, warned against taking the food. The woman said it be their pride, a pride that sustained those men, but was killin' the children and those young enough to need food to eat and not hate. Just about every woman and child died by daylight of poisoning. Writhing in agony, but they had their meal, their moment of joy, when the hunger was gone at last that evenin'. I had no one left, by this time anyways, so . . . there was no one to tell me to eat that night. My father had taught me to fish in the shallows by hand, a small dam of rocks covered in pine branches. If the smell of pine was too fresh, I'd know the fish would be poisoned or wrought with shit in the small pond. All covered up again with fresh snapped branches. That night, all was well, and I ate my fill of raw fish. I had traps hidden all along the bay . . ." Emmett stopped, as if running out of words.

"We'll not eat here first thing, Emmett. You and I will go out and find a small diner and you can have your fill without concern, we'll be leavin' tomorrow afternoon, bein' the meeting is for the mornin'. Oh, and Emmett, call me Seamus when we're of ourselves or with my family, which is now your family. It would have as that of a distant uncle, but family all the same . . ."

"That means the world to me, it does. In public and all things business, what moniker might I use then?"

"Mr. Sullivan . . ."

"Aye . . ."

"It's settled then, try yourself a full bath in your suite, Emmett. The tubs are large enough to accommodate even a man of your size, Mr. Johnston has left nothing to chance."

"Another concern of mine, Seamus O'Suilebhain . . ."

"If there be any concerns, they'll be mine to deal with, Little Emmett. You've given an oath to follow me to hell if need be. I want you to speak your mind, but don't speak in riddles that leave a man wondering." It was then, Emmett saw the colt revolver on the shaving tray that spanned the tub, as James lifted a washcloth to wipe his face.

"I was speaking my mind, Seamus. My concern is for you—my life I gave to you. Your gun nor the thought of death does not scare me. The thought of disappointing you is worse than death, I've already died a hundred times in this world . . ."

"Aye, each of us must be who we are, friend. Our dear sweet mothers would be slappin' us both, they would . . ."

"Dear sweet mothers, Seamus. Can ya' imagine what the backhand of our dear sweet mothers might do to one of these Yanks?" And the two did laugh at the thought.

The men did not partake in the complimentary treats left by their host. The steak and potatoes and desserts were still heavy in their stomachs from the train's dining car. There would need to be separation, a time to build trust, not the trust of men, but the trust a man has for a strange dog. A vicious dog, to be sure, time was all.

Not even the beds were used, the two men of one mind rested on couches with an ornate wardrobe blocking the one door. A shotgun

DP Curran

on Emmett's thigh, they awaited the sun to pierce the end of the sea . .
.

CHAPTER 34

"Gentlemen, I trust your trip and stay here last evening was a pleasant one, be it a quiet one at that, undercover here at The Blenheim. You're not a man one can impress, Seamus, I admire that. Me? I'm surrounded with a fakeness that I despise. You are a complete man, sir. Unaffected by what seems to drive all others in this unsavory world that we have met in. We may never be friends, you and I, not in any conventional sense, but you have my admiration, full and complete.

"And you mine, Mr. Johnston. How a man sits atop this gilded heap is a miracle in of itself to me. So many demons guised as people, familiar though they may be, demons all the same. Judgement over trust, is all I know, Mr. Johnston. I can just suppose the same goes for you, sir. Pardon my observation being put to words."

DP Curran

Mr. Johnston held up his right index finger with a polite smile to signify a halt in conversation. A dark-haired man, speechless in his ways, provided a pitcher of water and two glasses, before unlocking the side entrance of an elaborate bar, complete with high back stools of leather and wood. The man looked to Mr. Johnston for approval and was dismissed with a nod. Leaving just the two bodyguards as interlopers of no concern.

"I took the liberty of ordering light, for breakfast. Seeing that you and Little Emmett had left out early for the more comfortable setting of *Larson's Diner*. Can't say I blame you, but those days are over for me. Trapped, it seems at times, Seamus. All of this splendor is nothing more than a prison if you can't come and go as you please. Enjoy all of it, every minute while you can, but I have to be frank with you. You might want to start thinking about being so carefree, it's what you don't see that can kill you now, Seamus. Gone are the days of face to face conflict, this is a sneaky, dirty game from here on out. All of the players are marked, including yourself, not for death by any special knowledge of my own, but you are noticed. For good reason, sir . . ."

"I'll consider this morning our last meal as free men, Emmett and I . . ." James glanced back at an emotionless expression.

"Unless you start packing your own meals, I suggest that you get used to eating with me, Seamus. I'm a loner myself, with the same concerns. Poison is a fucked-up way to go, I appreciate my food, having been raised with little of it. For what it's worth, you have nothing to be concerned about with me. You were brought to me, Seamus, we had no relationship whatever. You had your life and I mine. Time will prove me right, my words can't and shouldn't persuade a man such as yourself, but for God's sake, have a piece of sausage. If you start feeling faint or sick, I'm sure Lil' Abner over there will kill anything breathing. I'll cut one in half, you pick which half you want, and I'll eat first . . ."

And so, it was, James Sullivan and Patrick Johnston did eat together that morning and many times after, enjoying each other's unique company as no others might.

The conversation went back to the train, without feigned surprise by Mr. Johnston.

"What do you know of opium, and those that deal in it, Paddy?"

"More than I'd like, you'd have to be more specific, Seamus."

"On the train, on our way here last night . . ." James sat forward in a buttoned soft leather chair.

"Go on . . ."

"The compartment next to ours was occupied by an oriental woman, Chinese. Two men accompanied her. We were fortunate, she was stupid. She spoke of my departed Finbar, as though she did not know of his passing, and of opium. She wanted to make use of routes that have not yet been discussed. She wanted territory, and spoke of a partnership that would seem to any clever man impossible." James paused to feel a reaction from the limited, yet important information.

"Lijuan, a woman in over her head, though she does account for the best uncut opiates on the East Coast of America. She broke away from San Francisco ten years ago with the backing of her father. She and her two brothers were a thorn in his side, he should have killed the bitch. The two brothers together couldn't hold a match to her smarts and ambition. Lijuan kept a secret like she kept her legs closed, not often. She has powerful friends, none the less . . ."

"All of her friends are of the former variety, Patrick."

"What the fuck, you killed her?" Paddy said, excitedly.

"All three of em', no choice. Coming to me without an introduction or even a notion of her identity or intentions. All of this with guns drawn, no, Paddy, I can't have that. She was indiscreet, reckless . . ."

"How was it taken care of, in a packed train . . .?"

"I prefer the last few cars in any train, safer. Given my experience in Ireland with train derailments and unexplained explosions and the like, the front and middle are no place to be. They let their guard down and they got off the train early, from the rear. The train never slowed, lest stop. A single bullet each in the head, they killed an entire family to acquire that compartment. The Chinese were not on the manifest."

"I used a porter, it was his choice, cooperation or death. He was smart, he chose cooperation mixed with respect. That equals life . . ."

"There has been a contract out on her for eighteen months, your story is amazing. How does one even begin to account for such a fortunate turn of events? There was a price on her, Seamus . . ."

"Aye, how does one . . .? Not interested, as far as monies linked to any contract, Patrick. The woman and others underestimated the situation that was planned, no doubt. What's amazin' to me is that she made it as long as she did, and that anyone involved might think so little of myself and Little Emmett, of course. Be that no matter now, but any influence you might have with the police in New Jersey, well, the family name on the manifest was Wentz."

"I'll handle it from here, Seamus. Getting so a man can't take the train down the shore without his work interfering."

James put a large box of intricate design on Mr. Johnston's desk.

"What's this?"

"Yours, if you should want it. I want nothin' to do with it, not now or in the future. However, roundabout the offer might have been, regardless its conception."

DP Curran

Patrick Johnston opened the box as a man who knew of its content. Many pounds of the finest opium and fifty thousand dollars in unmarked bills, stacked with purpose, filled every inch.

"They say this is the future, Seamus. We could be ahead of our time, you and I"

"I have no such aspirations, Mr. Johnston."

"That's apparent, it speaks to your character bringing me this. You're more than entitled to the money, at least."

"I took from their pockets, to cover the cost and sacrifice of a good man. Consider this a gift, an amends for killin' an associate, perhaps."

"Not an associate, just another fool who was bested. I will work with people you may not approve of, be that no business of yours, Seamus."

"As long as we're straight, Patrick. I keep my side of the street clean, and this woman was, well, she was dirty."

"Refreshing and chilling all at the same time you are, Seamus O'Suilebhain of County Donegal, Ireland, and the King of Swampoodle."

"Now, what I came for . . .?"

"Now, what you came for. What can I expect and how soon?"

For the next four hours and another meal, Patrick Johnston and James Sullivan went over the fine details of a flawless operation, which included the trucks and men needed for distribution of Mr. McCann's liquid product. As the men rose to embrace—Patrick Johnston looked James in the eyes.

"I have something for you, Seamus, something you've waited long enough for." With that, James was handed four boarding passes aboard a legitimate cargo ship bound for Ireland in two weeks, for that exact amount of time. Two passes were round trip fares, the remaining two were one-way passages from Ireland. At last, James's mother and sister would be coming to America where they would be safe under the care of James Sullivan Sr.

"Thank you. There is nothing more that I might say to convey my thoughts, friend." James was elated, though weighted with the ever-present responsibility.

"You've more than paid your way with this oriental 'gift' box here alone, Seamus. We're people, too, no matter what anyone else thinks. There's room for a little compassion, as long as it gets put away in its place. Perhaps the two of us might share this compassion from time to time, on special occasions, no?" With that the two men of nefarious natures became friends, unbeknownst to each at the time.

"Aye . . ." James was satisfied.

"To recap, you'll not be involved in any drug trade, your end will be in the distribution and control of alcohol, which will increase to the entire Eastern Seaboard. New York will have to be negotiated in a separate arrangement, leave that to me. We have some time yet, so we'll do this right, Seamus. The next time we meet, you bring the wife to meet my better half, Lucille, so we don't look like a couple of jag offs over dinner . . ." Paddy put up his fists, which ended in a full-throated tobacco laugh, reserved for but a few.

"Until then . . ."

"Take my car to the Ferry across from the Pennsylvania Ferry Station in Philadelphia, Seamus. I'll have it picked up, do me that favor, no train rides, from now on." A pause fell over the men, as a net. James was reassured.

"I'll start it myself, Seamus, look, I'll fuckin' drive ya' myself, for Christ's sake . . ."

"Naw, just start it is all . . ." With that all four men, Seamus, Paddy and the two body guards, laughed in different degrees.

"And Seamus, if you'd be so kind as to visit our friend on the way back . . ."

Paddy handed the location and house number of a small seaside town, just east of Atlantic City . . .

And so, it was, Little Emmett drove a modest Packard, though a Packard all the same back to the ferry line across the river from Philadelphia. Not before a visit to a man possessed of the devil himself.

"Are ya' pleased, Seamus?" Little Emmett's eyes told the subtle story that every Irishman's eyes tell to those that are aware.

"Pleased to be goin' back to Ireland, Emmett, you and me? As far as everything else, content for now is all." Little Emmett smiled at the thought of returning home, if just for a while, though Ireland would still be wrought with peril for both.

"They find the need to keep changin' the name of this little island, Seamus. City of Brigantine City, now City East of Atlantic City. Change the name they may, but the green head flies on this island will tear the flesh from a person, large or small."

"The Reeds Motel, Emmett. Up on the right, it's Paddy's. Pull in back . . ."

In the reeds across a sand blown dirt road from the motel, stood a dilapidated dock. Its faded wood decking was beautiful to the eye, though the combined weight of the two big men gave pause.

"Emmett, creep out there and move around a bit." James laughed into himself, as Emmett gave him a double look.

Two paint chipped row boats, large enough for four men, sat high in the water with fresh rope ties, looped over pylons.

The dock was sturdy and the full smell of its seasoned wood, filled the men with a freedom reserved for those of the sea. The squint of Irish eyes said more than any words might ever.

"A man could live out here, Emmett. I mean it, really live—a clean life."

"Aye, that a man could, Seamus, if he were a free man . . ."

James shook his head, before taking in a deep breath. Water lapped the sides of the boat, as the men climbed down, pulling up the tie. The sound of dress shoes in the hollowness of the boat stole the wishful dreams of James Sullivan, though he did not mention it or try to take the words back he had spoken.

"Shoals, everywhere and nowhere, Emmett. Imagine the wrecks in this channel, with those famous Nor'easters storm whitecaps hidin' these sandbars. Treacherous waters by any standards . . ."

"Tails of many a wreck in these waters, better your chances in a storm that rages in sound seas, then traverse this stretch in mere darkness." Emmett spoke with the respect the salt water commands a man, no matter age or strength.

Oars struck sand as hard as dry ground, before the boat found its way to an open passage to an empty shoreline, surrounded by sea grass and windswept dunes.

"There's not but a boatful of folks livin' here Emmett, that's worse than a crowded city in my book. A brown shack with tomatoes and berries growin' up the backside of it, that'll be the one. He'll be alone if he's there, Paddy says, he does his evil elsewhere."

With the boat pulled up high into the tall grass, the men headed out to what gave the marking of a road. Howbeit sand, there was evidence of horse drawn carts leading south.

Twenty minutes passed when a row of shanties appeared out of the sun, the wind blew up the water and gave the makeshift road the makings of a dream. In silence, the men took to the side, close to the sea grass and drifts. Shoes filled with sand and the taste of the salt air gave the Irishmen strength that made up every chromosome of their bodies. Salt and sand stuck not to James Sullivan but to, Seamus O'Suilebhain's brow, and thick blonde hair. Emmett McGowan removed his American hat in favor of the wind and salt air that made him complete, the cropped reddish hair of the big man gleamed in the sun, freckles long since in remission, now bright and prominent as any a young man.

The silence of the two men in this place, this respite from all reality was about to come to an end. The brown shanty, with the numeral 6 painted to the right of the screen door that clapped in a prying cadence, snapping at those who might approach.

"Take the back-door Emmett, drop him before he can run."

James opened the screen door, which was all that separated him from the narrow rectangular shotgun house. He waved Emmett through the open back door. The faint melody of Country music played, as every curtain danced with the wind. Fly strips held both dead and frantic green headed monsters, awaiting death.

A rhythmic squeaking of bed springs brought the eyes of the two assassins together, in a mutual controlled rage. Emmett, shotgun at the ready, with James easing out his Colt revolver moved closer to the bedroom doorway. With a nod of head, Emmett filled the entrance of the room, he continued forward in silence. James entered, revolver pointed at the head of a slender, naked man in the act of self-gratification. The man grinned, toothless to a climax.

"Wesley Rowland, your about to meet your Creator, and even I can't let ya' be seen like that. You'll be cleanin' yerself now, and quick like, take your drawers from around your ankles and do as I say, now, Wesley."

Emmett collected two long barrel shotguns from either side of the bed of fresh white linen. Bedding unbefitting a man of his deviate nature.

"You had the wrong gun in your hand, you'd have to admit that, Wesley Rowland, surely now, you'd have to admit that . . ." James looked around the room, noticing the clean tendencies of a man possessed by the devil.

"Good enough, lay back down on the bed, you might want to grab a hold of the mattress." James didn't care that the man never spoke, his toothless grin was worse than any words he might utter.

The man complied, still in an odd state of arousal, and grinning all the while. The occasional smack of saliva was an added last act of beguilement.

"Your makin' my job too easy, much too easy. Tie him down, Emmett, spread him out and gag him." With that, James turned his back and took out a velvet necklace box from his front pocket. In it were two glass tubes, the length of the case. He took one out and returned the box to his pocket. Still not a word from their captive, who of all things was now at full staff, writhing on a bed of white linen, the sun itself exposing the man in the once shaded room.

"Now then . . . ." Without warning James slid the glass tube into the man's penis as far as it would go, and snapped it, breaking the glass tube. Tears poured down the face of the man, as James began to speak. James squeezed his hands together, between the fingers, making his black, skin tight, rubber gloves, even tighter.

"We're gonna' take our time, Wesley. I want you to count the babies, each one. Then, recall the faces and cries of all the little children ya' had yer' way with." James pulled a wooden chair across the wide planked floor and sat down, rolling up his sleeves.

"Is it gotten hotter, Little Emmett? Given the heat here in summer and the frigid cold come winter, I think it best to reconsider movin' here. All in all, Emmett, Ireland is the place for us, that's what I'm thinkin', I am. That, and the fact that I've wasted about two inches of extra glass tube on Wesley here. Well then, have ya' counted all of the children? Sure ya' have . . ." James stood over his prey, looking into his eyes. "Don't be passin' out on me now, you'll shame the devil."

Emmett was quiet, but not shocked at what he was witnessing, he knew now first hand that James Sullivan was capable of anything, if you were what he deemed an enemy.

"Your straight blade, please, Emmett . . ."

James cut an incision down Wesley Rowland's chest and torso, exposing the ribcage. Still awake, eyes bulged and red with shock, the carnage continued. Taking a small bone saw from a leather bag, James sawed through the ribs, pulling the cage apart. He then pruned the heart loose, still beating as promised, as Wesley Rowland died a foul death. With the genitals now removed and shoved in the man's mouth and throat with the help of a wooden spoon, he was wrapped in the crisp white linen, he found so comforting in life.

James was methodical, as he washed the tools of his trade in one of two rain barrels behind the shanty. Washing and drying each instrument with equal attention, before then washing himself from head to waist in the opposite rain barrel.

James and Little Emmett made their way down the desolate road, each holding an end of twisted linen, walking side by side. Once in the boat, they navigated in silence back to the waiting dock. Carried to the road, the man's mutilated body was unwrapped and displayed for the clerk of the hotel to see.

After the two men were long on their way to the ferry, did the clerk call the newspaper men on Patrick Johnston's payroll, and then the police. In every headline from New Jersey to Boston, the name Wesley Rowland had become infamous. The message was sent to what happens to child molesters in the great state of New Jersey, in Atlantic City.

That night, back in Philadelphia, James Sullivan and Emmett McGowan sat in McGreevy's Diner eating grilled ham and cheese sandwiches and drinking iced tea while, reading the box scores and talking baseball.

"Emmett, do ya' have the salt water taffy we brought from the Atlantic City Boardwalk for my children?" James asked, Emmett nodded.

"Tomorrow, I'll take the boys to the game . . ."

Again, Emmett nodded in agreement, as he ate.

DP Curran

<u>BOOK VI</u>

'The Lion'

"Before you embark on a journey of revenge, dig two
graves."

~Confucius~

CHAPTER 35

Two steamer trunks sat open and empty in the bedroom of James and Bridget Sullivan. Silence is a pain that tears at true love, a ripping, discarding pain, that cannot be endured.

"I'll be back with my mother and Lilly, Bree. A dream that sustained me thus far, support me, lassie, I can't leave without confidence, your faith." James was for the first time unsure of his wife's disposition.

"You'll leave all the same, with a vengeance that has sustained ya' for these many years. How many days, Seamus, how days have gone by without the face of the English captain in your thoughts? You've killed him a thousand times already, husband, is that not enough? I've done all that I could to erase this man from your mind, a man who will suffer by the hand of God for rape and the killing of innocence. Leave it to God, Seamus, I beg of you—don't deny your

Creator His revenge, or you will suffer your own, by the Lord's own hand." Droplets of tears unseen before by James dropped from her large crystal blue eyes, made more so by the welling of her tears.

"My promise is to return, Bree."

"Send for them, as any man of means, then . . ."

"You know that I cannot do that, you know it in your heart, as you know me."

"I'll not see you again, for that I'm sure. I had a dream. A dream of your death, at the hands of *'The Lion'*. There was a peace made and then it was broken by treachery and lies."

"We've faced danger our whole lives, Bree. A dream doesn't change a man's fate . . ."

"Listen to me, Seamus. It was more than a dream—it was a vision. The same type of vision that I had a week before our Alice's death. There have been others as well, they've all come to pass, each one. You'll not go, tell me you'll not . . ."

"There was nothing you or anyone else could have done for Alice, don't bring her name into this, she was defenseless, an innocent. I'm neither."

"There is something you can do, and ya' know it. Send for them, Seamus, please . . ." Bridget whispered the last.

"You would geld me then?"

"No . . ."

"We go on forever, no matter when or where I may live or die, Bree."

Bridget clung to James's torso, regaining herself.

"We were together before we were born, and so it will be long after this life. I know that, Seamus, I know that as well as I know you, husband. There will not be another for me, I've sworn myself to that. I will come to you in the life ever after, as you see me now."

"No more such talk, woman. You're a bit overdressed for a forlorn widow to be . . ." James smacked his wife on the ass and the wicked smile of the headstrong girl that he married returned in full.

"Take the clothes from me, Seamus. See me as I am, ripe and wet with nectars, waiting to be parted and eaten as a peach." She backed away to the bed as she spoke the words, biting at her lower lip.

"You are as wild to me now as ever you've been, woman. You are the most powerful force I've ever known, nor ever will . . ."

Each piece of clothing was taken from Bridget with the reverence and abstraction that a most holy act produces. Man, and woman, a universe away from all else of this world, nothing relevant but the two as they became one. They melted together as molten iron, hardening into on solid being that would last the ages. An unimaginable torridness, reserved for those written in the Book of Life. They would be together for eternity, in a locked embrace of pain and ecstasy. Both emotions of equal proportion, tortured passion and love that could end in sorrow or an unbroken current. They battered one another in an obsessed frothing of wild untamed rawness. The choice was now, and it was to be unbroken, so said God, Himself . . .

There was nothing mortal that remained about either, husband or wife—truthful spirits both, no longer bound by the fears of men.

Steamer trunks packed, the children were lined up by age to say their goodbyes, unaware of their mother's visions. Owen stood fast, next to Bridget, before closing the front door and motioning from the porch.

"I'll speak to her, Seamus—I know how to talk to her, I always have. Leave here with a clear mind. Let me smooth things out . . ." Owen was calming in his words, and James did appreciate each word that he spoke.

"Do that for Bree, Owen. For your sister, not me. And Owen, be it that I don't return, if you and Aengus would . . . with Jimmy and Shane that is . . ."

"If that be the case, there needn't be much in the way of rearing, guidance is all. Your Bree knows her boys', all of her boys, Seamus. Besides you'll be here forever, Seamus O'Suilebhain. *Deo . . .*"

"Forever, now there's a thought, indeed." James shook the hand of his brother- in-law, with the pressure that implied a promise be kept.

James left into the night, Little Emmett by his side, with a heavy heart that rests in the back of a man's chest. Owen's subtle, yet soothing remarks held James as his journey took him through the streets of Swampoodle, with all of its smells and sounds to the docks in Center City. The deepest fresh water harbor in the entire country, deep enough for luxury liner and battle ship alike.

The Delaware River had its advantages, the City of Philadelphia, one of its beneficiaries. Midnight struck with the ship already moving from the dock, the Philadelphia skyline evaporated into the fog that separates summer and fall. Ships conversed by way of horns and signals of old, as the *'SS American'* made its way from river to open seas.

Passports were as official as any man's might be who played by the rules of governments. Though cargo vessels are loose with their passenger manifests, all documents were in the finest order, down to boarding passes and secure accommodations once arriving in Ireland.

The trip was multi-layered—James was given the opportunity to have his wish fulfilled, and Ireland would receive arms and gold to continue their fight for justice and independence. A trip that was futile in both ambitions by many a powerful man in America and Ireland. Bets were procured in Atlantic City by the highest officials and organized crime families, whose best interests went with James

Sullivan across the sea. Lloyd's of London had a line on the voyage for its most prominent criminals of means and influence.

"You know as we set atop the sea, men bet and scheme on our return to America." James spoke to Little Emmett, as he took off his jacket in a small yet posh cabin with two bunks.

"Our friend in Atlantic city, Seamus . . .?" Emmett spoke out of knowing.

"Be as you wish to seem—Socrates said that, he knew men's nature."

"Do you rely on this man, Seamus?"

"Riamh, never . . ."

"I rely on myself, Johnston thinks of himself, granted not an altogether thoughtless man. He has a sense of justice concerning children, that is enough for me to do business with him. A mutual respect has been built, though not out of full disclosure, no man would be so foolish. A man who does not respect himself, cannot respect others, it is impossible, it cannot be done."

"Then why do you allow such a trip to be known?"

"To achieve our goals in Ireland, we first had to leave America in plain view, in safety. This assured the protection of my family and interests in Philadelphia. All other promises made, concerning the rest of the east coast, depends on the outcome of this voyage. This I am sure of, Emmett, may my judgement be sound."

"Our lodgings in Ireland then, are they safe?"

"That, they will be, and under surveillance by our friends in America. The money spent on this trip came with a string attached, a string that is attached to the finger of Patrick "Paddy" Johnston. We'll check in at the South Bend Bed and Breakfast in County Cork, just long enough to make those who are bent on shadowing us."

"May the dead eat well tonight then. Kill an Irishman on his own soil—a stupid lot to be sure, Seamus. Death awaits each, slow and delicious."

"We can lose the men, though we cannot kill the men, Emmett. Not straight off, and not by our hands. They will be expected to send word back—dead men have no way of making that happen. Days will pass before they say they've lost our trail, and when they do send word, they'll be told to find us. More time will pass, and we'll have done what we came to do. This keeps everyone safe, my family, Emmett."

"Aye, you've got eyes that see the pasture as a whole, while I see just the barn."

"You know who's barn it is, Little Emmett. That's all that matters . . ."

Rough seas took the two men topside to the decks of the newest of great ships, as other affluent passengers went below to heave the remains of their supper. In woolen sweaters, Seamus O'Suilebhain,

DP Curran

and Emmett McGowan, faced rain, wind, and sea barefaced and free. They held their arms to the heavens and cried out as ancient Viking warriors traversing turbulent seas on their way to conquest.

CHAPTER 36

The storm shown itself far across the ocean, its smell of salt and sense of rebirth filled James. The wind pushed still at his face with a familiar cleansing that he knew as a boy, and until this moment, did not realize how he missed it so. An animal of land knows not the joys of the sea—it was taken from James, as he did the deeds of others on dirt and concrete.

The two men, now as close as any men might be in life. Circumstance and duty, mistaken for honor will bind similar men together in a way that is both dangerous and magnificent in its delusion.

"The night at Taylor Street, my two boys, Jimmy and Shane—it wasn't the first time they've each followed me, though it be the first time together, to my knowledge."

DP Curran

"I'd have been surprised if they hadn't followed ya', long before that night, whether it be separate or together. They wouldn't have been followin' ya' if ya' were workin' the graveyard shifts, a slave in some factory, Seamus. The two are of the same mind, they are." James sighed in agreement with Emmett.

"Do you remember what I told Aengus, Little Emmett, about the future and how near it may be . . .?"

"Aye."

"Aengus and Owen, are they a *'hundred percenters'*, tell me from the part ya' keep from all others, Emmett—are they *'hundred percenters'* . . .?" Little Emmett sat back against the heavy coil of rope, tilting his head to the stars.

"Bein' neither is of your own bloodline, no. Not in the way I think your askin', Seamus."

"Would they do right by my family, my blood?"

"Your boys will do right by ya' Seamus. Meanin' Jimmy and Shane, no disrespect to Padraig and Rory, but we know who will have to keep things goin'. Aengus and Owen are Bridget's blood and thus, your children's blood. They will do right enough by those two, and they will be the gargoyles that protect the house of your wife, of this I have no doubt whatever, in that sense they are *'hundred per centers'*." Little Emmett paused and turned to James.

"Pretty much all, except for you, Seamus O'Suilebhain, you've managed to keep the perfect amount of trepidation between yourself and even your staunchest supporters." Emmett laughed and put out his large paw to James, and they shook hands.

"You're in good shape either way, Seamus, of course Swampoodle will have to live with a hornet's nest of Sullivan's and O'Boyle's for a time, but everything has its season, so says the Lord, himself." The men settled back, two sparks of light lit the face of each. The match of a cigarette for James and a solid pipe for Little Emmett.

"I had a talk with Deidre, about one month ago, Emmett. She's not like me or her ma, I'm grateful for that, though it may sound wrong to another's ear."

"She's more like the two of ya' than either can see, ya' don't see the finer points of your own children, ya' see and feel the things that bother ya' about yourselves. Your Deidre is both you and your Mrs. The girl was raised up in a different way, different circumstances, structure and the like. Deidre Sullivan is as tough as she is responsible, it's plain for all to see, Seamus. All except for you and her mother. She's the pride of the bunch, Seamus. Talk about *'hundred percenters'* . . ."

A pause fell over the men as the causal talk of strangers had ventured above, just to turn and return below at the sight of James and Little Emmett.

DP Curran

"The night at Taylor Street, when I wrote out what I wanted done should anything happen to me, sooner than imagined by myself even. Aengus . . . he hesitated, though he agreed. That stuck with me, Emmett."

"The two of ya' both have a way of takin' things in that aren't as subtle as either might think, it's just no one is so fool hearted as to mention it."

"Though you've mentioned it now, Emmett. Why is that?"

"Because we both know that this is the time for truth, and not regrettable silence."

"Ya' believe it, too then?"

"That the odds are slim of us comin' back, back to Swampoodle? Aye . . ."

"At what cost does a man keep his word, Emmett?"

"All cost, for you, Seamus . . ."

"And what of you, Emmett McGowan, be it not the same?"

"I've lost my wife and children, Seamus, this trip is a privilege, howbeit my last act, I've my own promises to keep, for the sun is setting for me. As you, I can taste vengeance—delicious as it is wrong, but you, you have much to lose. I have nothing . . ."

"I've left a bounty for the future, Emmett, and you've been part of that. That makes us somewhat even, no? Others will feel the pain we've felt . . . my mother and sister are dead, Emmett, I've known this for seven years. Few people know of it, Aengus, of course, Owen, and Jon Hirsch. Bridget . . . I've not told."

"Mother fuckers, they are, Seamus. I'll take heads for this, I've got a galley full of em' in County Cork, not far from port. I would have been surprised if they were still alive, God forgive me for sayin', Seamus. Why the German safe maker?"

"He's true, Emmett, true as any I've met. Solid in his ways—he has all of my confidence. I've had Jon build a separate safe, unbeknownst to anyone, save himself and Bridget. Built right out from the foundation walls of *'The Lehigh House'* cellar. Filled with enough gold and cash to keep Bridget for two lifetimes. We used the old stone from an arson fire on Emerald Street, four years back. Impossible to tell, even to my eye, which is so keen to find fault in the most meticulous of craftsmanship. Bridget has had the keys and combinations since its completion."

"You give your loyalty to a German?" Emmett said, shock showing on his face.

"To a man, Emmett, a family man who knows the value of such things as a man's word and the sanctity of marriage. That's the difference between he and Aengus, even Owen, who is to me a good and faithful cousin to Bridget, but his values are not of my own. Not in the end . . ."

DP Curran

"You asked if I thought Aengus and Owen were *'one hundred percenters'*, is this man to you, Seamus, is he what you would consider a *'hundred percenter'*?"

"Without question, no hesitation whatever . . . as are you, my friend."

Little Emmett laughed and smiled again before, looking back up to the stars.

CHAPTER 37

"Mid-point, boys," said a seaman in passing to James and Emmett. His voice fading as he made his way across the deck, saying the same to anyone topside.

With Ireland in their grasp, James uttered a sentence that at first had the effect of a shrug from Little Emmett McGowan.

"Lorcan Finn, you remember the likes of him, do ya' Emmett?"

"The rat bastard, that was on Finbar's payroll?"

"That'd be the one, well he's dead and gone. Shot himself in the head, left a suicide note, containing every disloyal man to the Sullivan's and O'Boyle's alike, working under Finbar. Specifics, damning words to be sure . . ."

"Lorcan Finn, fuck em'. He was a bit of a nance for his line of work, showed too much flare in his duties, as it were. How long before he shot himself?"

DP Curran

"I gave him a good half hour, let em' write a note to his mother, a drop of whiskey. He wailed as a sick baby. I had Jimmy and Shane with me, Emmett . . ."

"That's a stiff affair, that is, Seamus."

"Fourteen and thirteen years are the boys now, a making up of the minds needed doin'. Now, it's done. All the while thinkin' about bein' a fuckin' gangster, the two of em'. Well, they saw first-hand what a man might do to another. They saw Lorcan Finn put a gun to his own head and spatter his brains along the floor and wall. The boys would have seen plenty worse if Finn hadn't done what he was told by me. I'm not proud of it, no, not one bit, but it needed to be done. Better they find out now, I'd hoped one of em', at least, would have showed a weakness for it. Not the case, Emmett . . ."

"They showed no signs of fear for the deed itself, or for you alone, Seamus?"

"None that I saw, and I wanted to see either one, Emmett. Fear of either would have meant their freedom. My father gave me no such choice, it was all about when, never once about any if's. Some men, take their son's huntin' for pure sport in America, their son's look forward to that special day. A day when they cross over into manhood, well . . ."

"Do ya' think they'll continue, the both of em'?"

354

"I'm thinkin' so, Emmett, but at least they'll know what's real. That night, the three of us spoke in the study until dawn. The questions came like a thunderstorm, I kept it honest and cautionary, yet they were hungry for more. Aengus and Owen both know, I want things done right, and who better than 'The Ghost' himself?"

"All of this assumin' ya' won't return . . .?"

"Aye, otherwise there would have been more time, time to put off the inevitable. There's never enough time though, is there, Emmett?"

"Not for men of a certain breed—any man of action and not words alone. The world's not for the weak, they bemoan the strong, be it man or woman. People lookin' for sympathy in a cruel world is all, Seamus. You'd no sooner see those two boys go off halfcocked than be trained in what lies ahead for each, should they still choose to do so . . ."

"Well, what's done is done. I've used my best judgement, those that can't understand, won't be needin' to. Let's go below and check on the munitions, Emmett. We've got a job ahead of us, we do."

"Our man, Leary, and his one-eyed son, is he down below?"

"With a Tommy-gun, sittin' atop every crate of handguns, rifles, grenades, dynamite and gold—like a mother hen. He never once set foot on American soil after the ship docked. Says it's a curse of some sort or another."

"It just might be at that, Seamus . . ."

This would be the largest cachet of funds and munitions ever sent to the Emerald Isle. A feat which stands as one of the greatest accomplishments of any patriot to Ireland. All done in her defense against English oppression and slaughter against people of a sovereign nation.

The full magnitude of the sacrifice and blind determination of a small group of men, would prove to be the difference between greed and duty. A bloody harsh reality that most free people take for granted, the murderous deeds and ruthless execution of a man's will, cannot and will not be comprehended.

"You'll not be smokin' a pipe whilst keepin' watch now, will ya' Jack?" The wiry old man nary smiled at James as he approached.

"Now why the fuck does ya' suppose I'd be doin' that now, Seamus O'Suilebhain, are ya' as mad as they say ya' are, man?" The old man was a rod of steel.

"The fact that there's a pipe hangin' from yer' mouth, Black Jack Leary."

The Irish tongue was spoken in all manner of foul usage for if the old man could muster a syllable.

The voyage took ten days, to reach the port cove of County Cork, Ireland. Foul weather and the ever-present danger of unexploded mines at sea, made for a tenuous passage.

Ferry boats lined the cove as James, under the careful watch of Little Emmett, looked for their transport . . .

DP Curran

CHAPTER 38

Emmett grunted at the sight of Black Jack Leary, so nasty a man to ever claim satisfaction in life.

"Do ya' even know what the fuck yer' lookin' for, either of ya'?" Jack leaned over the rail and spit.

"I'm lookin' for the colors of Donegal, ya' old wife beatin' son of a bitch . . ." Emmett looked to Jack, as he spoke, though Jack didn't exchange a glance.

"Guilty as charged, your grace. Will it be the gallows for me then?"

"Don't imagine it'll be that quick for the likes of you, Black Jack. You'll be tellin' tales of bullshit, long after everyone else who ever knew ya' is dead."

James stepped to Jack Leary, the deck of the ship moved with him.

"Who's guardin' the shipment, John?" There was no room now for dryness now.

"My boy, Marty. He's as good as they come, Seamus. There's no cause for concern . . ."

"Not for me there isn't, John. Best to identify our ferry for us and do your best not to run that whiskey soaked tongue of yours. Do as I've asked and get below." Seamus commanded.

"To be sure, Seamus. No need for violence now, you've got a friend in me, your da and I go way back we do, or did, as it were. Well, then, there she is straight ahead, and damned if she isn't flyin' the colors of Donegal, too. I'll be readying the cargo, if you will, Seamus."

James stood, face frozen with conviction. His head dropped to his shoulder to glare at Little Emmett, and the seriousness of the moment was now upon all involved.

James took a green cloth from his pocket, a cloth with a stone tied to its center. He made eye contact with the captain of the ferry, and held up the cloth, before dropping it to the sea. This to a short pull of the ferry's horn.

The transition was flawless, paperwork, the experience of the ferrymen, right down to the cooperation of the local officials. If there was ever a doubt about the professionalism of this plan, it had all but evaporated.

DP Curran

Long bed trucks were loaded with the precious cargo. Crates of weaponry, munitions, and monies was split into two trucks. Both trucks were identical, with high wooden rails and heavy sailcloth that covered each load with an ease and straightness reserved for a formal military operation.

James and Emmett rode with the gold and paper monies, while Black Jack and his son, Martin drove the munitions.

"Follow close, yet . . . not too close, Emmett. We go from one side of the road to the other, once more. I can't tell what country we're in when your drivin . . ." James's laugh was as wind through his nose, yet it brought a levity back that the two hadn't bargained for.

The streets and shops filled James with the shock that childhood brings unawares. Memories of trips and adventures flashed with the passing scenery of familiarity. James would sit the back of horse drawn dairy wagons to the south, where he and his friends would spend the day—lifting bread from the local outdoor shops and wading into the Cobh Cove, as it were known, as the ferries and tugs guided ships and moved travelers with their steamers and merchants with their goods.

The green was as painful as it was beautiful, the truck in front of James remained in focus, though his mind was traversing the annals of his early youth before the responsibility of saving a country that showed no will for it. The deep emerald hills rose and fell along the sea, as a life was playing out in the dark jade hues of home. The sea air was different than America, a full breath of salt and vigor that changed a man's views of any further travel abroad. Should he live, James had, at this moment, made the decision, the future . . . the promise to return to his homeland with his family for good and for all. He pictured his children growing from the emerald pastures, healthy and strong. He saw Michael as a grown man, Rory without the burden of polio. Jimmy, Shane and Padraig with a fresh start. Little Alice sat on his lap as the truck rolled on and his Bree was waiting for them all in Donegal. The feeling stayed with James, until he runneth over with joy. He was drenched for a time—guilt came as a thief, tearing the joy from his heart and filling it with a guilt and remorse that a man close to redemption or death might feel, save the common drunkard.

"We had a dog, not a special dog, no such sheepdog or pure breed, a mongrel. My father named him Benny, on account of a bum named Benny who always seemed happy. My da would say ya' couldn't sneak up on 'Benny the Bum' and find him to be sad. Turns out his name wasn't even Benny—it was Oliver or Olibier, dependin' on the day of the week. Benny just went better with bum, hell of a thing to change another man's name without his consent." James just listened to Little Emmett talk of a time gone by, yet he was back there as sure as the two were sittin' in a truck full of money and gold.

DP Curran

"Anyways, the two Benny's were more alike than just a name some man gave em' both." Emmett stopped talking as the wind from the sea washed the two men in the fields of fresh lilac that covered countryside for a time.

James spoke, under its spell. "What of the two Benny's, Little Emmett . . .?"

"The two Benny's . . . the joy of living left each, not all at once. A little at a time, till they both disappeared within days of one another. They left all that they loved about the people and things in life that made each happy and went off to die alone. We found em' both, we did, me and my da. 'Benny the Bum' in an alley, covered in trash, curled up as a man might sleep. The dog, our Benny, well, he went to the barn and lay behind it, sleepin' all the same. So, said me da, though I was with him when we found both. He told the same story until his own death, that the two Benny's went to sleep and never woke up, but I knew better . . ." Emmett looked again to the sea and took in a full breath.

"What was it ya' knew that your da didn't tell?" James feeling the truck keeping the cadence of the story.

"Both of their eyes were open when we found em' both, they never went to sleep, they just died alone. I don't want to die alone, Seamus, if it be in your power, don't let that happen to me. That thought has crossed an ocean with me and back—walked with me every day, a lifetime . . ."

"If we die, we go together, side by side, back to back to the end, Little Emmett"

"Do ya' think less of me for such thoughts, Seamus?"

"No, I don't. No . . ." James put his hand to Emmett's shoulder and repeated himself.

CHAPTER 39

Dusk fell upon the two men, with the adrenaline a thousand years probing through their hearts. Producing images, fractions and feelings besetting each man separate in degrees of satisfaction and discontent. Fleeting happiness melted to hot pain.

The lead truck moved past a line of tall hedge grove onto finality of gravel. Breaks squealed, gulls screamed out to the sea, as men jumped from the cover of tarpaulin which concealed a stockpile of fresh death.

"Dean deifir . . ." Shouted an old man from an out building, that was as dilapidated as he.

"Hurry, the old sod yells, look at the poor storage for such weaponry, Seamus."

Without retort, James exited the truck. He headed straight for the man, arms outstretched as if to grab both hands of the stranger.

"Mr. Morgan, sir . . ."

"Seamus O'Suilebhain, well, now . . ." The men transferred the hardness of one man's life to the next in an embrace of the hands and wrists. "Let us be quick about concealing this, your most welcome of all prayers, lad. If ya' would take your truck up to the house and pull alongside. I'll be there in a shake." James waved for Little Emmett to assist in offloading the various sized crates, still fresh with the smell of fresh cut pine of *'The Tinkers'*.

James left the man to the hustle, as Emmett approached donning an Irish cap, no longer wearing the brimmed hat of an assimilated American.

"Who might that be, Seamus?"

"Jessie Morgan, a friend to my father, and a servant of Ireland." James stared at the man, as he went to and fro, with the limp of a seasoned man of action. "Pull the truck up to the house above, Little Emmett. Let's get on with it." The wheels of the truck went from the traction provided by gravel to wooden planks over dirt and weed.

"Jessie Morgan, some said he was killed, killed some time ago, Seamus. His age is its own disguise now."

"To some it must be, but when you watch a man change day after day, you recognize him alright. His appearance has changed much, Emmett—I'll not argue that, though his shadow is that of a giant." The grinding of gears pulled the truck along the wooden pathway up the steep incline to the side of a stone house.

"A fine stone house, shutters drawn. Is there no suspicion concerin' this place, Seamus?"

"The home of a wealthy Englishman, Emmett. He wants to stay that way . . ."

Men followed up the wooden tracks of wood, in a steady pace of purpose and pride.

"Into the house, Mr. Morgan?"

"Neigh, Seamus. Follow me a bit further." The men walked several paces beyond the house, and stood in silence next to an old well.

"An old well, sir? I don't see your meanin'." James was not a man to be crossed up with riddles and the like.

"Though the stone be as old as the house, the well is new. Completed just two weeks prior to your visit, just in time, I'd say. Leave it to the Irish, Seamus—the last minute is the best minute . . ." The old man took off a woolen cap, revealing a thicket of white hair.

The crank was turned as men, men who had led extraordinary lives to this point, waited, looking down into the darkness. The waiting produced further questions, as Mr. Morgan raised a rope ladder that fastened to an iron hook, imbedded into the masonry.

"The original well was brought down to the earth and covered with a stone slab, besieged with thorn bushes and evergreens. It's still accessible and rather ingenious, if I dare say." Mr. Morgan spoke without regard or need for any approval or opinion in the matter.

James stared to Little Emmett in a way he wasn't accustomed to—in a position of powerlessness, for now it seemed. He held his tongue and looked to Mr. Morgan, for what was without a doubt, just the beginning of a well laid plan.

"Now, then, come inside the house and we'll get to it . . ." Morgan led the way, motioning for two of his men to stay with the truck, men laden with rifles.

The inside of the house subsisted of ornate furnishings, along with expensive oil paintings, that were the pride of its owner. A man of considerable taste, though the scarcity of such furnishings and art made it apparent to James that the house was staged. A precondition of his duties in America, which gave James both the insight of a professional murderer and a fine detective as well.

A refined kitchen table set atop a narrow throw rug was lifted and moved to the side. With the rug removed, Mr. Morgan pulled an iron ring that extended a chain, lifting the hatch in the floor. Propped with a measured length of oak, a lantern led the eyes to a makeshift cellar, fortified with heavy beams and stone pillars. All which stretched to a constricted tunnel, leading to the base of the well. Two more lanterns were lit from pegs lining the top of the tunnel.

"That rope designed with the likes of Little Emmett and myself in mind, Mr. Morgan?" James pulled at the ladder to empathize his point.

"Aye, all of this was designed with the two of ya' in mind, whether it be for one night or be it a thousand." Mr. Morgan's tone was clear on the matter.

"This rope line is from the shipyards of Glasgow, it holds the mightiest of ships to port, I suspect it'll hold your large friend here just as well. You go first is all, Seamus . . ." For the first time a smile appeared on the face of Jessie Morgan, howbeit amused by himself alone.

"And the gold and monies, sir?"

"That must go where it must go. Few men hold my respect as you do, Seamus, but you'll have to part ways with the contents of that truck. Not just in a physical sense, but in your mind all the same. Makes no difference, you've done your part, you're not to concern yourself with any such talk or thought of gold and monies, Seamus. It's my responsibility now, son."

"This by your word alone, sir?"

"Aye, by my word alone. Simple and true, Seamus. We'll all have what we need, one way or another. You've come back for more than one reason, your presence in Ireland is known, by now. There's no time for anything but truth between us, I'm afraid your stuck with me, lad. You and Little Emmett McGowan, who acts as if he knows nothing of me. Your father and I fought together at Cork Harbor, Ireland, twenty-five years past. This will be our grave here or our sanctuary, what of it, Seamus?"

"I've not come this far to interfere, though there were certain questions that needed askin', now that I'm satisfied, well . . ." James smiled, while two men appeared in the shadows from above.

"You've stayed true to your reputation, Seamus O'Suilebhain. Now, if you would be so kind . . ." The weight of time was upon James, with an internal ticking, reserved for he and his oldest son, James Jr. Neither knew that they shared such a trait with one another, their similarities so apparent to all but themselves.

"Emmett, the key to the truck, including the one found hidden beneath the seat."

Out of stones moving it shadows walked Black Jack Leary, rubbing his hands together, and wiping his clothing down.

"I've parceled out the weapons between the outbuilding and the house, Mr. Morgan, sir. Will there be anythin' else, my services are available, but should ya' not need me, I'll be headed for the pub. I've got a wee cough, a bug perhaps, drainin' me strength in a time of great need no less. I feel a spell comin' on, I do . . ." Jack put his hand to his throat and conjured up a cough.

"All the food and drink you'll be needin' is right above us now, Jack. Not you or your son, Martin, will be leavin' here this night." Morgan kept his eyes upon James, as he spoke the words to Black Jack.

"Sir, the Mrs., she'll be frantic already that me and her one livin' son haven't returned to her after such a long voyage to a foreign land of heathen's, no less. What'll befall her poor heart bein' us to be gone even longer?"

"Another good night's sleep will befall her, more than not, Jack. Go above and stay put."

"Drink ya' say then? Well, tis' me duty to me country to serve when asked."

Emmett held two truck keys in his sausage size fingers and thumb, he held the keys out to Mr. Morgan, leaning to him without stepping.

"Peter, take the keys and deliver the truck and its freight. See that ya' get a mark on paper upon delivery. I'll not ask Mr. O'Suilebhain if the first place he looked for a spare key was under the truck's seat . . ." Morgan's eyes still not averted.

James and Emmett smiled to one another, despite Mr. Morgan's disapproving tone.

"Seamus, you've been away too long, you've forgotten your manners here in Ireland concernin' your elders, ya' have."

"No, sir. I've remembered the lazy habits of my elders here in Ireland is all. You'll do well to show some respect, sir. I didn't do the things I've done to be scolded by a man who feels something owed him by mere longevity. Don't fuck about with me, Jessie Morgan, be straight up like, man to man. I've paid my way through service, not with the pious demeanor, fit for a long-suffering widow of the church. Oh, you've done your part alright, yet the whole way ya' carry yourself sickens me. Win or lose, your type stays miserable, I'll not speak of it again, though it pains me to watch."

"Your stay in America has produced that level of contempt for those who made it possible for ya' to go there in the first place. That's what you've learned?"

"Your agreement of my passage was a nod, a yay, perhaps. I know who made what possible, sir. I'll say the name if ya' like, we'll keep everything above board here. There's too much at stake for me to be thinkin' you my enemy, neither one of us can afford that, sir."

"You've changed, and I can't say for the better, Seamus. You'll find no quarrel in me, just a disappointment that I'll shoulder myself."

"No doubt, ya' will at that . . ."

"Let's go up and get a bite to eat and go over the plans that have already this day been set in motion—it was more than just a nod, as ya' say, Seamus. I lost my two sons that night, that night you made your way. They were slaughtered aboard the ship in the Bay of Donegal, so . . . I have selfish reasons for your successful return, as well. My pious nature will die with *'The Lion'* howbeit, your efforts prove fruitful this evening."

A long oak table was cleared so that the men might eat and discuss the events that lie ahead this night. Mr. Morgan had a most capable bodyguard at his side, capable of murder without the hesitation that a conscience might burden a man. Black Jack and his half-wit son were relegated to the kitchen for the remainder. Marty Leary was of a sound mind, and did cause James to wonder how his possible involvement could befit anyone. He could not help but to loath the boy, for in America, James knew all manners of boys that were considered retarded. Pug McCann took these boys into his gym, and treated each as a 'whole' child. Perfect in the eyes of the Lord. So, said Pug, and he meant it. James thought that his sister, Lilly would someday benefit from Pug McCann's gift, as it were. There was not a more protective man than James concerning these little children. Marty was a sorry sight to James though, a wasted mind that led to excuses, though he was born with just one eye. James blamed Black Jack, the boy's father, though he hated the thought of his son—a boy used oft times as sympathy for a drink at the local pub, a trip for which he was denied this night.

All that was needed unfolded before James and Emmett across the large oak table. Coordinates and times concerning garrison movements and the whereabouts of . . . *'The Lion.'*

CHAPTER 40

Darkness proceeded a light meal and a gentle reinforcement of the night's objective. A party of seven men, including James and Emmett, would encircle a gentlemen's club for officers of the English Army. Captain Edmund Wainwright was to be celebrating there after an accommodation and promotion to commandant, thus taking him out of the field, and out of Ireland. He was return to England in two weeks' time, anytime left would be to cause as much ranker and lasting impressions as possible.

Aengus O'Boyle knew this would be the last reasonable chance to make good on his promise to James. Not one to waste a situation, Aengus pulled together the impossible, the largest cachet of weapons ever brought to Ireland from The United States. He also added a huge amount of gold and monies to a free Ireland's coffers. Nothing of this scale had been a success to this point. Two promises made on a ship in the Port of Derry those many years ago came true in one swift operation. No matter the outcome, Seamus O'Suilebhain and Aengus O'Boyle were men of their word. Each knowing now for certain.

"Black Jack, raise yourself up . . ." Mr. Morgan shook Jack by his coat, as he slept drunk on a wooden chair in the kitchen. His son, Martin, laughed and drank from a bottle of whiskey, the smell of which hung in the air.

"What is it, sir? Unhand me or I'll . . ."

"You'll what? Listen close, John Leary, I'll say this but once for you and Martin here. Dillion will be stayin' here with the two of ya'. You'll be bound and kept below, should a garrison come to this residence in my absence. Any trouble whatever and you'll both be killed on the spot, at any length. You're a fine a seaman as there is, Black Jack, though the whiskey has drowned the better part of your brain that once controlled your tongue, and your son, well . . ."

"Ah, reconsider, Mr. Morgan. Me and Martin here are a harmless sort, we aim to keep to ourselves what we know, bein' how we're involved in plenty of our own misdeeds concernin' the Governor. I wouldn't have it any other way, if I had things to do all over again I wouldn't."

"Now ya' know I can't take any chances, John. Why, if somethin' were to happen to you, I'd feel responsible myself, a terrible thing to have weighin' on a man's mind for the rest of his days. Now, be a good couple of lads and cooperate with Dillion, you'll be where ya' belong in no time . . ."

"Alright then, bein' as I can finish off this bottle of whiskey first, with me boy?"

"Fair enough it is John. Drink up . . ."

In a matter of minutes, the bottle was empty and Black Jack Leary and his son, Martin, were led, bound and gagged down through the hatch in the kitchen floor.

"Would ya' do me the honor, Seamus, and show me what all the fuss is about in America, of *'The Viking.'* Morgan stood in the light of one lantern, illuminating just himself and James.

"You'd like me to kill a son of Ireland, for your own amusement? A defenseless man in cold blood, Jessie Morgan?"

"Better than that, I'd prefer ya' kill both father and son . . ."

"Kill em' yourself, man. Why the curiosity, you'll see soon enough what I'm about, no?"

"He's already given ya' up, Seamus."

"That remains an unanswered question for me still, Mr. Morgan. Be it, I find it were not Black Jack Leary and say someone else, it would be a slow death for that man, and that sir, I will enjoy. I assure ya' . . ." With that, James snapped the neck of a drunken man in disbelief, and followed suit with breaking too the neck of his son, Martin.

"You were warned once today, not to fuck about with me, Mr. Morgan. There won't be a second time." Little Emmett stepped to Dillion in a space too small for either men of ill will.

"Wicked, Mr. O'Suilebhain. Impressive and wicked, sir. You'll not have cause to doubt me this night or any other, of that I can assure you."

"Assurances are for those already dead. You, sir, will not assure me of anything, ever."

"Aengus O'Boyle does not disappoint, no, he does not . . ."

"Your closer than you've ever been, sir. Shut your fuckin' mouth, unless it concerns what we're here to do, and that, friend, that time is now." James was now in the face of Mr. Morgan, the buttons of James's shirt cuffs popped in unison, as he made two fists in anger, blood pulsed from his forearms to his shoulders. This was death's precursor.

"Seamus, easy now . . ." Little Emmett's voice cooled James in a manner to which brought his mind back to order to the task at hand. James sighed, stepped away from Morgan and looked to Emmett with an unspoken expression of gratitude.

The men returned to the living quarters without words, short drinks were poured, and each man drank, again of one mind. Three knocks in rapid succession, *'The Trinity'*, cut through the stained glassed door. Mr. Morgan looked to his pocket watch.

"That would be Joseph Lynch . . ."

In the doorway stood a tall, yet paunch man. His hair was curled, as a woman or perhaps a man of means might present himself.

"Mr. Lynch will be playing the part of Sir Lyndon Branton. The subsequent owner of the house we now find ourselves in, Mr. O'Suilebhain. A thespian by trade, and a fine one at that, or so I am told. An Australian penal colony has sharpened his passion for our cause, as well as a handsome salary. He has all the necessary paperwork, including identification and proper lineage, which has already been vetted by our English counterparts. In short, there is no Sir Lyndon Branton, we've taken the liberty of creating him. Alas, Joseph Lynch."

"Pleasure, Sir Branton . . ."

"The pleasure is mine, sir."

The accent and mannerisms were perfect, again the faith of his countrymen enveloped James Sullivan who, with each passing moment, was morphing back into Seamus O'Suilebhain of County Donegal, Ireland. Swampoodle seemed a lifetime away . . .

CHAPTER 41

Four men climbed up the heavy rope ladder into the night, with three more men waiting in the dark clean air. The olfactory senses heightened, the distinct contrast of America and Ireland was one of wonderment to James. Ireland had a raw scent, wrought with the taste of salt and pine needles, while America had an overriding smell of factories, fresh cut lumber, and all manner of progress.

"We'll head off down the edge of the main road, Seamus. The English have men throughout the wooded areas . . ." Mr. Morgan led, the sound of leather straps and slight rattle of rifles set the mood.

It had all returned to Seamus, the feeling of righteousness and justifiable rage. The contrast was stark, as compared to his duties in America. To James, he killed no more than gutter rats in America, stupid men, who dabbled in danger, putting their own mark on it first, signing their death warrants without either predilection or common sense. Men who had it coming, and James was more than glad to oblige. This, now . . . this was what he was born for, Ireland with all its troubles and strife at the hands of the English, the oppressor. This was meaningful, this was his destiny.

Seamus O'Suilebhain was alive, even vibrant. Bridget was the one equivalent, the one exception to what he again felt this night. He could not afford nor bear the thought of her, not now, not here. They would be together someday in eternity, perhaps, after all. Maybe Bree was right . . . yes, she must be, given the feelings that overtook him now. There had to be a God, a guiding force for good, the world was harsh, so must men be, but eternity would be there for both, no matter the harshness of man . . .

The lights of the town ahead were as immediate as a headache, the smell of burning wood rose from the smoke stack of the local chimneys. The loud drunkenness of men, along with the squealing of whores, women who James had an unspoken respect for, those making the decision, the hard choice to feed their families. To James, these women gave their dignity, something which no one else can feel, but each woman knew it. The men they laid with were foolish, weak for treating another person with a false advantage. These men, enjoyed a reputation that none of them deserved. It was a whore who showed James compassion, where he had guilt and fear, the night he gave his virginity to a large breasted redhead. She was kind and without judgement. So, James as a man would show the same kindness due another human being such as this, both here and in America.

"The third building, beyond the corner . . ." Hand signals were used by Jessie Morgan to direct his men.

Two soldiers stood guard outside the Bedford Inn, where they grabbed and cajoled the women who dangled their product in a knowing tease of satisfaction.

Men moved into position, backs against shopfronts with rifles to their chests. Two whores, one young, one older made eye contact with James. The younger, about to cry out was stopped by the older. The soldiers still busy with the women were unawares. James put the index finger of his left hand to his lips, all the while his right index finger on the trigger of his rifle. The older of the two nodded, and pushed the younger, no more than a girl toward the soldiers, blocking the view of the amorous young men in uniform.

The signal was given, three men to the rear of the building, while the remaining four, Jessie Morgan, Dillion MacDonald, Emmett McGowan, and Seamus O'Suilebhain took to the entrance. The women parted without so much as a raised voice, as the two young English Soldiers were over powered, mouths covered, and throats cut through the larynx. Both left unable to cry out in warning, blood poured as wine from the two necks, and slowed with the thickness of syrup. The two were put seated, backs against the stone facade, the women stayed without notice and talked and laughed as before. Now, conspirator's all, they performed with the honor of true women of Ireland.

The door opened, revealing officers of the English Army, some engaged in close talks now surrounded with women. The older whore emerged with dagger in hand, plunging it into the neck of a shocked and dumfounded officer. The sharpness of a whistle, was stifled, as shots were fired, alerting the men above. Officers donning pistols shot from a half wall second floor hallway into the crowd with precision, killing Jessie Morgan, a bullet striking his head, the full weight of the man dropped to the floor.

All the officers still seated on the first floor were dead, attention turned to the second floor, as men and women from the town converged on the shopfront, blocking the entrance, even beating the dead soldiers as they were dragged into the gutter. Stripped of their belongings, and all manner of inhumane acts ensued by people, howbeit young, old, man, woman, and child alike. Years of bound hatred unleased in a frenzy of degradation.

Returning gunfire ceased from the second floor, James and Emmett took to the stairs, as Dillion moved Jessie Morgan's body in hopes of reviving him.

Women, naked some, gathered in the hall, nodding or shaking their heads. They seemed in shock. James and Emmett would have to check each room. Every man who lay in the hallway was shot through the heart, prompting one officer to raise his hands from his back unarmed. Coward, English coward. He was about to speak when he, too, was shot through the heart.

Each room was searched by both, James and Emmett, no man was found. The man known as *'The Lion'* was nowhere to be found.

Several of the women stood before James, unabashed in their nakedness. Something for which James saw a sense of purity in, not vulgarity—simple, without pretense . . .

"Have any of you seen this man?" James held out a silver daguerreotype image of Commander Edmund Wainwright. Two girls started to speak at once, they smiled and one continued.

"He was here tonight, though he left under guard with more than a dozen of the girls."

"Look at me. Do you have any idea at all where he might be at this moment?" James's face told a story of revenge and justice to every woman present.

"His Majesty's Ship 'Tripoli' . . . she's docked in the bay of Donegal. A hand carved pleasure ship for the bastards own evil inclinations, most all here have been on it at one time or another. It's not so close to land as it is this night, a full moon no less, but for the captain's promotion and the celebration to follow, she sits in the bay accessible by the dock. Any other occasion and she would be out to sea, we'd have to be rowed out. This might make things easier for ya', sir." James had a glancing vision of his last night in Ireland, before focusing once more.

"Out to sea would have been better, thank you, thank you all . . ." James took from his pocket a pouch of gold coin and handed it to the girl that spoke to him. "Be fair to one another with this . . ."

"Are you goin' to kill him, sir? Kill *'The Lion'*?" The girl clutched the cloth sack, as the others clamored for its contents.

James paused, yet did not turn nor answer the girl . . .

James and Emmett took to the stairs, rifles pointed. The mob outside was getting louder, as the oldest of all the women sat at the bar, blood soaked, sipping the finest of wines. She smiled and laughed to herself, causing her body to move as she did.

"This, this is for you. You deserve more than gold, but I can't change the past, not for any of us . . ." James placed a cinched pouch into the woman's open palm, a hand as beautiful as any woman of royalty.

"Thank you . . ." James spoke the words in a low tone reserved for gratitude, this produce a short smile and the raising of a wine glass. She spoke not.

Dillion presided over Mr. Morgan's dead body, staring at James.

"What do ya' think of him now, Mr. O'Suilebhain?" There was nothing to be said, Dillion had asked a question that contained within it the answer, as well.

"Bring him outside, the people will know what is right. They will see to him . . ." With that James lifted Jessie Morgan as one might a sleeping child, and carried him outside. "Behold, a hero is in our midst." The people stopped and came to James, in silence, until one elder man spoke up.

"We'll take him from here, Seamus O'Suilebhain. There is more than one hero among us this night, and your night, well, your night is long from over, sir." Several grateful men took Jessie Morgan from the arms of James. The elder spoke again.

"Dillion MacDonald, you'll not mourn Mr. Morgan. That's for his family, your job is to go with Mr. O'Suilebhain, for he's lost more than any of us here, yet he not cries nor sulks. Respect for Jessie Morgan will be in your coming deeds, not the lack thereof. Go . . ."

The three men from the rear of the building stood with the crowd, blending in, rifles concealed in the brush. Three men struck out together to Donegal Bay, committed to both life and death.

CHAPTER 42

Pines surrounded the sharp enclave of the bay. The men paused to take in the sight of the royal vessel, His Majestey's Ship 'Tripoli', as it rose and dipped with the water. Soldiers, much older than their two unfortunate comrades stood watch, some took to the trees in constant motion.

"The three of us against this lot, Seamus, what of the three other men?"

"That's as far as they were paid to go, Emmett. They got me to where Wainwright might be, I'm thankful for that much. This is my score to settle, though, some might like to do the same, here I am. Emmett, there's no cause for you to go on, that goes the same for you, Dillion. You both have my respect either way ..."

"Why don't ya' just call us a couple of bitches, instead of whatever that was?" Emmett sat back against a large pine tree and let out a sigh. James smiled back to him, and shook his head in amusement.

"Emmett, I'm thinkin', you and I take to the water, while Dillion covers us from the tree line. Fire and move, Dillion, keep movin' . . . save your own skin, if you can. Be smart with your ammunition, and make your way to safety, once Emmett and I get aboard. On the other hand, you could keep firing at the dock, to keep reinforcements away, no pressure, either way . . ." James smiled, once again.

"That's the main difference between you and the rest of us, Mr. O'Suilebhain. You love this shite, and we just do it out of duty is all."

"Got me all figured out, do ya' Dillion? Lucky one ya' are, just in time ta' die . . ."

The trees and underbrush stirred just behind the three. *"Cara . . ."*

"Who the fuck is that?" Dillion, whispered and pointed his rifle in the direction of the voice, that sifted through the pine needles.

"Don't fire, Dillion, aim, but don't fire." James moved to a small clearing yet saw no one.

"Cara..." The voice continued.

"Hold," whispered James.

"Cara . . ." This time no closer than the last two.

James scrambled back to Emmett and Dillion.

"Wait, just wait, keep your eyes on the ship, Emmett."

"What are we waitin' on, Seamus?" Emmett spoke, as he trained his rifle back toward the dock and ship.

"Until now . . . *Cara.*" Cara in the Irish meant, friend. It was their safe word, a word that would be said three times, *'The Trinity'*, and Seamus had not forgotten. With that the sound of fallen needles got closer until the face of a stranger was upon the three. Two rifles pointed to him, the man pointed.

"What the fuck are ya' up to, the three of ya'?" Aengus O'Boyle stood with a dozen other men in the thick of the pines. "My cousin married a crazy fuck, that's a fact. I blame myself for that, I do. I've counted twenty-four soldiers on foot, and there's no way of tellin' how many below, in the ship. There's four dead men walkin' the deck alone, Seamus." Aengus tossed Seamus a sack of coal dust.

James knelt, and spoke without surprise in his voice, smearing the blackness to his face and hands before tossing it to Emmett and Dillion.

"I've got a plan, Aengus . . ."

"I've heard your plan, Seamus. By the way, Dillion, is it? Well, you were as dead as dead is red with that plan, son. Hitch your wagon to Seamus here and there's just two things that can happen. Most times both, unless you're him, so far. As follows, folks are gonna' die, and there's a more than fair chance that you'll be one of em' . . ." Aengus gave the sign for all men to kneel, as he surveyed the surroundings.

"We'll need to neutralize some of the English, thin the herd, Seamus. Hand to hand, at first, then storm that ship without fear nor mercy. Stay up here, any of ya' and you've got no chance whatever, none. I'll have archers further up, the ship will be ablaze, so beware of stray arrows. The men are good, but no formal military training, so, well, be careful is all. Seamus, you, Emmett, and Dillion, take to the water. I'll take my men to the soldiers on ground. I'm best at guerilla warfare, I'll be freelancin'. Let's move before word of that shite show you left behind makes its way here." The men blackened with coal, moved in silence.

The ship itself was illuminated by the full moon, everything about the sea and pines was a bluish color, the same color that Seamus recalled on the night of the massacre, those many years before.

The chilly water stiffened his bones, as he, Little Emmett, and Dillion slid into the bay. Rifles about their chests as they glided to the ship's bow, then separated around the ship. On land, the sound of shaking branches alerted the soldiers on the dock, though they looked with curiosity, more than concern. The coldness of the bay was numbing, the three had to hold out until they saw Aengus's men.

Seconds were minutes, as Aengus appeared on one knee just beyond the dock. A tremendous bang shook the trees about the bay.

DP Curran

Seamus then fired his rifle from the water, killing one soldier. He moved and shot another, before three flaming arrows hit the ship. Men took to the deck and water. The moon provided enough light to tell friend from foe, as Seamus pulled himself aboard from rope netting left dashed to the water for smaller row boats to shore. A mistake that would prove enormous.

The ship ablaze, the fighting was now hand to hand on deck. Seamus had three loaded pistols in a water tight kit on his back along with bullets he'd not have the chance to ever use. Smoke rose from the deck, though sight was not a problem, breathing was. Seamus pulled down the black mask of death over his face. A mask used in Ireland to conceal identity and protect families of freedom fighters. This night they would serve as protection from smoke inhalation, as well as putting the fear of God into less experienced English soldiers. Two more arrows struck the ship, men cried out in pain and in warning. Seamus made his way below, but not before a burning hammer like thud struck his left thigh, he had been hit, A rifle's bullet had taken the strength from his leg. He no longer felt anything, his leg had no feeling whatever. He fell to the floor of the galley, looking up he saw the face of a young soldier, rifle pointed at him. The young man's hands shook as he readied himself to fire, though not before James put a single bullet between brim and brow of the soldier, no more than a boy.

Murmured voices came from a closed-door cabin. More shots were fired as soldiers made their way below. Seamus, sitting against the ships wall boards, raised a full pistol and shot four soldiers, each tying to overtake him. They came one by one until there was nothing. Seamus struggled to his feet, his leg useless, covered in the thick blood that preceeds death. Again, the hot thump of pain grazed his back from a rifle barrel that showed from above. The soldier followed the blast, end over end. The young man lay dead by the hand of a friend on deck, fighting for his own life, as well, whoever it be.

The one remaining closed door below swung open and Seamus felt the same pain once more, this time his abdomen. Seamus returned fire, killing an officer. As others scrambled to the door, two more officers lay dead by Seamus's hand.

Behind a thick oak desk, the head of a man appeared, the strap of the helmet tight to the chin. Tight beaded grey eyes peered straight at Seamus. Before any words were spoken, a blast came through the desk, hitting Seamus in the right shoulder, his pistol fell to the deck. Then a voice, the voice of . . . *'The Lion.'*

"I'd rather it had been Aengus O'Boyle, though you, Seamus O'Suilebhain, are no ordinary man yourself. I knew you'd be back, though I thought it sooner. I killed your mother and sister in your absence, blame yourself for that. I got tired of waiting for you. Your mother, she was of no interest to me, none whatever. She had the nobility of a widow, that has no appeal to me. Lilly was as smooth a thoroughbred, once bathed and groomed, oh and she cantered as a thoroughbred, and how she worked her way into a gallop . . ."

He continued, "That did surprise me, I thought perhaps you were already dead, but reports from America said otherwise. Quite the dangerous man in America, Seamus, and busy, as well. Pity, you've come this far just to die with the sound of my voice being the last voice you shall ever hear." The bolt action of the rifle prompted Seamus to speak.

"For many years now, you considered yourself a soldier. The brave men that fight for you above on the deck, they are soldiers. The men who shot me, they are soldiers. You? You're a strange one, is all. Neither man, nor soldier, least of all a lion. You gave yourself that moniker, and had it spread about, no man does that, not even a boy. Nicknames are earned, no matter good or horrible they might be. No, you're what my associates would consider . . . a little bitch."

Instead of another bullet, Edmund Wainwright stood and clapped, the holster of his side arm unclasped. "Bravo, Seamus . . ." His words cut short, Seamus fired from his left hand, straight into the chest of Commander Wainwright. He fell back against the multipaned window of the cabin, breaking three of the panes.

Seamus crawled nearer, close enough to utter the words into Wainwright's ear, as he clutched his chest in a surge of adrenaline.

"Your mother, in England, in Essex. She's dead, her right hand severed while she lived. Here, a present for you, Commander." From a blood, soaked pack, Seamus reach in and placed the hand of Wainwright's mother on his chest.

"Ahhhh, ahhhh . . ." Wainwright expended his rage, and fell silent, save long breaths, that grew slower.

"Your fiancé, Miss Emily Parker? Correct me if I'm wrong, no? Well, she's alive, Commander, though she's pregnant, and living in Ireland. You're not the father, though you would already know this since you've not once consummated your relationship. She was a virgin, pure as could be, just waiting for you, Commander. Rest easy, sir, Aengus O'Boyle, my brother-in-law is the father, and he would never neglect his child. Here, Commander, take hold your mother's hand . . ."

With that, Seamus fired a bullet into Wainwright head, before Seamus himself faded to black, his body lifted high above the troubles of man to a bright all-encompassing light that erased the darkness.

Through the cabin door staggered, the bullet riddled body of Little Emmett McGowan. He fell to his knees before collapsing next to Seamus.

"We'll not die alone, Seamus. The hills are so green, so beautiful . . ." With a blood-soaked hand reaching his friend's hair, Little Emmett gave up his life . . .

DP Curran

Fighting raged on, though the sound of sword had taken the place of gunfire. Aengus searched the skewed galley, wet with sea water that forced dead men to gather in gruesome tangles.

Aengus found the two men, leviathans in life and evident death, yet he was not so sure, not so convinced that Seamus O'Suilebhain could be killed. Smoke filled the listing ship, stagnant with the screams of men not so fearless as to die when mortality shifted in sea and ship. Hardened men in life, now weak when death revealed its hand. Aengus knelt, boot over pantleg, seeming as to pray, if not in dire reflection. He rolled Little Emmett McGowan's arm from Seamus O'Suilebhain. The blood of each was mixed, so much blood flowed, dripping from Emmett's clothing and hair.

In one motion, Aengus lifted Seamus over his shoulders, and made his way to the steepening deck of the ship. Lifeboats with dead English soldiers provided transport to County Derry for Aengus and forty of his men, the precious cargo . . . Seamus.

"Dump the dead to the sea, and help us aboard . . ." Aengus shouting from the tipping stern. Irishmen moved in the sea, as if walking on land. Shoulders above the water, each man followed orders, without fail.

Less than a dozen English retreated into the comparative safety of the pines, firing into the sea without success, drained of all accuracy and strength. Men lay dying in shock. English blood soaked the needles beneath the men. No man lay haste for assistance . . .

In quiet cadence, Aengus O'Boyle stood at the bow of the lead rowboat, his brother-in-law and dear friend, Seamus O'Suilebhain lay just behind him. The boats hugged the sharp coast en route to County Derry, where help in the manner of concealment and healing could take place. Most of all, where deals could be made.

CHAPTER 43

Bridget O'Suilebhain was informed of her husband's death by her cousin, Owen, on the stormiest winter night since her arrival in Swampoodle decades before. An early spring snow drifted against houses and buildings alike. Cars took the place of horses and the sound of children in the white echo . . . that was Swampoodle. It made their voices seem as daggers, icicles piercing her heart.

Days passed, as pages fanned in a book, still no progress could be made to transport fifty-five men in all back to America, back to Swampoodle, until now. Aengus thought of spring in America, and his mind drifted to baseball, and the joy that Seamus took from it, he and his children. More American than Irish now, perhaps, Bridget and Seamus O'Suilebhain. Aengus's mind plunged deeper.

In Ireland, trucks were readied in intervals for the drive south to County Cork, and the Port of Cobh. Deals had been struck and plans

changed, so that men might leave the place of their birth without welcome of their return. The guaranteed safety of their leaving was all
. . .

Foghorns filled the damp night air, music to men of the sea, men of an emerald island.

Aengus O'Boyle lay in a bunk for the first time in twenty years, the heavy rope lines were undone. The ship, 'Landsing' was headed from the Port of Cobh, County Cork, Ireland to the open seas. A week's voyage, at least, to America, time to think and time to sleep. Something Aengus O'Boyle had little time to do in his life until now.

Aengus had fifty men strong that were making the passage back to America, young men of impeccable training and loyalty. Trained all by Aengus himself, they would be the men counted on to keep the prohibition bootlegging operation in Philadelphia and Atlantic City running as it should, without the need to count on untrained *'The Firsties'* and other misguided, malevolent fools.

Things would be done right, and he gave his word to see to it, and that was, well . . . money in the bank. His word was as another man's signature.

Four hours was enough sleep for Aengus, he stretched and tended to knife wounds sustained in the Bay of Donegal. The pleasure ship of Commander Wainwright sat at the bottom of the bay. The bodies of English soldiers and the body of *'The Lion'* were taken from the water with the respect and reverence reserved for such men serving the throne of the English. The Irish, who lost their lives, were left to a dark watery grave, no public displays, or speeches were made concerning the battle, as it were. Generals in England had cautioned that too much exposure of the incident would embolden others, other Irish to do the same. The fact was, no one in this lifetime would ever conceive of such madness. The legend and story would carry a nation and its children for decades to come.

There was one exception concerning exhumation from the sea, Emmett McGowan was taken from the burnt wreckage and given a proper burial. This was negotiated at the highest levels, all condition based. Emmett lay atop the hill on the farm he grew up on, all around him was the greenest, softest, thickest grass a man might ever see. The rolling pastures that led to the sea—beautiful, as the most beautiful of emeralds.

Soon, Irish resistance would later come in the form of targeted strikes, none of the daring 'devil may care' attacks that Aengus O'Boyle and Seamus O'Suilebhain had undertaken, and been so infamous for. The money that was sent to do just that was skimmed and hoarded by men of weak character. Much of the guns and munitions were sold for profit to splinter groups which made any effort of solidarity more fruitless than ever. No. Things were now to become political, men with money bargaining with men of money, and the people suffered for it. As Aengus O'Boyle wrote in a journal found long after his death in a safe on Taylor Street, 'Swampoodle, Philadelphia,' he wrote, *'Without the warrior class, the politicians will slay their own people in Ireland, with a quill.'*

For now, there was still optimism, or perhaps a man's personal satisfaction that he had achieved all that he might for his country.

In the wee hours of the voyage's first night, Aengus O'Boyle turned to Seamus O'Suilebhain from the top deck of the ship. A large coffin, draped and swathed in an Irish Flag, sat atop blocks of dry ice, tied and secured for the entire journey, no matter the weather, just as Seamus had instructed. Aengus kept his hand on the coffin, both men moving with the sea, in a rhythm all their own.

"Bridget has written that Padraig has signed a letter of intent to the seminary, to the priesthood—well, Seamus, I suppose there's always that strange one in every family that cannot be accounted for." Aengus look out and grimaced into the mighty winds of the Atlantic . .

.

DP Curran

CHAPTER 44

At port in New Jersey, the flag draped coffin of Seamus O'Suilebhain sat aboard a ferry, surrounded by eight pallbearers, including Aengus O'Boyle. The Irish Flag was removed in place of an American Flag to no objections. The decision made, after careful thought by Aengus, during the passage to America.

Across the river in Philadelphia sat two black Irish Draught Horses. They stood at seventeen hands each, and were hitched affront a meticulous wooden hearse, crafted by *'The Tinkers'* themselves, in honor of their beloved Seamus O'Suilebhain.

The entire Sullivan family, wife, children, family, neighbors, friends, and debtors alike followed the procession by horse drawn carriages, and most by foot. The difficult journey took them through Swampoodle, where hordes of people lined the streets, bridges and rooftops, to catch a glimpse of the man who protected and oversaw

Swampoodle. A man loved by his friends and respected by his enemies in equal measure.

Throngs of people filled Saint Columba Church, and lined the grounds and streets outside. Police officers and civilians wept, each to themselves in the open. Church bells rang as Monsignor Ryan blessed the body of Swampoodle's, James Sullivan Sr., where he lay, already given a Mass of Christian Burial at Saint Columba's Chapel in Ireland. The monsignor encircled the horses and hearse, sprinkling holy water, and then repeating his steps with incense from an ornate thurible. Prayers for the dead were spoken in Latin, before the procession ambled its way up Broad Street for the final journey to Holy Sepulcher Cemetery on Cheltenham Avenue. The final resting place for many Catholics, from every end of Philadelphia. A large swath of plots was purchased for the Sullivan and O'Boyle families' years before by James Sullivan Sr., after Little Alice's death. A man, an avid reader of books, who knew just one thing for sure, that all stories, when followed through, all end in death.

DP Curran

BOOK VII

Keys to the Kingdom

"Let the one among you who is without sin be the first to cast a stone."

~Jesus~

CHAPTER 45

The sun beamed through the stained-glass windows of Saint Columba's Church, as Bridget Sullivan took her place in the first pew with her youngest son, Michael, who looked so much like his father that it was a source of great strength to his mother. More than anyone might ever know, Mrs. Byrne cried, as she always had in church, she cried for her husband, for her son, Stevie, recently killed in a shootout. Innocent Stevie, she would say, though far from the truth. She cried for her sin of fornication. More than that, Felicity Byrne cried for James Sullivan Sr.

Bridget's cousin, Owen, at her side with his wife, Sarah, and two children, Kevin and Lilly. Today she was also joined by her daughter, Deirdre, her husband Jack, and their three sons, Seamus, John, and Rory Brady. Rory, being named after her brother who had contracted pneumonia and died, just two years prior. He was buried alongside Alice, and his father.

Today was a special day for Bridget, a day that she hoped her whole family would share. She would have her prayers answered, she turned to see her sons, James Jr, his wife Maura, their children, Bridget, and Padraig. Behind him walked Shane, with his wife, Keira, and their son, Aengus. Their lifestyles mirrored that of their father, as did an unbreakable loyalty to their mother, Bridget.

To Bridget's great surprise was a man she hadn't seen often, since the death of her husband, James, her brother, Aengus O'Boyle, married himself now, with a wife twelve year his junior, and a daughter named, Orla. He smiled a grin that projected life and death, without fear of either.

At the altar of Saint Columba's stood a tall young priest, with thick blonde tresses of hair, with the gait and build of a man not forgotten.

Father Padraig Sullivan looked out into an overflowing church, about to say his first Catholic Mass. The young priest's eyes searched the crowd, until he found his entire family. Aengus sat far from Padraig's mother and siblings. He stared into the eyes of his Uncle Aengus, and smiled. Lifting his head upward, Aengus O'Boyle nodded to his nephew, and the young priest was glad.

Today's homily would be about redemption . . .

Every Sunday, Bridget Sullivan made the arduous journey to Holy Sepulcher Cemetery. She went with the full and true notion that she was in fact still married to Seamus O'Suilebhain. Though few brave men tried her hand over the last ten years, she, with a laugh, would refuse any offers of marriage.

A stunning woman of beauty and strength. Bridget was in conscious contact with Seamus, through every trial and joy in the years to come.

Each night, Seamus came to her in a splendor that just two entwined souls might ever know. He was young and powerful, and she was his strength, an open vessel that let him return each night. The power of love, said she . . . written in the Book of Life.

The End.

DP Curran

Swampoodle Devotional Pages:

The loving memories of these families do not all reflect the era in which this novel was written during the time my grandparents, mother, and her siblings lived in Swampoodle. All the people below, and thousands more, are and will always be 'The Heart and Soul of Swampoodle.'

Kerrigan Family-Lehigh Avenue

Holland Family-Silver Street

Marcellino Family-22nd Street

Clauser Family-2731 Oakdale Street

Welsh Family-23rd Street

Parents of Jim Welsh-Stillman Street

Thiroway Family-Seltzer Street & 25th Street

Tom DeWitt-Bambrey Street

Thorson Family-Bambrey Street

Kelly Family-3002 Ringgold Street

Schroth Family-Firth Street

Stem Family-2800 Bambrey Street

Rowland Family-Oakdale Street

Cubbage Family-2554 W. Silver Street

Fogarty Family-2815 N. Stillman Street

Frank Gallagher-2735 N. Garnet Street

Slavin Family-3135 N. Pennock Street

Shields Family-2514 Silver Street

Fullam Family-Bonsall Street

Doraz Family-2711 W. Oakdale Street

Marzano Family-2122 Toronto Street

McQuillen Family-2742 N. 24th Street

Coll Family-2835 Ringgold Street

Lonergan Family-2727 N. Croskey Street

Black Faily-2729 N. Croskey Street

DP Curran

Sferides Family-2733 N. Croskey Street

Schmidt Family-2831 N. Judson Street

Higgins Family-2767 N. 25th Street

Walsh Family-2500 W. Huntingdon Street

May Family-2242 W. Huntingdon Street

Walsh Family-2501 W. Huntingdon Street

Schafer Family-2224 W. Lehigh Avenue

Crozier Family-2113 Somerset Street

Rabl Family-2220 Oakdale Street

Wildasin Family-2703 N. 27th Street

DeCarlo Family-Oakdale Street

Nagel Family-Oakdale Street

Hammond Family-300 Block of Bambrey Street

Hammond Family-2900 Block of Bonsall Street

MacClay Family-2736 W. Sterner Street

Roberta DeCarlo & the DeCarlo Family

McClernan Family-2729 W. Oakdale Street

Wright Family-3119 North 26th Street

Passamante Family-24th Street (owned Billy Passans Steak Shop on 22nd & Somerset)

Kathy Miller-2821 Taylor Street

Frances Szafran-2537 W. Sterner Street and 2713 W. Lehigh Avenue

Gerry Sposato, Glynn Family-2051 West Somerset Street

Cutillo Family-2904 24th Street

Rose Lee Armstrong-2612 W. Sterner Street

Lee Family-2612 W. Sterner Street

Edmond & Pat Cubbage-2554 West Silver Street

Brown Family-19th & Somerset

Smith Family-2548 W. Sterner Street

Reed Family-Bambrey Street

John R. Shields-3020 Ringgold Street

Farabelli Family-3144 W. Stillman Street

Woods Family

Phil (brother of Frances Szafran)-Seltzer Street

Sweeney Family-Taylor Street

DP Curran

Sweeney Family-Haggart Street

Curran Family-Silver Street

Magee Family-22nd Street

O'Neil Family-Somerset Street

Keane Family-Haggart Street

McFadden Family-Seltzer Street

Ferry Family-Lehigh Avenue

McGowan Family-22nd Street

Dougherty Family-Bonsall Street

Breen Family-Bambrey Street

Phillip, Donald, & Thomas Pello-2537 W. Sterner Street

Passante Family-22nd & Clearfield

Marzano Family-22nd & Clearfield

Ragno Family-22nd & Clearfield

Bill, Nancy, & Steve Gibbs-2909 W. Lehigh Avenue

Walter (Bob) Peel, Deceased

Eva (Greer) Peel, Deceased

Annamay (Peel) Austin

John Peel, Deceased

Rosemary (Peel) Mitchell

Elizabeth (Peel) Hagerty

Rush Family-2727 N. Bosnall Street

Conboy Family

Conway Family

Bill Lee-2616 Sterner Street

Lee Family-2616 Sterner Street

Kiefer Family-3107 N. 24th Street

McConnell Family

Anita Hoster

William Dugan

Betty Tata

Denise O'Sullivan Farrell

O'Sullivan Family

Holland Family

Dot & Bob Brooke

DP Curran

Kenney Family-2600 Block of Lehigh Avenue

Rickey Geiges

Nagel Family-19th & Lehigh Avenue

Chuck Nagel-26th & Lehigh Avenue

Eileen Kelly

Rilling Family

Byrne Family

Evers Family

Egan Family

Cubbage Family

Gallagher Family

William (Bill) & Catherine (Cass) Dornisch, plus their five children Bill, Jack, Bob, Paul, & Joann-2726 N. Garnet Street

Tom & Mary O'Sullivan, plus their ten children-Stillman & Somerset Streets

Made in the USA
Middletown, DE
10 April 2018